ALSO BY GILES BLUNT

The John Cardinal series

Forty Words for Sorrow
The Delicate Storm
Blackfly Season
By the Time You Read This
Crime Machine
Until the Night

Other novels

Cold Eye
No Such Creature
Breaking Lorca

THE HESITATION CUT

RANDOM HOUSE CANADA

GILES BLUNT

PUBLISHED BY RANDOM HOUSE CANADA

Copyright © 2015 Giles Blunt

www.penguinrandomhouse.ca

Random House Canada and colophon are registered trademarks.

Library and Archives Canada Cataloguing in Publication

Blunt, Giles, author
The hesitation cut / Giles Blunt.

Issued in print and electronic formats.

ISBN 978-0-345-81597-2
eBook ISBN 978-0-345-81598-9

I. Title.

PS8553.L867H47 2015   C813'.54   C2015-900717-8

Book design by Five Seventeen

Cover image: © Roy Bishop / Arcangel Images

Printed and bound in the United States of America

10 9 8 7 6 5 4 3 2 1

Penguin
Random House
RANDOM HOUSE CANADA

For Janna

I am inhabited by a cry.
Nightly it flaps out
Looking, with its hooks, for something to love.

—Sylvia Plath, "Elm"

ONE

THERE ARE MANY farms amid the hills that roll from New York City to Rochester, and on one of these farms a bell was ringing at the unconscionable hour of 4:45 a.m. It was a small operation, fifty acres to be exact, located just outside Corning and barely a stone's throw from the Pennsylvania border. The bell rang every morning at this hour. All farmers are early risers, of course, but at 4:45 it is too early to be milking cows, and too dark to be doing anything else. Yet this was the hour at which the monks of Our Lady of Peace routinely left their beds to begin their long, long day of work and devotions. This was the bell for vigils.

There was nothing medieval about the monastery—not in appearance, anyway. The chapel was a plain, angular affair of red brick; the refectory and dormitory were squat rectangles. The outbuildings were no different from any other farm in the area, with one notable exception. The barn—very old, very weather-worn, and noticeably listing—was adorned on one side with a vivid white cross. The monks' cowls and tunics, their prayers and their daily routine had changed very little over the last thousand years, but Our Lady of Peace was not a Gothic, cloistered place.

Brother William, thirty years old and bleary with sleep, hung the bell pull back on its hook and left the belfry. He knelt in the chapel as the other monks arrived, footsteps echoing with the swishing sound of robes.

Father Michael whisked in through the side door, followed by the much taller, much slower Brother Conrad. Except for their cowls and tunics, both men looked completely normal—capable men who would have made a good life for themselves anywhere. This was not true of all the brothers. One who now took his place nearby was stricken with leukemia, currently in remission. Another suffered from a hunchback, and crossed the chapel toward his kneeler in a crablike, scuttling motion. And as for Brother Martin, a great barge of a man who was in charge of the farming operations, he wore a patch over the hollow in his face where his right eye used to be.

Of the sixteen monks who lived at Our Lady of Peace, only three had physical deformities. Brother William knew it was uncharitable, but part of him considered these wounded creatures as a separate category. He identified himself with Father Michael and Brother Conrad—strong, capable men who had come to the monastery purely out of choice, men who had left worldly futures behind them. He pushed this unworthy thought away as Father Michael gave the signal to rise and, once they began to sing, forgot about it entirely.

When vigils were over, William stopped off in the sickroom to see Brother Raphael, a very old man—over ninety, some said—who was dying of cancer. The ancient monk was lying on his back, hands clasped over his chest. For a brief moment William thought he might actually be dead, until he noticed the tremulous rise of his chest. Brother Raphael exhaled with a rattling sound, as if a dry leaf were trapped in his ancient lungs. William sat beside him and prayed.

For weeks now, Brother Raphael's waking and sleeping had come independently of night or day. He was like an eager traveller who has already set his watch to the rhythms of the country he is soon to visit. The old eyes were sunken, and the thin, papery skin had turned dull grey. Day by day the flame of his existence grew smaller, gave off less light, but showed no sign of imminent expiration. William looked at the face where the skull became ever more visible beneath the skin— the ridge of bone over the eye sockets, the skeletal rictus emerging beneath the cheeks. It was the ambition of every young monk to die an old monk; William was looking at himself, sixty years on.

He made the sign of the cross, about to leave, when the old man's eyes flickered open. He spoke as if he had just nodded off in mid-conversation, and in a voice startlingly clear for one who had suffered so long on the narrow ledge of his own extinction.

"Christmas soon," he said.

"Oh, it's two months yet," William said. "Nearly three."

"Always my favourite, Christmas. More fun than Easter."

"It's just the presents you like."

"No, no. I like the songs." The old monk sighed deeply, and the leaf rattled again. "The presents are good too."

"Can you sit up a bit? I've brought you some tea."

William slid an arm beneath the frail, bony back and tilted

the old monk forward. He could have lifted him with one finger, he weighed so little. Brother Raphael sipped tentatively, then lay back with a gasp. William thought he had fallen asleep, but then that voice, so unsettlingly clear, emerged again.

"Chaos in the gift shop, I suppose."

"Don't go worrying about that. Brother André has everything under control."

"Does he have the cards on display? The Christmas cards?"

"Bit early, don't you think? There's still three months."

"Got all the same ones last year. Not one box of assorted. People want variety, I told him, but he doesn't listen. Bit of a featherbrain, truth be known."

"Brother André is very new. He'll get the hang of things. Would you like more tea?"

Raphael nodded.

William propped him up with one hand and turned his pillow with the other. The old monk took a few small sips from the proffered cup and leaned back with a sigh.

"So difficult, these Internet monks. Television monks. Can't tell them anything."

"We don't have a television."

"Born and raised by the Web. That's why he can't count, can't think ahead. Has he got the cards out?"

"I'm sure Brother André has everything well in hand."

"I forgot I already asked. Sorry."

"It's all right. Is there anything I can get you? I have a few minutes before lauds."

"Now? I thought you meant for Christmas."

There was no chance Brother Raphael would live into December, but William was not going to point that out.

"Yes, for Christmas. What can we get you?"

"New pair of boots. A good sturdy pair, this time. Hole in mine size of a door."

"Really? You want new boots?"

"A barn door. How can I work in the fields?"

"Boots may take a while. Do you need anything right now?"

But Raphael was asleep, as absent as if he had left the room.

William was closing the infirmary door when Father Michael came breezing down the hall. An athletic character, Father Michael, with the air of a man in a dash to get out of the rain. A pair of Adidas poked out from below his habit like a witty remark. He raised one finger and said, "The library," as if announcing a lecture on the subject.

"Yes, Father?"

"You can expect a visitor. A writer of some sort, a woman. She's researching something to do with medieval monasteries, I forget what."

"A woman? Will one of the Sisters be accompanying her?"

"What would the Sisters know about our library?"

"Nothing, Father. I just thought—"

"She'll be on her own. I want you to be as helpful as possible."

William felt a slight tremor.

"Father, maybe Brother Conrad should help her. He knows the library almost as well as I do. I'm not very good with strangers. Besides," he added with relief, "I'm supposed to help Brother Martin with the sheep this afternoon."

"Brother Martin can manage without your assistance. I'd rather have you in the library while our visitor's here. Not that she'll be any trouble. Her references were very favourable."

"Father, could you please ask Brother Conrad? It's just ... I don't know. A woman ..."

"You're not worried about temptation, are you?" Father Michael looked at him with something close to scorn. "After ten years? Have more faith in yourself, William. I certainly do."

A word began to repeat itself in William's brain, over and over: *obedience.*

"I'm sorry, Father. Of course I'll be glad to help her. If you tell me what she's researching, I could have materials ready ahead of time."

"It won't take you five minutes to find anything she wants. We're not the Library of Congress."

"No, Father." William cast his eyes down in the monk's humility; he mustn't imagine he was the world's greatest librarian, when he was so utterly insignificant, a nothing.

"Frankly, I'd be surprised if we have anything that isn't available on the Internet." Father Michael jerked his head toward the infirmary. "How is he?"

"The same. I don't think Brother Raphael realizes he's dying."

"Nonsense. Of course he realizes."

"He wants a new pair of boots for Christmas."

"Did he say that?" A slight smile crossed Father Michael's face. "I expect our good brother was just teasing you. It's his way of saying he needs nothing. Needing is over for him."

"Oh. Was I being literal-minded again?"

"There are worse faults."

Father Michael flashed another smile, then swept along the hall to the infirmary, his robe flapping around him like a personal storm.

William picked up a towel from his cell and went to the lavatory to wash. The other monks were already in chapel; he had all twelve sinks to choose from, but he stood before the same tiny mirror he had used every day for ten years.

A woman.

Maybe she would be ugly, he thought, then immediately castigated himself; it was not a kind thought. He had taught himself long ago to look on the bright side of any task he approached with reluctance, and this one had a side that was very bright indeed: he was getting out of sheep duty.

William hated working with the sheep. They were exasperating creatures, and accident-prone—always discovering new ways to kill themselves: ambling off cliffs, or cutting their throats on barbed wire. Disgusting too, with their mange, their abscesses, their incessant worms. William had never expressed his disgust, but somehow it was no secret that he was happiest in the library. He was no scholar anymore—his previous interest in history was long forgotten and, apart from religious works, the only books he read were mystery novels. But he still knew his way around a library.

He shaved quickly and joined his brothers for lauds. Singing the daily office was the core of a monk's existence, and the brothers of Our Lady entered the chapel at least six times a day: for vigils, lauds, sext, none, vespers and, of course, daily Mass.

There were eight monks on William's side of the chapel and seven on the other. On his right, Father Michael sang in his clear tenor, a sweet voice for so brusque a man; on his left, Brother André sang in his shaky, uncertain way. But it didn't matter, they were praying, not performing.

> *This God is our God for ever and ever;*
> *he shall be our guide for evermore.*

Phrase by phrase, the world began to recede, and William's heart became lighter than air.

When the monks were filing from the chapel, Brother William waited for Brother André, who was attending to the sanctuary lamp. This was the lamp found in all Catholic churches, a simple oil lamp encased in a hanging red globe, burning day and night before the altar to symbolize the presence of God in the tabernacle. It was one of André's duties to make sure it was always filled with oil. If it were not alight, that would mean God was not present.

Brother William held the door open for the young postulant.

"You're looking so cheerful," André said. "How do you manage it every day?"

"Drugs, Brother André. Drugs. A small injection every morning before lauds."

André grinned, showing bad teeth, and the two monks entered the stainless steel clatter of the kitchen.

William poured corn flakes into a small tin bowl and carried it to an alcove where the other monks were eating in silence. Talk was not allowed at meals, but the alcove was cozier than the refectory, and William liked eating here. He ate quickly, rinsed his bowl, then hurried outside.

The sun was still not high enough to reach the courtyard. Brown leaves skittered across the flagstones as William made a brisk diagonal toward the library. He stepped smartly round a puddle of last night's rain, the edges filmed with ice.

Someone had left lights on in the library. It was only just 7 a.m.; he hoped they hadn't been on all night. The doors were never locked, but it was understood that the library opened when William got there and closed when he left. He would have to remind his brothers about the lights.

He pushed open the glass doors, and it was like coming upon a small animal in the forest. Behind a long table, a woman leapt up from her chair and stared at him with dark, alarmed eyes.

TWO

IN THIS FIRST moment of mutual surprise, William had time only to register that she was a compact, contrasty being, black clothes against very pale skin.

"Good morning," he said, relieved that he didn't sound as startled as he felt.

"I know it's early. Father Michael said I could set up in here. The door was open." Her voice was like a boy's, with a breathy buzz.

"That's okay. We get up pretty early around here," William said. "Welcome to Our Lady of Peace. I'm Brother William."

Her initial nervousness had vanished. She said her name as if it were a neutral fact, unconnected with her.

"Lauren Wolfe."

"Father Michael tells me you're a writer. That must be wonderful."

Her shoulders gave a little hop under black denim. "It has its moments."

She had a very direct stare. William directed his own gaze to the floor.

"And you live in Corning?"

"New York City."

"How nice. I have a brother in New York."

"Then you know what a dump it is." She tore a page from a spiral notebook. "Your abbot said you'd be able to help me."

"Prior," William corrected her automatically. "We're not big enough to be called an abbey, so we can't have an abbot. Father Michael is our prior."

"I'm looking for stuff by Peter Abelard," she said. "The medieval philosopher? Some of his work's not available in New York— not in English, anyway." A small hand rose to her mouth as if of its own accord, and she chewed on a knuckle.

"Isn't his work available on the Internet? He was a pretty important philosopher."

"A lot of it is. Some of it isn't."

The monastery did not have a computerized catalogue. William went to the card file and started flipping through the *A* drawer. The woman stood on the other side of the big oak cabinet and pushed a list across to him. Her dark eyes—sad eyes, he noticed—barely cleared the top.

William scribbled numbers next to her neat script, not looking at her. Such sleek hair she had—a bit darker than honey blond. And those eyes.

When he spoke, he tried for a businesslike tone. "We have some of these. They'll be this way, if you'd like to follow."

He went past the study carrels and down an aisle of theology that stretched to the far wall. The woman trailed behind him at a wary distance.

"We've got miles of Aquinas," he pointed out. "You sure you wouldn't rather do him?"

"No, thanks. I'll stick with Pete."

Peter.

Peter had been Brother William's name before he had taken holy orders. It was like hearing the name of a loved one who had died.

They stopped at the farthest aisle, and William stepped onto a small ladder. As he searched the top row of books, he became aware of a strange scent. Over the library smells of paper and glue, a dark, exotic fragrance bloomed. It evoked in his mind obscure images, dreams dimly remembered.

"Goodness," he said. "What is that extraordinary smell?"

She tilted her face up to him. Her nostrils flared almost imperceptibly. "I don't smell anything."

"It's wonderful. Like incense."

She plucked at the lapel of her jacket. "Maybe it's my perfume. I'm not wearing any, but it's probably in my clothes."

A blush burned its way up William's face, and he pretended sudden absorption in the books.

"You have a good sense of smell," she said. "It's myrrh. They do use it in some incense."

The purpose of perfume was physical attraction. A monk should not notice such things, and William was mortified that he had commented on it, even innocently.

He extracted Luscombe's translation of the *Ethica* from the shelf and blew the dust off, found a second volume, handed them down to her, and climbed down from the steps.

She followed him back out to the front and sat down with her trophies at the long reading table. She opened one of the books and leaned over it so that her hair swung across her face. She tucked it behind her ear, picked up the pencil and clamped down on it with small, perfect teeth. It was as if William had ceased to exist, she was immediately so absorbed in her reading.

He watched her from behind his counter. He was feeling a little edgy, as if the myrrh had crept into his blood. Myrrh, he knew from the gospels, was associated with death, with mourning.

He busied himself sorting the trolley and steered it around from stack to stack, reshelving books. His visitor didn't stir. She chewed her pencil, made a note and put the pencil back in her mouth.

An hour later, William had finished restocking the shelves and went on to cataloguing a stack of prosaic acquisitions: *Successful Sheep Raising, Goat Husbandry, The Modern Way,* that kind of thing. His visitor never looked up. She remained motionless except when she jotted something in her notebook. She was left-handed, he noticed—though why he should absorb such a trivial detail, William couldn't fathom; he would never have noticed it in a man. Those sad brown eyes were getting to him. He said a little prayer to the Virgin to keep his thoughts pure, and resolved not to look at Miss Wolfe again before next bell.

He kept his resolve: he didn't look at her, but it seemed hours before he was released from this miniature vow by the nine o'clock bell.

"Excuse me," he said. "Will you be joining us for Mass?" She might have been deaf for all the response he got. William cleared his throat loudly. Still she didn't notice. He shifted in the light and cast a wedge of shadow across her book. She jerked upright.

William waited for the look of fear to leave her face.

"I'll be going to Mass now," he said gently. "You can stay here if you like, or you're very welcome to join us."

"I'll stay here, if it's all right."

He indicated a stack of five books on the end of the table. "More Abelard for you."

"Thanks," she said, but made no move toward them.

As he was crossing the courtyard, Brother André caught up to him, reeking of sheep and disinfectant. "Is it true you've got a woman in there?"

"I haven't *got* her anywhere. She's visiting from New York. Using the library, that's all."

"She came all the way here from New York? Is she young? Old? Fat? Thin?"

"Please don't talk about it, André. We have more important things to think about."

"You're right. I'm sorry." Brother André stopped at a stone outside the chapel door and scraped field muck from first one boot then the other. "It's just I've never heard of a woman in here. Is she nice, I hope?"

"Nice enough," William said, then added, "Not very happy, though."

"Oh, well. She'll feel better after Mass."

William smiled at the young postulant and opened the chapel door.

Half an hour later, he was making the reverse diagonal across the courtyard, whistling through his front teeth. Sunlight slanting over the refectory roof cast a razor of shadow across the flag-stones. It was astonishing to William that there had been a time in his life when Mass was not important. But that had been a life utterly without proportion, a life of chaos. Now, Mass always restored him, as if it somehow adjusted his sense of balance: the horizon swung level, the planets clicked into place, and the day, no matter what the weather, was rinsed clean.

William had offered a brief prayer after Communion that his visitor might find peace; sorrow clung to her like the scent of myrrh. He could hear it in her voice. Maybe if he could make some small contribution to her work, it would cheer her up a little.

But when he entered the library, she wasn't there. Her absence at the table made a still life: her books and papers were spread open, the empty jacket, small as a child's, hung from the back of her chair. Abelard's *Yes and No* was propped up against other books, with her notebook and yellow pencil at angles beside it. He was close enough to see her neat, square handwriting, but he did not try to read it. A hint of her perfume rose to him from her jacket. Instantly, the scholarly paraphernalia, even the pencil, became female, alluring, and William retreated behind the safety of his counter, where he ordered a dozen books one after the other without so much as a pause.

He was finishing up the last of these when his visitor's boyish voice wreathed through the noise of his keyboard like smoke.

"Excuse me ..." She waited for him to stop and look up. "Do you mind if I ask you a few questions?"

She was leaning over the counter, notebook in hand, eyebrows raised in inquiry. Her arms were thin; the slight biceps, where they emerged from the sleeves of her T-shirt, were even paler than her face.

"I thought Abelard would answer all your questions."

She shook her head. "He's just background to something else I'm writing. How does your prior decide whether someone really has a vocation?"

It would be best not to talk to her—an attractive woman, best avoided.

"Father Michael would be the one to ask about that."

"I know, but what do *you* say?"

Really, he didn't want to get into a discussion. Something about her—he could not have said what, exactly—tugged at his heels like an undertow. But there was obedience to consider. Father Michael had told him to help her in every possible way. So he told her that judging one's vocation was up to the individual person; no one else could be certain one even *had* a vocation.

"But what if the individual is mistaken—or lying, even?"

"Lying?"

"Héloïse says in her letters that she fooled her abbess and everyone else into thinking she was holy."

"Maybe she *was* holy."

"She didn't think so. She couldn't think of anything but Abelard. Even when she was supposed to be praying, even during Mass."

He explained to her how holiness could take different forms, that a lot of the saints were passionate people, and that Héloïse had almost certainly had a vocation, stronger than she knew.

"But she was so miserable. Isn't there some test, some rule the abbess could apply to weed out someone like that?"

God is testing me, William thought. He not only makes her attractive, he makes her inquisitive. His instinct was to run for the hills, to keep running and running until Lauren Wolfe was long gone from the monastery. And yet, *Not my will*, he thought, *but Thine*, and patiently explained the stages of cloistered life. He felt as if he were babbling; he hadn't uttered so many sentences together in years.

"So you have this progression," Miss Wolfe said. "Now, the guy wearing regular clothes..."

"That's Clement. He's a lay brother."

"And the one wearing the blue robe?"

"Brother André. He's a postulant. If he chooses to renew his vows—I believe he's due in a couple of months—that'll be for two years, and that's called the novitiate. It's only after those two years that you decide if you want to take final vows."

"And those are for life."

"For life, yes. But it's much safer than marriage. People who get engaged can't really know what they're getting into—there aren't enough steps to the altar. We lost two men, just last year, in their novitiate."

"Was it their decision, or were they asked to leave?"

Was there no end to her curiosity? He explained to her in general terms how one fellow had just decided he couldn't stand the monastic life, and Father Michael had felt the other man's personality was unsuitable.

"Was it a sexual problem?"

"Um. No."

Blushing was another thing William had not done in years, and now he blushed for the second time in one morning. What power in this slight entity, that she could affect his circulation, bring this sudden heat to his skin, without so much as touching him.

She gave him that direct stare again. "It must have been traumatic, losing two guys in one year. There aren't that many of you."

"Well, there are sixteen of us, so it's not so bleak, really. And we have Brother André coming along."

Meeting her gaze for a moment, William was drawn to the sad eyes, the pretty face. He looked down, disengaging himself the way he would have turned from a pagan ritual, no matter how compelling the words, how gorgeous the art.

"Thanks," she said, and snapped her notebook shut. She left the counter, and William swivelled around with relief to resume his work. The clicking of his keyboard nearly vanquished the hum in his ear, the appealing buzz of her voice.

When the bell rang for sext, he left her at the table without repeating his earlier invitation.

The monks were singing their second Psalm before he noticed her at the back of the chapel. His heart gave a little chime of happiness. She wasn't singing, but seemed to be reading the Psalter with concentration; her eyelashes were tiny dark crescents.

He didn't give her another thought until sext was over and he was heading with the others into the refectory for lunch, their main meal of the day. Male visitors were allowed to take meals with the monks, but women were expected to eat at St. Bridget's convent up the hill or make their own arrangements. He wondered what arrangements she had made.

When the monks were seated, Brother Conrad climbed the stairs to the corner lectern. A radio announcer in his former life, Brother Conrad had a deep, clear voice that made anything he said sound extra important. He read from the Rule of St. Benedict while the food was relayed silently along the table from one monk to the next. The noon meal always began with a paragraph from the Rule.

"The sixth step of humility," Conrad read, "is reached when

a monk contentedly accepts all that is crude and harsh and thinks himself a poor and worthless workman in his appointed tasks."

If I had kept that in mind, William thought, I would not have sounded off in that pompous way to Father Michael, going on about needing to know what their visitor was researching.

"He must say with the prophet, 'I have been brought to nothing, and did not know it. I have become like a beast before You.'"

Brother Martin pointed to the butter, and William passed it to him. *A beast, a nothing, that's me all right. So pretentious to think I could help a writer from New York.*

Brother Conrad's bass continued through the overhead speakers. "*The Vatican Bank*, Chapter Five." A work highly critical of Rome.

William loved being read to. Silence at mealtimes was not, as outsiders might think, an isolating practice. With everyone listening to the same text, the same voice, you were all focused on the same wavelength. The absence of idle chatter freed the air of static, kept the mind precisely tuned, and, as with most aspects of life at Our Lady, it was an efficient use of time.

Afterward, William and André stood outside on the refectory steps and stretched. Brother Martin hove up beside them, large and bald, grim as a destroyer. The black patch over his right eye enhanced the nautical effect. "We could use another hand in the field this afternoon," he said darkly.

"I know," William said. "But Father Michael has asked me to stay in the library."

Martin fixed him with a glittering blue eye. "It's no picnic dipping those animals."

"Maybe you can get Clement to help."

"Clement isn't strong enough. Can't this woman find her own books?"

"It's not my choice. If she finishes early, I'll come and help you."

Brother Martin cruised slowly away into the sun and growled over his shoulder, "We'll be in the south quarter."

"Don't mind him," Brother André said. "One of the rams kicked him this morning." He pointed to a small figure coming up the orchard road. "Would that be our visitor?" Her black clothes moved like an ink blot across the tortoiseshell hill.

"Yes, that's her," said William.

"She's all in black. Like a nun."

"Hardly. Nuns don't go around in jeans."

"Maybe she's in mourning. You said she was unhappy."

William started toward the library. "See you at none."

"Did you manage to get some lunch, I hope?" he asked when she came in.

"Yes, thanks." She went straight to her table without so much as a glance at him, and William had a fleeting sense—a huskier tone in her voice, a tenser set to her shoulders—that she had been crying. But she settled easily back into her books, switching on her concentration like a lamp.

His visitor worked on in silence, sometimes scribbling furiously, sometimes chewing thoughtfully on her pencil. William hadn't enough work to keep himself busy. He tried to read Cardinal Newman's autobiography, but his mind kept wandering. A detective story might have held his interest, but monks were expected to read only serious books until after vespers—then out came the Clive Cusslers and Dan Browns.

The library was still, except for the pleasant hum of the fluorescent lights and the occasional sound of a turning page. A crow was cawing in the courtyard. One hour went by, then two; William began looking forward to none. He was aware from time to time of a faint ache in his chest.

At three o'clock, he left her and went to the chapel: three short Psalms, over in ten minutes. When he came back, she hadn't moved. He spent the rest of the afternoon dusting shelves. The ache in his chest came and went like the feeling of an oncoming cold.

At five o'clock, he said, "Normally I start putting things away about this time. Are you finished with the books, or shall we leave them out for tomorrow?"

"You can take them," she said. "I'm going back to the city tonight."

He felt the floor shift slightly, as if the tiles might suddenly open. He managed to say, "Perhaps you'll visit us again sometime."

"Not likely. Monasteries aren't my kind of thing."

William picked up the books. There was one missing. "What have you done with the Gilson biography?"

The change in her expression was instantaneous. The brown eyes went black. "I didn't steal it, if that's what you think."

William stammered, "I didn't mean to sound so accusatory—it's just, you know what they say."

"No, I don't know what they say."

"'A misfiled book is a lost book.'"

She dropped her bag on the table and headed into the stacks. She came back with the book, offering it in evidence, an attorney approaching the bench.

"Really, Miss Wolfe, you mustn't think—"

"Take it."

She thrust the book at him. He noticed a scar across her wrist. Her skin was transparent, showing delicate lilac veins. The scar crawled over them like a livid worm.

She knew he had seen and jerked her hand away the moment he'd taken the book. She slung the bookbag over her shoulder and strode toward the exit.

William watched through the window as she crossed the courtyard, all but hobbled by the bookbag. It was far too heavy for such a small person.

THREE

ENTER *LAUREN WOLFE* into a search engine and it will garner several hundred thousand hits. Although she has no website or Facebook page, anyone consulting the Directory of American Authors—or even Wikipedia—will find that she was born thirty-two years ago to Dr. Laurence M. Wolfe and Rachel Leightman, that she received an MA from Harvard, and that she is the author of three novels and one volume of poetry.

The entry is more interesting for what it leaves out. It does not say, for example, that her father, Dr. Wolfe, is Head of the Pancreatic Oncology Department at Cedars-Sinai hospital. Nor does it say that her mother is one of three heirs to the Leightman Department Store fortune (originally Leightman Furriers). It certainly does not say that Dr. Wolfe left the heiress for a younger woman when their high-strung daughter was only eight years old. And it most emphatically does not mention that at the age of twenty-two, and following a relatively trivial disappointment, Lauren Wolfe took the bus to her mother's place in Southampton and opened a vein in her wrist.

Lauren was trying not to think about that now. She had been

doing fine until that librarian monk had stared at her scars. Now she was lugging her bags across the parking lot of the Shady Pine Motel, having just checked out, and was anxiously hoping the bus would arrive swiftly and carry her back to civilization.

The only indication that the motel parking lot served as a bus stop was a tin sign, one foot square, with a picture of a skinny dog on it. Lauren let her bags down on the gravel near the sign and pressed the snaps of her jacket together. It was getting chilly; the sun was pasted above the hills, a grey wafer smudged over with clouds. The hills surrounded you up here, and exhaled a clammy vapour that Lauren supposed was fresh air.

She had been looking forward to the monastery. The truth was, she probably could have secured permission to use Abelard translations at Columbia University, but she had wanted to get a sense of the monastic life first-hand, even if she ended up not using it for the book. The monastery had turned out to be so prosaic it was disappointing. She had expected row upon row of monks to be studying obscure texts, but they had mostly been out in the field or in the barn. And she had expected them to be more severe; she had been surprised to learn that they spoke to each other. She'd read somewhere about an order that never uttered a word, and slept at night in their coffins.

Lauren considered her own life quite monastic, although she numbered among her virtues neither obedience nor chastity. As for poverty, well, she didn't much care about owning things, and these monks looked pretty well fed. But their abstention from the trivialities of daily life seemed admirable, as did their self-sufficiency. And it looked a peaceful life. On the other hand, all that praying would have bored her to death.

She lit a Marlboro, wondering vaguely if the monks were

allowed to smoke. Fresh air spoiled the taste, but you couldn't smoke indoors anywhere these days, and she had a superstition that lighting up would make the bus come sooner. The wildness of the surrounding hills was making her nervous. She imagined a woman fleeing through the woods: steel jaws snapped shut, and a scuffed white Reebok filled with blood.

Two cars sped by, small as cats, not the snarling predators of New York but miniature, tame cousins.

A few minutes later, the Greyhound appeared around the curve and Lauren raised her hand. The bus rolled into the parking lot and stopped. Lauren had to walk a gauntlet of eyes, feeling every glance like a blow, before she found an empty seat.

Across the aisle, a woman with a face like a Gila monster flicked her tongue out to moisten a finger and turned the page of her *Cosmopolitan* magazine: "Ten Ways to Keep Your Man." All of them healthy and dignified, no doubt. Not, Lauren thought, that health and dignity were her own strong points; she was too fond of sex. One of her major revelations at university, next to the works of Virginia Woolf and Sylvia Plath, was that when she was really depressed, sex was the only drug that worked. Perhaps it was being away from home for the first time that had made her so susceptible; she didn't know, and her therapists had not proved a huge help either. All she knew was that when the world turned cold and black, the identity of her partner—male, female—even her personal safety, paled into insignificance. She was not proud of it, but she did not hide this truth from herself.

She put in her earbuds and fiddled with her iPod. The bus was pulling away with a grinding of gears and a hiss of brakes. Outside, a monk hurried up the road from the monastery, cloak flying, almost at a run.

It was the librarian, whatever his name was. He saw the bus pulling out and stopped running. His shoulders sagged, his face went slack. He ran a hand over the brown fuzz that bristled on his scalp. He squinted as the bus went past, trying to make out the passengers through the tinted glass. The medieval garb looked surreal beside the highway, as if he had just materialized from the fourteenth century, having crossed oceans of time on some frightening, urgent mission.

Lauren riffled through her bag. No, she hadn't forgotten anything. She turned and watched him grow smaller and smaller, still looking after the bus. Unlike some of the other monks, he was not a bad-looking man. In normal clothes, and with a little more hair on his head, he might even be attractive. And he had a gentle, soft-spoken manner that had made her feel at ease. (Except for the episode over the book, but by now she had put that down to her own paranoia; she was prone to sudden outbursts of anger.)

A sombre adagio throbbed over the iPod. Long, damp hills rose and fell across the road, and Lauren wished it were snowing. The bus's heating system gave off a tinny smell that dried her nose so it hurt. She wished she had an iPod that could play back a weather system of her choosing. The hills would vanish behind the blizzard she would dial up.

Lauren's thoughts drifted to Brother William. What had gone wrong in his life? she wondered. What had driven him to commit his own form of living suicide? He had been all in a flutter about the missing book and then suddenly he'd gone still and pale, seeing her wrist, as if he were having a vision.

Most people didn't notice that jagged white line, but Lauren noticed it every day; she saw it first thing in the morning when she washed, and often found herself tracing the scar absent-mindedly with her thumb.

She fingered it now.

Even though ten years had passed, Lauren knew all too well that she was not over the suicide business. When she was blue, the memories came back—the note, the blade, the waking in hospital.

And lately, for no reason readily apparent, she would open the bathroom cabinet looking for an aspirin and find herself staring fixedly at the battalion of vials ready to kill her. Just last month she had come home from the drugstore and was astonished to find among her purchases of dental floss and unscented soap—among the toothpaste, tampons, mouthwash and emery boards—a pack of Wilkinson razor blades. She had no memory whatever of buying the blades, didn't even know you could still get them.

"Are you all right?"

It took Lauren a moment to remember where she was: the bus, the trip home from the monastery. The bus must have stopped somewhere, because there was a boy sitting beside her now. She hadn't even noticed him get on. He was looking at her with a worried expression.

"Can I do anything?"

"No. Thanks."

Lauren squeezed by him and made her way unsteadily to the back of the bus.

The lavatory was hardly more than two feet square and everything in it was stainless steel. Even the mirror was steel. Lauren's reflection swayed in its depths, dim and underexposed, a prisoner trapped in a steel oubliette. Even leaning forward, she could hardly see the tears that rolled in hot twin tracks down her face.

FOUR

BEFORE HE DISCOVERED his vocation at the age of twenty, Brother William had been Peter Meehan, a lonely student at an undistinguished college on Long Island. His mother was dead and his father, a former homicide detective, had taken to drink, walling himself up in a fortress of silence from which he rarely emerged, unless it was to rage at his boys over some perceived sin. For much of their childhood, Peter and his older brother, Dominic, had been raised by a maiden aunt, a well-intentioned woman of plain face and iron-bound virtue, who did nothing to sweeten their father's temper. Peter endured his rages the way a faithful dog waits out a storm, nerves shaken but loyalty intact.

Going to college was Peter's first time away from home. Before that, he had not even been to a summer camp. Drink had forced his father to retire early on a half pension, and what little money he had left over after mortgage payments was squandered on alcohol. Peter chose Luce College because it was the only place to offer him a full scholarship. His continued enrolment there depended on his achieving the respectable if unremarkable grades he had managed all through high school.

His aunt, having raised no children of her own, had become overprotective of her two adopted sons. Dominic had responded to her restrictions with anger and resentment, Peter with absolute compliance. He had never attended a school dance, and although several girls had made his heart flutter with no more provocation than coming within a range of twenty yards, he had never had a girlfriend.

As a remedy for loneliness, he adopted constant study. He had no passionate devotion to any particular field; his courses were a mixture of the humanities, with a slight bias in favour of history. While other students were dancing at parties, or skiing in Vermont, Peter remained in the library, often until midnight. Ensconced in a carrel, he didn't have to endure the sight of couples kissing, of couples walking hand in hand; he didn't have to endure the envy he felt of those other boys, who were always accompanied by girls.

When the library was closed, he alleviated his loneliness by helping out in the college chapel. He was too old to be an altar boy, but they found volunteer work for him: organizing various fundraising activities—raffles, book sales and dances in which he did not participate. He became friends with the pastor, Father Gage, a balding, pot-bellied man for whom the college chapel was just a pleasant distraction. Father Gage's full-time work was at the parish in nearby Southampton.

Hard study did not quite vanquish Peter's loneliness, but it did pay off where grades were concerned. After mid-term results were handed out, a classmate, Cathy McCullough, caught up with him in the hallway. "You have to tell me how you pulled it off," she said cheerfully. "It certainly wasn't your class participation."

Peter could hardly bear to look at her. Cathy had a sunny blond face that was an accusation against his own unhappiness.

"It was luck," he said. "I must have just said the right things."

"A three point four is not luck. Your papers must have been terrific." She tugged on his sleeve. "I'm not asking for the fun of it. I really want to know. Why don't we grab a coffee in the cafeteria?"

Five minutes later, he was sitting across from this blithe vision, sipping coffee and talking in just the way he had seen other people do. How many times had he envied such conversations? He wondered now if any of the solitary young men at the other tables envied him. Cathy was a little plump, but she was so pretty and so chipper, how could they not? Sunlight streamed through the windows, and her hair shone like cornsilk.

"It's really very simple," he told her. "You see this, here?" He pointed to a footnote in Cathy's history text.

"Footnotes are so distracting. I never read them."

"Well, the professors do." He reached into his satchel and pulled out Huizinga's *Waning of the Middle Ages*.

"That's the one in the footnote. You actually went to the library and took it out?"

"And you see this, here?" He pointed to one of Huizinga's footnotes and reached into his satchel again.

Cathy laughed. "You're like a magician."

"There's no magic. It's just a matter of putting in the time. Books are like this great chain of knowledge. You read the texts, then you read the books mentioned in the footnotes, then you read the books mentioned in *those* footnotes, until you've pretty much read everything on the subject."

"Good God. That would take forever."

"In a general history, maybe. Not with particular issues, though. Particular battles."

"You must know the library inside out."

"Yes, well— there's not much else to do."

"Peter, there's *everything* else to do! There's always some kind of fun thing going on around here. My problem is, I hate to miss any of it." She touched his sleeve. "But would you show me some-time? The library? I ventured in there once, but it was just so intimidating, I turned and ran."

"It's easy. You can come with me right now if you want."

"You probably think I'm real dumb, right?"

"No," he said solemnly. He wanted to tell her she was won-derful, but the words caught in his throat. The single syllable was all that came out.

That first day, he did indeed show Cathy around the library, the computer catalogue, the reference room, the stacks, the cor-ners most conducive to quiet study. He walked her through aisle after aisle of European History where students, bored or hun-gover, slept in the study carrels, heads down on open books.

Cathy waited a couple of days, perhaps not wanting her inter-est to seem obvious, then she began to show up more and more often in Peter's favourite corner. She arrived at the table with an enormous stack of books, as if true diligence required they be read all at one sitting. She smiled at him but did not talk, and went home long before he did, leaving a pleasant botanical smell in her wake.

The day came when she asked him again to join her in the coffee room, and he accompanied her shyly, bearing three vol-umes of Gibbon for protection. They chatted about their essays for a while, and something Peter said made her laugh hard. She bent forward over the table, and her shining hair spilled around her face with an innocent glory that Peter had until that moment associated with angels, not with human beings. Feeling as bold as a Crusader, he asked her if she would like to go for a walk.

It was late fall; the air had the chill of winter but the smell of autumn. They walked in their scarves and sweaters, kicking leaves along the campus path. From time to time a roar from the sports field would interrupt the stillness, but it could not distract them from each other. They talked in a way Peter had never talked to anyone in his life. He wanted to know everything about her; wanted her to know everything about him.

One night he told Cathy how his mother had died. He was sitting beside her on the hard, smooth bed of her dorm room. "Oh, Peter," she said, and held him like his vanished mother against the swell of her breast. "That's the saddest, saddest thing I've ever heard." She hugged him tight, and won his heart completely by bursting into tears.

By then they were well into one of those campus romances that one remembers years later as having lasted a year but in reality may have been an intense three or four months. They were together all the time. They held hands between classes, and stayed outside in the freezing cold and kissed until their lips were sore. They did not sleep together, however—not even once—because Peter had a dim sense that sex was a high explosive the purity of their love would not withstand. Over the weeks, Cathy became more and more upset about this; she was insecure about her looks, worried endlessly that she was too fat, and finally accused him of finding her undesirable.

Peter did not understand his own feelings, but explained his reticence to Cathy (and to himself) as part of his Catholic upbringing. He thought that she had come to accept this, but one day he returned to the dorm to find she had left him a note. The two of them had exchanged the usual affectionate e-mails of young people in love, but this was the first time she had left him an actual note in an envelope. Somehow, he knew this envelope would not contain good news, and he opened it with dread. What it said shattered him. Cathy had found someone else who cared for her in *all* ways; she would not have time to see Peter anymore.

What a joyless, wretched creature he had become after that. He could not eat, he could not sleep, and in a very short time he could neither read nor think. He ceased to function. For a time— or so he told himself years later—he had even ceased to exist. At the suggestion of Father Gage, he had made a retreat at Our Lady of Peace, and it was here, surrounded by simplicity and fellowship, he had first heard the call.

That was how, shortly after his twentieth birthday, Peter Meehan had died to this world (as the language of Catholic vocation would have it) and his life as Brother William had begun.

Gradually he became known in the monastery as the most gentle monk, the most compassionate, the monk in whom others confided, often when they should have been confiding in their prior. And he prided himself on his gentleness—to the extent that he was allowed to pride himself on anything—and struggled not to let it become a *sin* of pride, but only an accurate self-assessment.

Within a few weeks of his coming to Our Lady of Peace, he had recognized it as the wisest choice he had ever made. He had found happiness, and when the time came, he had no hesitation in taking his final vows. He would never, ever leave.

•

Now here he was, reading in his cell—the cell that had been his home for ten years. His desk was a plain painted board, with an equally plain shelf on which sat his rosary, his breviary and his Bible with the coffee stain on the cover. The side of the desk formed the headboard of his bed, on which a hard, flat pillow bore the indent of his head, but there was nothing in the cell that identified it with William personally. That's what a monk's cell was—the place where you ceased to be you.

He was reading a poem called "Thin Ice." It seemed to be about a girl, a ballerina on skates, performing for some unnamed male figure. Her smile never falters, even as her skates fill with blood. Sitting at his desk, William underlined the final passage:

> *Part of me*
> *Wants to kill me*
> *That's the part*
> *I want to meet.*

He turned the book over and stared for the hundredth time at the photograph on the back. Lauren Wolfe was standing outside, a fire escape behind her. The black-and-white picture made her hair look much darker. She wore a black tuxedo jacket (William wasn't sure if that was a current fashion or a personal eccentricity), and beneath the fringe of her hair the eyes looked out with the wary expression he remembered so well. It drew him in, made him want to comfort her. How could a person with such a pretty face want to kill herself? What a senseless murder that would be.

He flipped back to a grisly poem called "Leg-Hold Trap," in which one girl tries to cheer up another who is caught in a steel trap, her leg torn and bleeding. *He doesn't hate you*, she reassures her friend, *He only wants your skin.*

William rather wished now he hadn't ordered the book. She was a morbid person—even the title proclaimed it: *The Hesitation Cut*. He wouldn't have known what it meant, except that there was a poem with the same title about a practice run at suicide.

He still felt bad about her day at the monastery. He had run after her to apologize for their misunderstanding about the book, but the bus had pulled away just as he got there. He hated the idea that she might harbour ill feeling toward him or, even worse, toward the monastery. He had tried to make up for it by ordering one of her books for the library.

Owing to some obstacle in the online ordering process, the book didn't arrive for six weeks, and in the interim William had thought about Lauren Wolfe less often. But the poems brought her vividly to life; her unhappiness was like a hook in his flesh. He appropriated the image from a poem called "Nervous Systems," in which a father patiently explains to his inconsolable daughter that fish don't feel pain the way we do. Fish have different nervous systems.

> *According to him*
> *She's just trying to swim.*
> *She's just trying to swim*
> *In the air.*

William marked the last two lines with the pencil. He wondered if the fishing story was true. For that matter, had no one told her it was all right to stop skating if you got tired?

He examined the pencil under his desk lamp. He had found it under the reading table the day after she'd left. He had slipped it into his pocket, refusing to consider what such an action might mean. The eraser end was pitted and scarred with Lauren's toothmarks. William clamped it lightly between his teeth, turning it first one way then the other, trying to fit his canines into the tiny dents. It was frustrating in the way one of those pocket mazes is frustrating, where you have to sink several ball bearings into separate notches. And yet putting this pencil in his mouth gave him a queer thrill in the pit of his stomach.

He thought about mailing it to her, but that would look silly: it was just a wooden pencil, not even worth the postage. He wasn't going to keep it, he told himself, he would just look after it for her, until she came back.

He flung the pencil across the desk and left his cell.

Halfway up a hill at the edge of the woods that surround Our Lady of Peace, there is a small triangle of land set apart from the orchards and fields by a white wooden fence. It is the quietest spot in this quiet place, a quarter mile from the nearest dirt road and a ten-minute hike from the chapel; even the bleating of the sheep does not carry this far. The grass is weedy and thick and far too long, and several of the white metal crosses lean at severe angles, but for a monk who has taken final vows, this patch of ground is the only conceivable exit from Our Lady of Peace.

William was among the fifteen monks who gathered there one iron-grey November morning. All were hooded against a flurry of fine snow. A grubby, yellow backhoe was parked nearby.

Now and again the wind plucked sharply at the monks' robes and sent a toy blizzard spinning across the graves.

They had said a requiem Mass in the chapel, and had just now assembled in a tight semicircle beside an open grave. Father Michael stepped forward and turned to face them. "David Tinnick died to the world forty-seven years ago, when he took up his life as Brother Raphael. He brought to Our Lady of Peace his guidance, his sense of humour, and his devotion to God. And now Brother Raphael, too, has died to this world ..."

It made William think of his own name, his own past as Peter Meehan, who had died to this world ten years ago. Where was Peter Meehan now? Was he truly dead to this world, or did he live on, deep inside William, waiting to be called forth?

Father Michael talked on. He spoke of how a monk learns to become nothing. How the process begins with the vow to *own* nothing. Indeed, Brother Raphael lay beside the grave on a plain wooden pallet that was propped across two sawhorses. The ancient monk would take to his grave the habit he had worn for so many years and nothing else—no coffin, no keepsakes, and certainly nothing so vain as brand new boots.

Father Michael stopped speaking and nodded at William. William stepped forward with three other monks and each took hold of a limb. William grasped Brother Raphael's right arm; he had never felt anything so cold. The four monks carried the body in an awkward sidling motion into position over the grave.

They stooped toward the earth like movers lowering a couch. Brother Damian, because of his girth, could not bend over this way without ceasing to breathe. He dropped his leg too soon and the corpse lurched to one side.

André lost hold of the other leg, leaving Brother Conrad and

William to ease Brother Raphael down by his wrists. They let go, and Raphael's right hand flipped back over his head in a carefree wave goodbye. The blue-grey face disappeared.

By the time the graveside prayers were over, William was cold through and through.

Brothers Damian and Conrad stayed behind to fill the grave; the others made their way out through the cemetery gate in a ragged file. Brother André fell into step beside William.

"Poor Brother Damian," he said. "You could see he felt terrible about it."

"He could stand to lose a few pounds."

"It's working in the kitchen does it. It's hard for him, surrounded by temptation like that."

"You're supposed to recognize your weaknesses," William said, thinking guiltily of the book on his desk, the pencil. "You're supposed to take them into account."

"What if your weakness is not recognizing your weakness?"

"Then you must rely on your brothers to point it out for you. In a helpful, constructive way, of course."

"I hate criticism," said André. "That's my weakness." The young monk kept his gaze on the ground. "How long do you suppose Brother Raphael will spend in purgatory?"

William laughed. "How on earth would *I* know? He can't have too many sins to repent."

"When I was in grade school, one of the Sisters told us that a famous saint—I forget which one—was granted a vision of purgatory. He recognized one of the suffering souls—it was a man who had died sixteen years before. Sixteen *years*. And the thing is, this particular man had been a bishop. A bishop! At that rate, I'm going to roast for three centuries."

"I'm sure you'll get time off for good intentions."

It was the talk of weaknesses, and not the talk of purgatory, that stayed with William. He retrieved the book of poems from his cell and went straight to the library, where he behaved toward it with exaggerated detachment. Whistling under his breath, he typed up a call number—he used a gigantic old typewriter for this purpose—and fixed it to the spine with glue and tape. He wished one of his brothers were in the library to see how brisk and businesslike he was being, to note his jaunty whistling, the smart clack of his Underwood.

He typed out a lending card and pocket, which he glued inside the front cover. Then he typed out cards for the Author and Title files.

When the paperwork was done, he slipped the book into place on a shelf of American poets. He returned to the front, switched off the lights and left the library.

He enjoyed a couple of good days after that. He did not even peek at the book. He volunteered for extra duties: he scraped vegetables in the kitchen, pitched in with the cider press, he even helped with the sheep—anything to keep busy. And of course, he prayed: he knelt in the comforting red glow of the sanctuary lamp long after vespers and prayed to the Virgin to keep him pure, to Jesus to help him resist temptation, and to the Holy Spirit to inspire him with exalted thoughts.

Even when he returned a volume of Merton's poems to the shelf and *The Hesitation Cut* crept into the corner of his eye, he didn't pull it down. He was tempted: he wanted to look at that photograph; he wanted to read her words. Several times he found himself staring at the chair where she had sat and had to force his mind in other directions.

Gradually, the ache in his chest dwindled to a smaller, sharper pain, as if a diamond were lodged in his ventricle. People suffered from gallstones all the time, kidney stones too; he could survive this sharp, hard thing in his chest.

Three nights later, William sat on his bed doing a crossword puzzle. He clicked the button of his ballpoint and inked in a word.

Brother André rapped on his door.

"You forgot this in my room the other night." He tossed the yellow pencil onto the bed, where it slithered into the folds.

"That's all right. You keep it."

William had left it in André's room on purpose, hoping to get it out of his sight. Now it had reappeared like a rash.

"I have too many pencils anyway."

Brother André pointed. "But you're using a ballpoint on the crossword."

"It's just the *Post*. They're easy."

Brother André's face stretched into a voluminous yawn, and he wandered off to his own cell.

William took up the pencil and wrote the word in quickly. A pencil, after all, is just graphite enclosed in a length of wood. They paint it and sell it as the cheapest instrument of communication, even throwing in a handy delete function on one end. There was nothing emotional about such a common household item. He wished Brother André were still in the doorway to witness the normal way he could wield a normal object.

Of course, if the object were truly neutral, why would a grown man sit on his bed contemplating every nick and groove along its seven wooden inches? There were the roundish indentations where Lauren had pressed her teeth into it. Higher up, beneath the little tin collar, she had bitten so hard that the yellow skin was broken and raw wood showed through.

He remembered her small teeth, so white that the edges were almost transparent, and he knew that this pencil was anything *but* a common household object. This pencil was a powerful wand: wave it and an apparition materialized, with her wary eyes, her sherry-coloured hair. It had belonged to her, gone places with her, her thoughts had flowed through it, thoughts hot as blood. She had held it in her hand, touched it with her teeth, her lips, maybe the tip of her tongue.

William brought the pencil to his mouth and ran the rough, pitted edges over his lower teeth.

Later, in the dark, he lay awake for a long time.

Toward dawn, he dreamed he was kneeling on a frozen pond. The ice gave way and he plunged into icy black water and saw Lauren Wolfe sinking below him. He swam down and down through the frozen depths and grabbed hold of the rope around her ankle. Now he too was pulled down with tremendous force. He got his teeth into the rope and chewed through it, fibre by frozen fibre, until finally it snapped and Lauren shot to the surface. He burst through the surface a split second later into a brilliant, joyful light.

The bell for vigils rang.

He was still thinking about the dream when he entered the refectory for lunch. Brother Conrad was by the lectern slapping clouds of sawdust from his tunic. Fond of woodworking, Brother Conrad. William sat down, and two monks wheeled carts of food in from the kitchen and began to set hot dishes before the others. William passed the soup to Brother André, hoisted two slices of bread from a plate and sent that along too.

It may have had something to do with the sonority of Brother Conrad's newscaster voice, but even so, William was not prepared for how the words of the Rule would resonate.

"The fifth step of humility," Brother Conrad intoned, "is achieved when a monk, by humble confession, discloses to his abbot all the evil thoughts in his heart..."

Father Michael swivelled his chair from side to side. Every time he did so, a computer screen lined with columns of figures sprang into view behind him.

"Let's be clear about this," he said. "Are you telling me you're infatuated with this woman?"

"I'm not sure, Father."

"Come on, man, look at yourself. Be honest with yourself." Father Michael went still. "Is she the reason you're letting your hair grow longer?"

"My hair?" William touched the top of his head. "I'm just growing it a little longer for winter." But was that the only reason? He *had* been more conscious of his appearance lately, shaving with more care.

"Are you having sexual fantasies about her?"

"Not at all, Father. Nothing like that—it's deeper than that. In fact, I've been praying continuously for guidance from the moment these feelings began, and I believe my prayers have been answered."

Father Michael's eyebrows lifted in expectation.

William related his dream, how he had plunged through the ice and saved the drowning woman.

Father Michael tilted back in his chair. "I fail to see how this answers your prayers for guidance. The woman is on your mind; it's no surprise you dream of her."

"But it's the *kind* of dream, Father. Don't you sense a message here?"

The priest raised a warning finger. "You and I do not run our lives according to dreams. We run our lives according to vows and the Holy Rule. If I pray for guidance and then dream of killing my grandmother, am I supposed to take that as a sign?"

"Of course not."

"Why should you give any more weight to your dream? I'm no psychologist, but I know that dreams are made of wishes and memories and bits of random fluff. I don't like this, Brother William. I don't like it one bit. If this is heading where I think it is ..."

"I sensed her pain the moment I saw her. She's like an animal caught in a trap. I believe I'm called upon to help this woman."

Father Michael sat forward again, peering at him. "How can you help her, other than with prayer?"

"By going to see her. Talking to her."

"You will not. I forbid it."

"Father, she's lost. She's in a wasteland. Completely cut off from God. I feel her desolation—it's like death."

"I'm telling you: abandon any thought of seeing her. You are not this woman's personal saviour."

Clement Smith knocked on the door. "Excuse me, Father ..."

"Not now, man!"

Clement withdrew, and Father Michael jabbed a finger at William. "We are not Franciscans. Our duty is not to minister to those in need. Our duty is to our own salvation, to the contemplation of God, and to show by example that an unworldly life is not only possible but fulfilling."

"Yes, Father, but—"

"To see this woman is to threaten your vow of chastity. To leave this place is to break your vow of obedience. *Nothing* is more important than your vows. Think of all the people who know you, who know that you are sworn to this life. What will they think of you, of the Church, if you throw it over? And what of your fellow brothers? Each of us gives strength to the other by example: if one leaves, all are weakened."

"I wouldn't be going forever. I've no intention of breaking my vows."

"You've every intention. You sit here lying to yourself and to me."

"Father, I swear my intentions are good."

"No doubt when Eve ate the apple her intentions were good. How do you suppose evil presents itself? With green teeth and a foul smell? After ten years in a monastery, can you still be so naive? Temptation is pretty, temptation is charming. It has a soft voice and a sweet smell and it will always look like anything but what it is. Stripped of Miss Wolfe's engaging form, what do we have here? A man about to betray everything he believes in. What a triumph for evil over good."

"She's not evil."

"Of course she isn't. Neither is gunpowder."

William hung his head. Finally he said, "I've been blind, haven't I?"

"Worse. You've been willfully blind."

"Father, help me out of this. I think of her all the time. I ache for her. This has never happened to me before."

"Excuse me, but I believe it has."

How could Father Michael remember? It was so long ago.

"There was another young woman in your life," the priest continued, "before you came to us here. You were every bit as passionate about her. She was perfect, you said. She brought the first real joy into your life. She was lovely and sweet and good— but we both know how it ended. In fact, it's what drove you here. You can't have forgotten."

"I haven't, Father. But I was nineteen years old and I'd had no experience. I didn't know myself. I was totally unprepared for such an emotional involvement. But this is spiritual."

"William, I know there are priests—I've met them—who can be next to the most beautiful woman in the world and see her as nothing other than one more troubled soul. You are not that kind of man. Neither am I."

"But that's *exactly* how I see her. She's so unhappy."

"Let me finish. There are other priests, too many priests, who do not know the limits of their strength and who do not avoid the occasions of sin. You know the ones I mean. They teach in boarding schools, they run group homes, they surround themselves with exactly the temptations they should avoid—God help the children unlucky enough to be in their care. And all the time, you can bet they tell themselves they're helping the very people they harm most." Father Michael flushed with anger at the thought of such priests.

"This isn't lust," William said weakly. "Maybe I don't know exactly what it is, but it isn't lust, and it's not a boyhood crush."

Father Michael took a deep breath. "A man's duty is to find the place where he won't be tempted. And when he's found it, to thank God he's found it, and stay there. To do anything else is asking for trouble. Do not stray from the very place where you are at your best, William."

William looked at the floor.

The priest resumed quietly. "Strength is measured by the tests we pass and fail. This is one you must not fail. I want you to go on a fast, William. Fast for the next three days and pray constantly for clarity on this matter."

"Should I stay in my room, Father?"

"No. This isn't a punishment. You may have soup and juice. Naturally, you will come to daily office, but you are excused from work. I will explain to the others that you have a personal crisis to deal with. You will be in our prayers, and I'll hear your confession the moment you feel remorse. This is a serious matter, Brother William. Very serious."

Back in his cell, William snatched up the offending pencil and broke it in half, then he snapped each of the halves into quarters. He went down to the basement. He inserted a metal bar into the small Gothic door of the furnace and pulled it open. Its heart was a shifting fold of flame, blue as the Virgin's cloak. He tossed the fragments of pencil inside, and they flared up in hissing yellow pennants.

William knelt in the chapel for that entire first day, praying fiercely: for forgiveness, for strength, and also in gratitude that, with the help of Father Michael, he had come to see his error before his vows lay in a shattered heap. When his brothers came in for Mass, he participated, but being embarked on his spiritual housecleaning, he did not feel at one with them.

By the middle of the afternoon he had missed two meals, and a surge of energy fountained from his solar plexus, making his extremities tingle; he channelled this energy into prayer. He prayed all afternoon and into the evening, and by the time he had missed supper, and his brothers came in for vespers, his body felt light and aerated. When he sang, his ears and the tips of his fingers buzzed as if constructed of some celestial alloy. He stayed for another hour after vespers, then left the chapel, feeling shiny and clean as a new blade. Later, he fell into a restless sleep that lasted until the bell woke him for the second day of his fast.

William's first thought on waking was that he had caught a ravaging case of flu. When he tried to stand, his legs shook beneath him. In the chapel, his brothers surrounded him like animated waxworks, figures out of nightmare. How had he ever come to be mistaken for one of them?

Brother André waited for him outside the chapel after sext. "You look like you've been run over by a very large truck," he said.

"Don't talk to me," said William. "Stay away from me."

The young monk's face clouded with hurt. William abandoned him on the flagstone path and crossed the courtyard to the dormitory.

He lay on his bunk feeling as if his innards had been scooped out.

"The others can come and get me if they want," he thought. "I don't care one way or the other."

He lay unmoving through the entire afternoon and into the night, hands folded across his chest. He no longer loved his brothers, he no longer loved his life, he no longer loved Our Lady of Peace. His cell closed around him like a grave.

The third day was his resurrection. He sat up in bed before the morning bell rang and switched on his light. The room leapt to clarity. Overnight, every object had assumed an exuberant individuality: his rosary gleaming on the desk, his Bible with the coffee stain, his cross with the chipped shaft. His cowl and tunic hung on the door; the frayed cuffs and loosening seams had the exaggerated look of a stage costume.

The tiniest objects were impossibly clear. Within the nubs on his woollen blanket, individual fibres snaked around each other like roots, and above the desk, the chipped cross shone like a Crusader's sword. He saw it as an intersection of two lines, Life and Time, a starting point: something momentous was about to begin.

No headache, no tremors, no dizziness now. He pulled on his habit and strode along the corridor with brisk good mornings to all.

"I'm sorry about yesterday, Brother André. Please forgive me."

"That's okay," said the postulant. "You were hungry."

"Hungry?" William laughed. "Hungry is not the word."

Images streamed through his mind as if he were drowning, his life passing before him. Possible futures flashed by: Lauren Wolfe smiling at him, holding his hand—by a river, in a park, on a hill—places he had never seen.

In chapel, he sang with his brothers as if he were still one with them, but he existed in two places simultaneously—with them, and above them. He was drifting over the monastery like a satellite equipped with magnificent lenses; he could switch from a wide-angle view of the sheep-studded hills, the river-creased woods, to a close-up of the worry lines on Father Michael's face. They made a single geography.

He stayed in the chapel all day, leaving only for drinks of water or to use the lavatory. He knelt before the statue of the Virgin, with her mild, heart-shaped face. There was no doubt whom that face reminded him of.

No hunger pangs now. And yet he suddenly felt it imperative to visit the refectory.

His brothers had not moved. Brother Conrad was still reading aloud about the Vatican banking scandal. Awareness of William's presence rippled around the U-shaped table like a breeze across a field of wheat. Heads looked up from tin bowls of soup, spoons halted midway to mouths.

William knew he was behaving oddly; he could see it reflected in his brothers' round eyes. But he was filled with benevolence now; the bitterness of yesterday had evaporated, and he looked at them with love. When Father Michael made a move to get up, William turned on his heel and left.

Twenty minutes later, the priest found him in the chapel.

"I've checked with the kitchen," he said. "They tell me you haven't set foot in the place. What have you eaten in the last three days?"

"Nothing at all, Father. Just water."

The corners of Father Michael's mouth turned white, the iceberg tip of a temper he had struggled over the years to control. "And who instructed you to embark on a total fast?"

"Surely you remember telling me, Father?"

"I told you to restrict yourself to soup and juice—a far cry from no nourishment at all. Are you trying to mortify the flesh? To make yourself sick?"

"Nothing like that, Father. I feel very well."

"Then what were you doing goggling at us in the refectory just now?"

"I felt a sudden surge of love. I wanted to see everyone."

"Fine. Take your surge of love into the kitchen and have some soup. Tomorrow you will eat a full breakfast." He raised a hand, palm out, to forestall objection. "No discussion, Brother William. One might expect such behaviour from a postulant, but not from a seasoned religious like yourself."

When William entered the kitchen, Brother Damian paid no attention. He was slicing up legs of mutton for the next day's stew and ignoring the chatter of Daniel Whaley, a good-natured old coot who helped out with the farming two days a week; his own farm grew smaller each year owing to the compassion of his bank.

Daniel had the habit of referring to himself affectionately in the third person. "So who gets the ticket?" he was saying. "Old Daniel gets the ticket, that's who. Come outside and find a yellow one under the windshield wiper. Up Rochester way that's good for thirty-five bucks. Thirty-five bucks. Guess those city fathers figure let's get rid of the deficit we got here, get old Daniel to make a contribution. Hey, Brother William, how's tricks?"

William nodded, ladling himself some soup.

"Oh, sorry. Forgot you can't talk while you're eatin'. Trust old Daniel, always do the wrong thing."

William sat down, and the first sniff of asparagus soup nauseated him. When this had passed, he tipped a spoonful into his mouth. It spilled over his tongue like hot cream, in a glory of taste and touch. A shudder of pleasure snaked along his spine. He had never tasted anything so wonderful. The sensation involved his whole being, a hot caress from inside. A groan of pleasure escaped William's lips, and Brother Damian swivelled an eye in his direction. Daniel nattered on with amiable derision about the sorry price a bushel of McIntoshes brought these days.

"It's criminal," he said. "When an honest farmer can't make a buck, what you have is a state of affairs that's criminal."

William consumed two bowls of jade-green soup, then floated dreamily off to his cell, where he curled up in a fetal ball and slept through vespers and into the night.

When he awoke, the rest of the monastery was asleep. The hall was dark except for the dull glow of a night light. A peculiar canine noise drifted in from the hallway—somebody whimpering in a dream. A white rhomboid of moonlight shone down the wall and across the tiny desk. The clock said three-thirty.

William got up and opened his curtain wider. A full moon was impaled on the prongs of a yew tree. He faced the room again. The rhomboid of light now flowed right across his desk and over his stained and curling Bible. Nothing seemed accidental—the angle of the book, the brilliance of the moon were full of intent. The cross on his wall hovered above the Bible, pointing to it.

William picked up the Bible. He closed his eyes, opened the book at random and pressed it flat against the desk in a patch of moonlight. He stabbed with an index finger and opened his eyes. He had marked this passage years ago, when he had learned it by heart:

> *If a man has a hundred sheep, and one of them has gone astray, does he not leave the ninety-nine on the mountains and go in search of the one that went astray? And if he finds it, truly, I say to you, he rejoices over it more than over the ninety-nine that never went astray. So it is not the will of my Father who is in heaven that one of these little ones should perish.*

William stood rapt, his skin pale in the moonlight. The room hummed with the solemnity of the moment. Now he moved quickly, smoothly. From his closet he pulled out a small knapsack. He took his toilet items from the shelf—brush, nail clippers, toothbrush—and stuffed them in the bag along with his Bible and rosary. He stripped off his cowl and tunic, rolled them up and put those too in the bag. Throughout all this, he took shallow, nervous breaths, as if his breathing might wake the whole dorm and bring his brothers charging out of their cells like Marines.

He was wearing a pair of beige trousers and a cotton undershirt. It was not cold enough for a winter coat, and he did not own a fall jacket. Except for socks and underwear, his closet contained only one item of clothing—a blue sweatshirt one of his brothers had given him last Christmas. It was a size too big, but it would be warm enough.

He zipped the knapsack shut and slipped it over one shoulder. Then he stepped out of the room and glided silently along the corridor. When he passed the night light, his shadow flared up like a black flame. Brother André whimpered in his sleep, Brother Martin snored, and someone else passed wind.

William stepped outside and shivered. The moon was over the barn now, a bone-white disc that lit the grounds platinum. He hurried across the courtyard, slowing only for a furtive bow to his Saviour as he passed the chapel. In the wash of moonlight, the place exuded peace: the chapel spire, the barn with its cross, and the rime of frost on the rolling hills might have been a scene from a Christmas card. But the peace seemed uneasy, the stillness unnatural.

His boots were loud on the gravel road. Apple trees on either side hunched in rows against the winter. Invisible crows cawed to each other across the dark. William tried to keep his mind blank, but all he could think was: I'm breaking my vow of obedience, I'm breaking my vow of obedience. He could almost hear it crack, as if it were a small bone.

It took him about twenty minutes to reach the highway. The Shady Pine Motel was dark and deserted, only two cars in the lot. A north wind funnelled down the road, and the sweat turned icy where it ran down William's ribs. There was no traffic at all for a couple of minutes. Then a tractor-trailer came barrelling toward him from the north, the headlights blinding. William stood at a confident angle and put out his thumb. The truck whooshed by at sixty miles an hour, stinging his face with grit.

He felt a slight panic. In less than an hour his brothers would be rising for vigils, his absence would be noticed. He didn't know what they would do when they found his room empty; such a thing had never happened before. He squinted toward a sign at the next curve. He couldn't read it from this distance, but he knew that it said "New York City 285 miles." He started walking—he would walk the whole way if he had to. And he might have to. No driver was likely to pick up a lone hitchhiker at four in the morning.

Before he had gone a hundred yards, another truck came round the bend. This one was a small panel truck. William put out his thumb and tried to convey his harmlessness with a cheerful smile. The truck zoomed by, but three hundred yards up the road the brake lights lit up as it slowed and pulled over.

William ran to it and yanked open the passenger door. He was well into an effusive expression of gratitude before he realized with shock that he was not addressing a stranger.

The driver shook his head and slapped the steering wheel with an open palm. "I said to myself, I said, 'Daniel, you're hallucinating! What in God's name can Brother William be doing by the side of the highway at four o'clock in the morning?'"

William climbed in and made three unsuccessful attempts to shut the door.

"Have to pull up on the handle, there."

William did so, and banged the door shut.

"Almost didn't recognize you without your livery. Thought I was seeing things."

"Yes, well—I have to go to New York all of a sudden. It's lucky you came along." It sounded like he meant it.

"Why the heck didn't you take the Blue Bomber?" This was the nickname for the brothers' ancient Taurus station wagon.

"It's not working. Something's wrong with it. The battery, I think."

"Battery? And you couldn't take the bus?"

"I didn't want to wait."

"Must be pretty darn urgent for you to light out in the middle of the night."

"A sick relative," said William, appalled at the ease of the lie. "My brother. He was in a car accident."

"Golly. Not life-threatening, I hope."

"Fifty-fifty, so they say."

"I'm sorry to hear that."

Daniel wrestled the gearshift into place and pulled out onto the highway. He jerked his thumb toward the back. "Just hauling the last of my Cortlands to green market down Binghamton way. They open at six. No point getting there much after, so I set my alarm for three-thirty. Hospital call you?"

"Right. Yes."

"How'd they get through at this hour? I've never been able to get hold of you fellas after suppertime."

"Brother André happened to be going by the office when the phone rang."

Where did all the lies come from? He had stepped through a mirror into a separate universe where truth did not exist, full of non-existent hospitals, fictitious calls, events that had not occurred.

Daniel jerked his thumb once more toward the back. "Help yourself to the apples if you're hungry."

William had forgotten his fast. He selected a medium-sized apple from a bushel behind the seat. With the first bite, the juice burst into his mouth like champagne.

Daniel returned to his opening theme. "And you couldn't take the ChevyVan either? Don't tell me that's out of commission too."

"Wasn't available," William said between ravenous bites. Half an hour out of the monastery, and how many lies had he uttered— five? Six? *Dear God*, he prayed, *don't let me flounder, don't let me lose my way.*

"Darn lucky I came along, Brother William."

"It is. I know."

"Side of the road? Middle of the night?" Daniel shook his head at this bizarre equation. "I said to myself, Daniel, I said, be careful. He looks like some kind of es-ca-pee."

THIN ICE

You loved me on skates
My taste for sharp objects
Pirouettes, figure eights
I knew you liked watching
You knew my feet bled

Part of me
Wants to kill me
And part of me
Is dead

Only once I fell
My smile never slipped
The crowd never guessed
I have a hot red wound
A hot glass heart
For girls
Well and truly doomed
Love is the transparent art
For certain girls
Thin ice is best

I was your daughter
You taught me how to bleed
If summer comes
I'll skate on water
But for now you can read
My crimson
Hieroglyphics

I'll skate away
Let me break
Let me make
Something ragged, something raw
Something difficult to take

I swear by the blades
Beneath my feet
Part of me
Wants to kill me
That's the part
I want to meet.

—Lauren Wolfe

FIVE

"LOOK AT THAT one behind you—an MD, at least. You can tell by the beard."

Lauren didn't turn to look. Naomi trained her sights on the target as she took a sip of wine.

"Guy with him's probably his accountant. I'll go by their table and pretend to faint. As soon as he revives me, I'll introduce you."

"I don't like beards," said Lauren. "Or doctors either."

"That rules out half the acceptable men in New York."

"Half the *Jewish* men."

"Well, excuse me all over the place." Naomi pressed a hand in mock *mea culpa* over her heart. "I didn't realize Brad Pitt had expressed interest."

"Naomi, I wish you'd stop trying to set me up with people. It's not my priority in life to find a husband."

"I suppose you've dedicated the rest of your life to what's his name—to Mick—that estimable man."

"I don't want to talk about it."

"He's so caring, Lauren, so *warm*. He's always *there* for you."

"Naomi..."

"Why are you pining for this brute? He just makes you miserable. What you need to do is find out why you always go for guys that hurt you."

"Naomi, I'm not going into therapy."

"Fine. In the meantime, find yourself a mensch, will you? Someone gentle—someone tender and devoted—that's what you need. And forget about Mr. Musclehead. A musclehead who disappears all the time."

"What's it matter? I'm not going to die without a man in my life."

"Sister Mary Immaculata, here. Speaking of which—I have to tell you, sweetie, a historical novel by Lauren Wolfe is not going to be an easy sell. Publishers don't think of you that way. For them, you're 'haunted,' 'dark,' 'witchy'—those are the words that come up."

"'Witchy'?"

"They mean it in a positive sense."

"I didn't know there was a positive sense."

"As in 'spooky.' You don't fit their bill for historical stuff. When it comes to history, they want someone flower-printy, someone scholarly, preferably someone fat."

"It's good to know they have such high standards."

"I'm just telling you the way it is, honey. That's what I'm here for."

Lauren pulled a Marlboro out of the pack and fiddled with it.

"You know you can't light that."

"Naomi, *stop*. I'm just holding it. And, by the way, it's not a historical novel."

"Bless your heart, I'm so relieved."

"It's not *about* Héloïse and Abelard. It's about a girl who's *obsessed* with Héloïse and Abelard."

"Obsession is good. Obsession I can sell."

"What about foreign rights on the monkey book—did you sell any more?"

The "monkey" book was Lauren's previous novel. The murderer-protagonist keeps three blind monkeys in his kitchen.

Naomi shook her head. "I still have hopes for Sweden, though. And Germany. Germans adore obsession."

"Naomi, I need money. I *really* need money. I owe rent. The landlord's hounding me."

"Why didn't you tell me, for God's sake? I can lend you money. It's not like you're just any client. You think I don't care enough to help?"

"I don't want *your* money. I want to earn *my* money."

"You will. In the meantime, I don't see why you can't accept help from me. You act like I'm going to hold it over you, or something. You think it's self-reliance, but it's rejection, and it's hurtful, and it's insulting."

"My, aren't we sensitive today."

"Oh, yes, Lauren—we all know you're the only one with feelings. Nobody else is allowed to suffer while you're in the room, right?"

Lauren sighed. "Let's change the subject, okay?"

"Like you've cornered the market, or something."

"You're giving me shit because I won't take your money, and it's just too fucking weird, all right? Now can we drop it?"

"Fine."

"You're already taking me to lunch, aren't you?"

"That's not the same. The agency pays."

Lauren diverted her attention by gesturing at the ceiling, which was festooned with tobacco pipes: meerschaums, briars, corncobs—pipes of every shape and size. "What is this decor? Neo-Gentleman's Club?"

"We'll wear tweed next time. Dress like a couple of dykes."

"Don't be mad at me."

"You just exasperate me, Lauren."

The waiter arrived with their food, and talk was suspended while he fussed over them with the pepper grinder. Naomi ordered another glass of white wine. Lauren was drinking mineral water.

"Hey, you never told me about the monk place, the monastery. Why did I never hear about that?"

"You were in Frankfurt or somewhere."

"So what were they like? Did they give you the creeps?"

"Not at all. Not really. They're quiet, they work hard, and they don't need anything."

"Aren't they awfully Catholic? Into the Body and Blood?"

"The prayers were actually pretty Jewish. 'Lead us out of the desert' and all that. It was like being back in Sunday school. I almost laughed out loud when they had a reading about Ezra."

Ezra was Lauren's cat—a keg-shaped tabby of lumbering gait and small ambition. "Apparently Ezra spake unto the people."

"Probably on the subject of Seafood Supper, if I know him." Naomi leaned forward confidentially. "Why don't we go get manicures later?"

"I can't. I have to work."

"My treat. Your nails look like they got caught in the Cuisinart."

"Thank you. But I have to work."

"You think you're suffering from existential angst. Your real problem is you don't do enough *girl* stuff."

"I do girl stuff. I went to Bloomingdale's with you, didn't I?"

"That was six months ago."

"I felt like a bimbo for weeks."

"Have some fun for a change. You could get your nails done all black."

"It makes them taste bad."

"God, you're a pain. Why do I bother? I hardly even like you."

"I know," said Lauren. "Me either."

When Lauren got home, she stopped in the vestibule to collect her mail then walked quietly up to the second floor. The hallway was not carpeted, however, and when she turned the key in her lock, it made a loud, echoing *clack*. The landlord heard and slid out of his apartment across the hall.

"Miss Wolfe. Good day."

"Mr. Zaleski, how are you?"

Mr. Zaleski was sixty, from some part of Europe Lauren hoped never to visit, and much given to self-pity. He had a thick, cylindrical body that tapered to a shining bald head, so that his overall appearance could be described as ballistic.

"How am I? I am worse, thank you." Two fingers, fat as sausages, wavered over the area of his heart as if uncertain of its location. "Every day it hurt me. And doctors…" He waved a hand as if fanning away a smell.

"I'm sorry, I still don't have any money for you."

"Today is fifteenth. First you say seventh, then you say fourteenth."

"I talked to my agent today. She's trying to speed things up."

"One thing you don't pay me. Another thing you lie to me."

"Mr. Zaleski, it's only two weeks overdue. I've been here for three years and my rent's always been on time. I don't understand why you're making such a fuss."

"Everybody else pay on time. Only holdout is you. You know property taxes? Property taxes is killing me."

"Don't worry, you'll get your money," Lauren said, and pushed open her door. "In any case, I'm sure you're raking it in from those horrible little closets you built downstairs."

"No one else owe me money. You are only one. I wonder why it's so."

"What do you mean, why? Because I don't *have* any money."

"Sure, sure, I know." He waved off the bad odour again. Then, sliding back into his apartment and closing the door, he muttered a single syllable: "Jew."

Lauren stared at his closed door, that single syllable reverberating inside her chest. She entered her apartment and stood over the kitchen garbage bin to sort her mail. Ezra butted his head against her ankles while she dropped catalogues, subscription notices and sweepstakes announcements straight into the garbage.

"Hi, Ez," she said absently, and he meowed for a head scratch.

Lauren did not care about being Jewish; she hardly ever thought about it, and had no interest whatever in Jewish traditions. Now, suddenly, it was a source of pain.

She hung up her coat in the closet, careful not to catch splinters from the broken door. She couldn't afford to replace it and wasn't about to ask Mr. Zaleski for any favours; he still hadn't fixed the radiator in the bedroom that blasted out enough heat to warm a stadium. She went to her phone and pressed the voice mail button. A familiar voice, Mick's voice, made her flinch.

"Laur. Laur, if you're there, pick up. You're not there? Listen, I'm sorry. I'm really sorry about what happened."

What happened. As if the smashed door had nothing to do with him, as if it had been an accident.

"I'm not in the city. But I'm thinking about you, and I'm sorry. I know you're sorry too."

Now it was supposed to be *her* fault. Mick always irritated her, but she stood in the centre of the room, transfixed. His Brooklyn accent was more pronounced, disembodied like this.

"I've been thinking, Laur. I've been thinking there's such a thing as the girl or the guy who's exactly right. Maybe there's also people who are exactly *wrong.* Maybe we're just, I don't know, wrong. That's all I'm saying. Maybe we're just wrong for each other, I don't know. Talk to you."

Not that he had left a number to call. And he wouldn't give her his cellphone number—*for your own protection, babe.* Always and everything, on his terms. They would talk when *he* wanted to talk. Lauren deleted the message and bent down to pick up the cat. She carried him to the desk, nuzzling her face into his fur.

"Don't be so smug," she said. "One day they'll come to kill the cats, and then where will you be?"

She sat down at her computer. The cursor was panting at the end of a sentence that brought her heroine, fifteen-year-old Coral, into the house after a date with her boyfriend. The girl was trying to be quiet, but her father waited in the darkened living room. Lauren knew what had to come next—her father bursting from his chair, the slap to her face—but she could not hold it still in her mind.

•

The first thing Mick LeMar had ever said to her was, "You don't look too happy."

They were alone in a small kitchen. The rock music was not as loud in here, and he had spoken quietly.

"What's the matter—you don't belong here?"

"Every once in a while I make an effort at human contact," Lauren had said. "I always regret it."

"Yeah, I don't belong either." He was wearing a work shirt and jeans; everyone else was elegantly dressed. He drank his beer straight from the bottle. "At least you *look* like you belong," he said. "You were probably invited, right?"

"Why, did you climb in the window?"

"As a matter of fact I did." He smiled. "Installing new gates. Big boss was worried about security."

A fat man dressed in baggy Armani entered the kitchen and clapped Mick on the back. "Mick! So happy you could stay!" Then he took Lauren by the shoulders and shook her as if she were a defective radio. "Cheer up, Lauren!"

"I can't, Franco. This is as happy as I get."

"I'm telling you, we are going to make this movie!" He released her and scooped ice into his glass. "We are talking to Columbia, we are talking to Paramount ... I told Thelma Schoonmaker about the project and she's very excited."

"Who's Thelma Schoonmaker?"

"Best movie editor in the world. She cuts Scorsese's movies."

Lauren didn't see what purpose a film editor could have at this stage. And as for talking to Columbia Pictures, well, anyone could call spirits from the vasty deep, but would they come?

"You're worried about the script, I know, but don't worry! We are talking to Paul Haggis, we are talking to Sofia Coppola ..."

"How exciting."

"I am *very* excited. And you must know, Italians make the best movies."

"I always thought Bergman was pretty good."

Franco made a face. "Bergman's dead."

"I like Matt Damon," said Mick from beside the fridge, but Franco ignored him. He raised his glass as he sailed into the other room emitting his battle cry. "We are going to make this movie!"

Mick had the kind of blue eyes you can see across a room. Lauren asked him, "What are you smiling about?"

"I was just wondering if you wanted to maybe shoot a game of pool."

He took her to a place on Nineteenth Street, with elegant cloth lamps that hung low over the tables. There was nothing smoky or tense or even particularly masculine about the ambience. There were two other couples bent over their games, and one table of Asians involved in a solemn round of snooker. Lauren hadn't been near a pool table since her days at boarding school.

Mick demonstrated the proper way to hold the cue without making the obvious move of putting his arm around her. He was patient and serious; he wanted her to enjoy the game.

Lauren had a good eye, and often sank the ball. Unfortunately, the cue ball tended to follow right into the pocket, losing her the point. Mick explained the concept of "English," but any attempt to get fancy caused her to miscue.

"That's okay, Lefty," he said. "It's the only way you get better."

When it was his turn, he would lean into the light, and his whole body would go still. He sighted along the cue with unfussy concentration, making slight adjustments in the crouch of his left hand where it guided the tip. Behind him, his right arm swung from the elbow, back and forth in a relaxed arc. When he shot, it was with a decisive, gentle gesture—a physical *bon mot*—that sent the target ball into the pocket and the cue ball into place for the next shot. Lauren couldn't wait to sleep with him.

After the third game, he set his cue in the rack and said, "Are you seeing anyone right now?"

"There's one guy," she said. "But it's not very exciting."

"Tell him to go away," Mick said. He reached out and tugged a lock of her hair. "I'm looking after you from now on. You won't be needing nobody else."

In the first bloom of romance, their vast differences of class and education had provided an essential element of mystery. They had enjoyed a few good months.

The last time she and Mick had been together, he had lain in the crook of her arm, his head on her breast, half asleep. She was wondering if she should give him his present now or wait until they had done it again. She lit a cigarette with one hand and gently stroked his shoulder with the other. Their flesh was pressed so close and unmoving she could not tell whose legs were whose, and only the sandpaper of his whiskers distinguished his cheek from her breast. The yearning in her blood was for the moment stilled, and she drifted in the gauzy region between sleep and daydream.

"Where did you learn to do that?" she asked.

Sandpaper scraped her nipple, and then Mick was looking at her with soft, bleary eyes. "Red Hook High," he said, his chin digging into her rib. "Had to take math, shop and muff diving."

Lauren tried to suppress a laugh, but her mouth curled at the edges.

"That Mrs. Gifford," he went on. "She was a real slave driver. Gave us a two-hour practical. I couldn't move my jaw for three days."

He looked down and traced a pattern with his forefinger. "The truth is, I read about it in books. I know you think I don't read."

Lauren touched his face. "I never said that."

"You think it, though, Miss Priss that you are."

"Yes, Mick. You're so familiar with my thoughts."

"Miss *Harvard*."

She took a deep drag on her Marlboro. She no longer liked it when he brought up their differences.

He nodded at her cigarette. "Nasty habit there, sister."

Lauren turned her head aside and exhaled the smoke before speaking. "Not as bad as some."

"I thought you were going to quit."

"Did you now?" She tugged at his earlobe. "*I* never did."

"You should. It's bad for your lungs, bad for your heart …" Mick was one of those self-destructive people who are always ready with healthy advice for others.

Lauren stubbed out the cigarette and sighed. "If I quit, all I think about is smoking. I can't see, I can't think, I can't write. And if I can't write, I may as well be dead."

"I quit *my* habit. You think that was easy?"

"You don't have to write." She pushed him onto his back and climbed on to his chest.

"Don't get started," he said. "I have to go."

"You can't escape." She took hold of his wrists and pinned him to the bed. "You're my prisoner."

She leaned down with all her weight, but he raised his arms easily and tipped her off. He got out of bed and disappeared into the bathroom. Lauren felt the sting of rejection, but she was not going to let him know it. Mick did not handle tears well; if she showed the slightest vulnerability, he would turn to stone.

She reached into the night table and pulled out his present, a small rectangle wrapped in paper with a William Morris pattern. It wasn't much, a Black Keys concert DVD, but Mick adored the Black Keys. Unfortunately, she was still smarting from his rush to leave and didn't much feel like handing him a present just now; it would look like she was bribing him to stay. His leather jacket was hanging on the back of a chair. On an impulse she reached for it and tried to push the DVD into a pocket. It was too big, and as she tried to make it fit, her fingers touched a soft plastic packet.

Mick came out of the bathroom and pulled on his jeans. Lauren was standing by the window in her dressing gown, keeping her back to him. It took him a while, but he finally noticed, as he was tucking in his shirt. "You pissed off about something?"

"You told me you weren't dealing anymore, Mick."

He sat on the bed to pull on his boots. "I don't know what you're talking about."

"You've got a pound of dope in your coat pocket. I was trying to shove a present into your pocket. I found it by accident."

"Oh, that. That belongs to Kevin. I was just holding it for him."

She had always imagined criminals to be expert liars. It surprised her how obvious he was; his voice always changed and he looked away with a sheepish smile.

"How many years is that good for, Mick—fifteen? Twenty?"

"I think you better back off, Laur."

"And if some creep decides you're trespassing on his turf, how long before you get shot?"

"I said I think you better back off."

He stood up and pulled on his coat, feeling in the pocket she had invaded. He picked up the present from the night table and unwrapped it, staring at it as if it were labelled in Chinese.

"I don't want to see you in jail, Mick, and I don't want you to die. Is that so hard to understand?"

He broke the package open over his knee and ripped it apart. A disc fell to the floor and he snatched it up. He snapped it into pieces, tossing shiny segments against the wall. He kicked the closet door with a tremendous bang.

"Don't you never—never—touch my things again."

At every other syllable, he kicked the door for emphasis.

"Don't you never—never—tell me what to do."

"Mick, stop," she said faintly, but he kept kicking at the door; he didn't stop until it was a splintered ruin. Mick had never hurt Lauren, not physically. So far, he had only taken out his temper on objects.

The memory released her, and she was once again facing her computer: Coral still tiptoed into the house, her father still waited in the shadows.

Lauren got up and put on her dressing gown. As she crossed to the window, objects in the room—the empty bed, the broken door—seemed to emit a knowing hiss: somebody was in for it.

Across the street, a lost-looking man stood underneath a street lamp. Lauren reached up to lower the blind. The man turned away and disappeared behind a Con Edison truck, and then the street was empty.

SIX

WILLIAM STEPPED BEHIND the Con Edison truck and caught his breath. Even though she had been little more than a silhouette, he had recognized her instantly: the wary posture, and the way she tucked a strand of hair behind her ear. Then she had reached up to lower the blind.

Lauren Wolfe—a strange name for a lost sheep, but he had found his lost sheep at last. His fractured vow of obedience, his midnight flight, had been worth it after all. Even his arrival in New York—a shrieking post-apocalyptic nightmare after the peace of Our Lady—had been worth it.

When the old pickup had finally rattled into Binghamton, kind old Daniel had bought him a bus ticket at the station and left him with twenty-five dollars and the promise of prayers for his brother's recovery. William had been asleep when the bus pulled into Manhattan and only woke when the driver switched off the motor in the Port Authority Bus Terminal.

The place stank of disinfectant, and the ceiling was so low he could have reached up and touched it. A cluster of rough men moved through the crowd ahead of William, drinking from bottles wrapped in brown paper bags. They shouted incomprehensible oaths at one another, and William felt the press of imminent violence, though none occurred.

"Excuse me, sir," a quiet voice said beside him. He turned to see a man lost in a heartbreaking cloud of filth. "Can you help me out? I really need money for food."

William reached into his pocket and handed him three dollars.

The whites of the man's eyes widened. "Hey, thanks."

"Do you have a church you can go to? A priest you know?"

"Oh, yeah, the Friars downtown are real good to us. I may head down there later." The man hobbled away.

William saw several more beggars before he found the exit. Fasting had taught him about hunger, but it struck William that his vow of poverty was a cruel joke. True, he owned nothing, but he had never wanted for shelter, a warm bed, hot food. He lived with friendship and the happiness of productive work, and these alone constituted fabulous wealth compared with the misery he saw now.

A policeman at the exit gave him directions, and William set out on a long walk downtown. During his college days he had made the occasional foray into Manhattan, but he had forgotten the frenetic swirl of the place, the dirt, the speed, the noise. Ceaseless activity everywhere you looked, and yet all disconnected, and endless torrents of traffic. Even though Seventh Avenue was a one-way street, the cars were at war with one another, cutting each other off, honking long and loud, drivers leaning out of windows shouting curses at each other and at the cyclists that were zooming by everywhere you looked. It was like stepping into the mind of a lunatic.

A filthy newspaper clutched William's leg and wouldn't let go until he spun around and walked backwards. A cyclist who nearly hit him yelled, "Asshole!" before pedalling away. Cyclists were everywhere—definitely a big change from his college days—and the Don't Walk signals seemed to bear no relation to the hordes of people crossing this way and that. It all seemed random.

At Herald Square, he crossed over to Fifth Avenue, switching his knapsack from hand to hand as he walked the endless blocks.

The curbs were thick with tin cans, paper cups, old hangers and even odd items of clothing: a sneaker here, a pair of pants there. The air tasted bitter. Pedestrians staring into cellphones collided with one another or stood at the corners, consulting their screens before stepping into the traffic. Everyone looked disgusted. Overhead, the fragments of sky were bright blue, but no sunlight reached the streets; shadows soaked into the pavement like ink.

An hour later, he found the building he was looking for.

The woman behind the counter had blond hair, but her face was severe, as if all the promises made to a woman with such pretty hair had been broken.

"Which officer are you here to see?"

"Dominic Meehan."

"He's with a client. What's your name?"

"Peter Meehan." It was the first time he had spoken his former name aloud in ten years. He felt he had committed an enormity. "I'm his brother."

"Dominic Meehan has a brother? He comes from an actual family?"

"I live out of town."

"Have a seat. It could take a while."

William-Peter sat down opposite a man whose forearms were covered with tattoos and pulled out his breviary. There had been nothing he could do about Mass, of course, but he had read his vigils, lauds and sext on the bus. He turned now to the Psalms for none. This contact with God comforted him, and he went on reading past the three required Psalms until his nerves were soothed.

He looked up when he heard his brother's voice. Dominic was guiding a small black man to the door as if he were blind.

"You have to be patient," he was saying. "You've only been working there two weeks. I'm sure you'll do fine."

"People don't understand. Expect a ex-con to know everything right off. Ain't right."

Dominic was a good eighteen inches taller than his client, with shoulders that sloped away from his head like planks. He had been a pretty good halfback in high school.

"Stay cool, George. Don't take things too personally. You'll be fine."

William-Peter stood up with a nervous smile ready on his face.

When the door swung shut behind the ex-con, Dominic turned and saw his brother. His whole body went still—for two seconds, three seconds, perhaps four full seconds—before he emitted his greeting, which contained neither characteristic sarcasm nor uncharacteristic warmth, but only complete, unfeigned surprise.

"What the fuck are *you* doing here?"

"I'm here to visit someone. A friend of mine is in trouble."

He had rehearsed this answer, but spoken aloud it sounded inadequate. He sensed his brother was ashamed of him, embarrassed by his being a monk; Dominic hurried him out the door.

•

"Since when do you guys hit the road on missions of mercy?" Dominic asked when they were in his car. "Doesn't sound on the up-and-up to me."

"It isn't. Father Michael refused to let me go."

"So you're AWOL. Aren't you in deep shit? What happened to obedience?"

"Yes, well. Things aren't always black and white."

"I find they pretty much are." They stopped for a red light, and Dominic turned to him with a sly face. "This 'someone'— you aren't going to tell me it's a woman, are you?"

"It's true I'm here to find a woman, but—"

"Jesus Christ."

"Dom, it's not what you think. I'm only here because she needs help. Not for any other reason."

His brother expressed skepticism with a snort. "I should have known. Guy suddenly ups and leaves years of sanctity for a trip to the Big Apple? Got to be a woman involved. Of course, in your case the motive is purely Christian."

"Well, think whatever you want. I can't stop you."

"Could never figure out why you joined up in the first place. Never made any sense."

"I've been very happy there. It's not like I've left permanently."

"Uh-huh."

Dominic rested one wrist on top of the steering wheel. A yellow cab veered in front of them, and he hit the brakes without comment.

"There seem to be an awful lot of taxis," William-Peter observed.

"Too many. Listen, how long you planning on staying?"

"I had in mind three or four days. But it may take that long just to find her."

"Find who? She have a name?"

"Miss Wolfe. Lauren Wolfe. She's a writer. Why are you smiling?"

"I can't get over it," his brother said. "First he's on a religious quest, now he's on a romantic quest. Explain to me how those two fit together."

"I told you, it's not romantic. She needs help."

"So you said. It's definitely the most *interesting* thing you've ever done."

"Well, that's never been my goal in life. To be interesting."

"No? My goal in life is to retire and spend the rest of my days hunting and fishing. Just a few more years and I'm there."

Tall buildings passed by the windows in an endless progression.

"Tunnel's backed up. We'll take the Triboro."

Dominic lived in Queens. It was a slow drive up a fume-choked expressway and then over a long, rusty bridge.

Later, they sat in Dominic's kitchen.

"Caitlin's not home from school yet?" William-Peter asked. "I guess Dorothy's still at work."

Dominic ignored the question. He poured himself a triple Scotch and asked his brother if he would like one.

"No, thanks. I haven't had a drink in years—well, wait, I had a glass of wine on Christmas. But other than that ..."

It was pleasant in the kitchen, watching the window darken above the sink. It reminded William-Peter of the alcove at home, except there, of course, there would be no conversation.

"Doesn't have to be Scotch," Dominic added. "Plenty of beer in the fridge. Lots of Coke."

"Coke, then, if you have it."

Dominic poured his drink and sat facing him across the corner of the table. He raised his own glass in a toast. "Give us this day our daily Scotch ..."

"That's a huge glass, Dom. Doesn't it affect your work?"

"It does. It makes work possible. It makes work conceivable." He swirled the ice in his drink. "What I am, Peter—can I call you Peter?"

"Of course. It's nice to hear it again."

"What I am, Peter, is an alcoholic—a *responsible* alcoholic. I hold a steady job, I do good work, and I never drink on duty. I keep this"—he raised his glass—"strictly within limits. Everybody's got their drug: some people like dope, some people like sex, some people like chocolate-chip cookies." He lifted his massive shoulders in a shrug. "You happen to like praying. I happen to like Scotch."

"It's not the same thing. Prayer is not an addiction."

"It's an escape," Dominic said, turning his glass reflectively. "Every escape is addictive. It's just a matter of taste."

"It's hardly an escape to be face to face with God every day."

"Sorry, Pete. I didn't realize he lived with you."

Peter let that go. "On the other hand," he said, "raising sheep, sorting books—it's not very stressful. I can see where it would get to you, dealing with ex-convicts—murderers and rapists every day."

"I like them. I plan to write a book someday: *Fun with Felons.*" Dominic laughed; the Scotch seemed to be having its effect. "*Pigs on Parole.*"

"You seemed very understanding with your client."

"He'll fuck up again. I give him two months max. People can't help themselves, Pete. They're hopeless."

Peter sipped his Coke; it tasted exotic after the cider he was used to. "How is Dorothy these days? Is she still working at the same place?"

"Far as I know. I only see her when I pick up Caitlin."

"Wait a minute. You're separated? When did that happen?"

"Couple of years ago."

"I'm sorry to hear that, Dom. You couldn't work things out?"

Dominic shrugged. "Marriage is a tough discipline. Dorothy's not cut out for it. *I*, on the other hand, am a major fucking saint."

Peter smiled. "I'm sure you did your best. Would you have a phone book? I'd like to look up my friend."

"A *phone* book? Haven't you heard of the Internet?"

"Yes, but it doesn't have her phone number, just an address—and even that's probably old."

"It's probably right up to date." Dominic picked up his cellphone. "What's her name again?"

"That's okay. Don't worry about it."

"What's her name, Pete? Jesus."

"Lauren. Lauren Wolfe."

Dominic started thumbing away at his phone. "There's fifteen of 'em in New York City. She have any initials?"

"I don't know."

"How old is she?"

"I don't know. I guess around thirty."

"She live in Manhattan?"

"Possibly."

Dominic's questions made him sound like the cop he used to be. Peter was beginning to feel like a suspect.

"Okay. There's six L. Wolfes in Manhattan. One's listed as

thirty-two years old, another listed as thirty. Rest are in their sixties and seventies."

He held the phone out so Peter could see.

"You want the numbers?"

"No, that's okay."

Dominic thumbed the screen again and pulled a tiny notebook from his pocket. He set the phone down and scrawled a number.

"That's the Third Avenue address. Ninety-eighth Street's unlisted."

"That's probably her. I get the feeling she's a solitary kind of person."

Dominic looked at his watch. "I'll call Rossi at the Eighty-first. He'll find out for you in five minutes."

"Dom, no. Not the police. I appreciate your help—but it just doesn't seem right."

His brother contemplated him, phone in hand. "Suit yourself, Romeo."

"Please don't call me that."

"Why don't you sit yourself down on the sofa and I'll make us some dinner. I got some spaghetti sauce in the freezer."

Peter went into the living room, where he was startled by his own reflection in the dark front window. That ghostly figure in civilian clothes—could that really be Brother William? He turned his back on the window and sat down. The brothers at the monastery would be finishing their evening meal by now. What a poor example he had set. When the two postulants had left the previous year, it had saddened him terribly. The monastery was an artificial environment, hermetically sealed; when anyone left, some of the oxygen went too.

And Dominic's living room oppressed him. A rack of rifles dominated the far wall, half a dozen of them gleaming behind a padlock. There were trophies too: a bear's head fixed in a silent roar above the television, and a gigantic fish arching over the hall door, its eye a perfect disc of fear. *Trying to swim in the air.* Over the stereo set, a moose head brooded like the bust of a composer.

The sportsman could be heard cracking open a tray of ice cubes, while Peter remembered the buzz of Lauren's voice, her flash of anger, the scar on her wrist.

The telephone rang. Dominic came in, sipping from a fresh drink. He picked up the phone and said his last name. Then he covered the receiver with his palm and said, "Father Michael."

Peter shook his head.

Dominic said into the phone, "He's here, but he doesn't want to talk right now." He muttered a few more monosyllables in response and hung up.

"What did he say?" William asked.

"That I should keep an eye on you. You're under a strain. They want you back when you're ready to come."

"He's being so understanding."

"Of course he is. He's a priest."

"Why do you say it like that?"

"He wants to keep you in the fold. He'll say whatever's necessary." Dominic tilted his head toward the kitchen. "I gotta finish the Chef Boyardee thing."

That night, Peter slept on the fold-out couch. Dominic had told him that Caitlin slept on it when she visited and found it more comfortable than her bed at home. Peter suspected she was just being kind to her father. The iron frame bisected the mattress directly under his ribs, and woke him every time he turned over. He was not used to so much food, either: the spaghetti had given him indigestion.

A glow from a street lamp made the stuffed animals ghostly. Their glass eyes flared with each passing car, then dimmed.

It was strange and not unpleasant to be wakened next morning by a human being instead of a bell. Dominic shook him by the shoulder and put a cup of coffee beside the couch. He smelled of toothpaste and aftershave.

"There's breakfast on the table, and I put some clothes on the chair. They're too small for me, so they should fit." He dangled a set of keys. "Very important: if you go out, lock everything."

The moment Dominic was gone, Peter grabbed his breviary. His brothers would be singing lauds by now. He stood beside the sofa and said the Psalms quietly. It wasn't the same as singing them in a group. The good cheer they usually evoked refused to come.

The bathroom seemed small and personal after the huge monastery lavatory. The face cloth was softer, the soap more fragrant. And the shower had real force: splinters of water stung him all over in the most delightful way; suddenly a shower seemed a device of great wit. Dominic had given him a fluffy red towel the size of a cape that made him feel like a hedonist. Showers and towels—he had forgotten they could be such pleasures.

The mirror reflected not just his head but also his chest and shoulders. He could see all the way down to his navel. For ten years, he had seen nothing more than his disembodied face. Once again he had the peculiar sensation that his own body was a stranger. It looked slack and unused, the muscles barely visible; a saddle of fat hung from his ribs.

He draped the towel round his shoulders. Dressed in red like this, he didn't resemble "Brother William." He recognized this person in the mirror; he knew him very well. His name was Peter Meehan. And yet *I*, he thought—this person out *here*—am not Peter. *My name is Brother William, I am a Benedictine monk, and I live at Our Lady of Peace.* He continued this interior chant right through breakfast, and it ran through his head as he made his way along Astoria Boulevard to the subway.

He walked slowly, the sun was warm on his back; clumps of dirty snow steamed at the curbs.

The official in the ticket booth yelled directions at him through bulletproof glass.

When he tried to change trains at Fifty-third Street, he got lost and frightened. He climbed the stairs into sunlight and a chaos of pedestrians. The noise was unbearable. He took a deep breath, told himself not to panic, and decided to walk the rest of the way. It was miles, of course, and by the time he reached the east Eighties he realized he still had to get across Central Park. He bought a hot dog from a street vendor and ate it in a patch of sun on the steps of the Metropolitan Museum of Art. It was pleasant sitting there, watching the people come and go. The buildings in this area were handsome and well-kept, exuding an aura of wealth.

He crossed Central Park, which wasn't nearly as frightening as he'd expected; in fact, it was beautiful and peaceful, alive with joggers, cyclists, roller bladers and women pushing prams. Didn't any of them have to work for a living? He emerged at Eighty-seventh Street and continued on to Broadway and up to Nighty-eighth.

It turned out to be a mixed neighbourhood, with down-at-heels townhouses scrunched up against low-rise apartment buildings. The address he was looking for was the last house before a dingy building. It looked as if it might have once been home to a large family, perhaps even a well-to-do family, but the grimy facade of painted brick, the broken lintels and chipped front steps said those days were long gone.

The street ended at Riverside Drive and Riverside Park. He walked back and forth from Broadway to Riverside, trying to seem casual, glancing every now and then at the address. A Con Edison truck was parked across the street near an open manhole that belched clouds of steam.

Finally, she appeared. His lost sheep.

After she pulled down the blind, Peter strolled to the end of the street and stopped at the edge of the park. The Hudson River glittered darkly in the distance. Footsteps approached behind him. He turned, and a woman walking a dachshund gave him a cold glance.

He wandered back up the sidewalk to stand right in front of Lauren's building. Something in the first-floor window caught his eye. It was only a piece of cheap thin cardboard, curling at the corners, but in the soul-deep thrill of the moment Peter could well believe it had been set in this window by a divine hand. It was a small black sign with red letters.

STUDIO FOR RENT.

SEVEN

THE ROOM WAS no bigger than his monk's cell. The bed, the knee-high fridge, the tiny hot plate—all were crammed into a space the size of a large broom closet. The landlord, Mr. Zaleski, pointed from one object to another, as if practising his English nouns.

"Got fridge, got hot plate, got bathroom down hall. Even you got little table."

Zaleski pointed from the fold-out table to a cot that dipped in the middle.

"Got table. Got bed. Table you can throw away, if you don't want. Is belong to previous guy."

"No, no. I'll keep it if he doesn't want it."

Mr. Zaleski fanned away the odour of this personage. "Four months he owe me. I don't believe he shows his face here more. All I ask is pay your rent and not destroy my property. You can pay two months' rent in advance?"

"Yes. Yes, I can."

•

By the time he got back to Queens, he had worked himself up into a high state of nerves about asking Dominic to lend him the money.

"Sure, I'll lend you the money. I'm happy to lend you the money."

"It'll take me a long time to pay it back."

"No it won't. We'll take it out of your share of the estate."

"What are you talking about?"

"From Gramps. You've really forgotten?"

"You mean from the house? I told you to keep all that. I signed it over to you."

"I know you did. And if you remember, I told you I wouldn't keep it. To tell you the truth, little brother, I never thought you'd last in the monkey house as long as you have. I put your share in a money market fund. This is not riches we're talking about; it was divided with our noble cousins in Ireland. But your piece has been sitting there ever since, waiting for you to finish with this religious crap."

"It's not crap, Dom. And I haven't finished with it. I just have something to do, here, that's all."

"Whatever."

Dominic dug out his chequebook with a tough, businesslike air, as if his brother were one of his parolees. He wrote a cheque for two months' rent. "They have to pay you interest on the second month's rent, once a year. This amount, it isn't going to come to much, but make sure you get it, and give me a call if you don't. I'm assuming the place is a total dump. Has to be, for that rent."

"It's small. But I'm used to that."

Dominic scribbled out another cheque. "For groceries. Apartment stuff."

"Dom, it's far too much."

"It isn't. You'll need every dime. You can pay me back when you get a chequing account up and running. Should only take a couple of days. You're gonna need clothes too."

Dominic got up and lumbered off toward the bedroom, Peter following.

"Got tons more stuff hasn't fit me for years. Everything shrinks in this world." He began slamming sports jackets across his closet.

"You're going to need a job. Fast. I have some thoughts on the matter, but I have to make a few calls. Let me get on the stick and see what I can do."

Peter tried on shirts as Dominic tossed them onto the bed. "Such a lot of shirts," Peter said. "It reminds me of when Ma took us to the department store. I don't know why it stuck with me—I couldn't have been more than three or four years old. She grabbed about fifty different things and—"

"Yeah, yeah. I don't want to hear it."

"She stood there tapping her foot, looking you up and down." Peter laughed at the memory. "It was like she was sizing up a work of art or something."

"I don't want to hear it, Pete." Dominic glared at him from the closet. "Every good thing she did, far as I'm concerned, got cancelled. Nullified. Expunged from the record—the second she pulled that vanishing act. Don't mention that woman to me."

"Dominic, it was so long ago ..."

"I don't want to hear about it. I know no such person. She does not exist, all right? Are we clear?"

"Fine. You're only hurting yourself, though."

"Exactly. So shut up about it. What are you in the waist, about a thirty-four?"

"I'm not sure."

"Try these on."

A pair of brown corduroys flew from the closet.

If Dominic had any inkling of the trepidation his brother was feeling, he gave no sign of it.

Peter spent the morning and into the afternoon of the next day opening a chequing account, which proved to be more difficult than one might imagine, especially when—as far as the financial world considers—you haven't existed for ten years. When Dominic came back after work they had dinner and then he drove Peter into Manhattan, dropping him off at Ninety-eighth Street with his two fat suitcases. Then, with a "See you later," as if it were just any ordinary evening, he drove away.

And that was how Peter broke his second vow, his vow of poverty.

He sat in the corner of the apartment and stared at his surroundings, sick with grief, until it got dark. As he was getting ready for bed, he was made even more lonely by sounds of life from other parts of the building. There was a grating over the bathroom sink through which filtered noises of fellow tenants gargling, or brushing their teeth. And what a peculiar sensation it was to hear footsteps overhead; it seemed somehow unhygienic. Within a few days, however, he was certain the footsteps were Lauren's. Then they had a sweet, inevitable sound.

His apartment may have been roughly the size of his cell, but it was dark and cramped and had an air of abandonment. Peter found a hardware store, where he bought a hammer and screwdriver and set about fixing small things: a light socket, a window ledge, a loose table leg. Then he banged two nails into the wall under the sink and hung his hammer there. It gave him an odd sense of permanence: my hammer, my sink.

It was frightening, this newly discovered power to do what one wanted, to have a dream and make it real, even if the reality bore scant resemblance to the dream. It was a capacity common to most human beings in varying degrees, but he had divested himself of it when he became a monk.

As two days passed, then three, then four, he thought about the monastery less and less. His thoughts were almost entirely consumed by his upstairs neighbour.

He looked out through the iron bars—*gates* the landlord had called them, as if they led somewhere. He looked out through the bars, waiting for Miss Wolfe. He had to speak to her. He had broken two vows for her sake. The couple of times he bumped into her in the hall, she had not recognized him. Why should she? They had only exchanged a few sentences at the monastery; she had barely looked at him. His hair was longer now, and he looked entirely different out of his cowl and tunic.

Mornings and afternoons, he spent hours at the window, but it was not until the fifth day that he saw her again. She came up the front steps, carrying a bag of groceries that looked enormous in her arms. Everything seemed too big next to her. Peter got up and pulled his jacket from the hook on the back of his door. He cleared his throat and, feeling like an actor making his debut, stepped into the hall.

She was dimly outlined through the lace curtain on the vestibule door. Peter opened it and nearly tripped over the bag of groceries she had set down in order to retrieve her mail. She extracted several large envelopes and closed the box just as

Peter stepped up beside her and slipped a key into his own box.

"Hello," he said, and the word sounded as complex and experimental as a new poem. Her interrogative look made him stammer. "I'm-I'm new here. I just … moved in."

"Oh." She received the information as one more burden on top of the groceries and the mail. "See you around."

She obviously had no memory of him. Should he mention the monastery? How they had met? She turned her back and put her key in the door.

"Can you tell me," he burst out, "where's a good place to buy vegetables? Around here, I mean."

She turned awkwardly, her key still in the lock. "The Korean on Broadway is closest. It's two blocks down."

"The Korean? That's the name of the store?"

"Of course not. It's the owner's nationality."

Peter sank into gloom after this encounter. It was most unsatisfactory, pathetic even, and he feared he would not get another opportunity for several weeks.

He was digging into a baked potato at his crooked table when he was startled by the sawtoothed noise of his door buzzer. It took him a moment to understand what the sound meant. He went out to the hall and pulled aside the lace curtain. He was greeted by a man wearing a shiny black helmet, his entire body sheathed in a black and yellow leotard. It was like being hailed by a gigantic bumblebee.

"Do me a favour," the man said when Peter opened the door. "You know the people in 2A? Wolfe?"

"Yes. Well, sort of."

"Give them this, will you?" He thrust a plump manila envelope through the crack. "Save me coming back."

It was a heavy, flattish parcel from a literary agency, and it sat on his table for the rest of the afternoon. A scenario played itself out in Peter's head, over and over again. He saw himself making a clever remark as he handed her the package. She would laugh and invite him in. He saw them drinking tea. He didn't know why he should imagine laughter. After all, she had a nervous, touchy disposition, and in her vicinity his sense of humour seemed to desert him.

When, around suppertime, he heard her footsteps overhead, he picked up the parcel and ventured out into the hall. He hadn't set foot on the stairs before, and he felt like a trespasser as he went up to the second floor. Instead of a long dark hallway with four doors on either side, as on his floor, there were only two doors. He knocked on the one marked 2A and waited. He could hear water running.

Her voice was muffled by the door. "Who is it?"

"Your downstairs neighbour. I have a parcel for you."

The door opened and she appeared before him in a white dressing gown. She held it together at the throat as she reached out for the package. Her thanks, the transfer of the parcel and the closing of the door took approximately three seconds.

Over the next few days, he kept remembering how she had looked in the doorway, her hair clinging in wet strands round her neck. The white robe, the pale face, came to him within moments of his waking and haunted him throughout the day. This image was so much on his mind that when he actually saw her in the flesh a couple of nights later, he did not at first realize that the figure crouched by the front steps was Lauren Wolfe; he mistook her for a stray child.

She was squatting beside the recycling bin, speaking in a

worried singsong to an injured bird. It was a fledgling pigeon, with a cartoon face, all beak and eyes. One wing stuck out stiffly from the tiny body. When Lauren reached out, it pecked at her and tried to hop away, pivoting on the useless wing.

Lauren sat back on her haunches. "It's in such pain," she said. "Can't we do something?"

"I don't think so," Peter said. "It looks done for."

"I'm scared to pick it up," she said, and he saw that she was actually quivering. "I read somewhere they get rabies."

"No, I believe only mammals get rabies."

The bird opened its beak so wide that its face disappeared, and the tiny pink tongue arched into a loop. Lauren stood up and clutched his arm, her eyes bright with anxiety. "We have to do something. Maybe we could mash up some food."

"Food's not going to help."

"We can't just let it suffer."

"Why don't you go upstairs," he said gently. "I'll look after it."

"Are you going to kill it?"

"Go on. You go along upstairs."

Her gaze shifted back and forth from one of his eyes to the other, as if she could only trust an emotion that read identically in each. She scooped up her bag and went inside. When she was gone, Peter looked around for a heavy object. The bird throbbed and struggled in his grasp; it defecated in his hand.

He knelt and lifted the edge of the garbage can. He held the bird underneath and pressed the can down so that the bottom rim all but severed the tiny head. He retrieved a Campbell's soup tin from the garbage, slipped the mangled cartoon body into this cartoon coffin, and closed the lid on a life that could only have been improved by its ending.

When he went inside, Lauren spoke to him from the landing, halfway up the stairs.

"Did you do it? Did you kill it?"

He nodded, not wanting to say the words.

"Why don't you come and have a cup of tea," she said. "You've gone all pale."

He followed her up the stairs to her apartment. She filled the kettle and invited him to sit down.

"Don't be so upset," she said, although she looked upset herself. "You did the poor thing a favour."

"I know, but it doesn't feel that way," he said. "It feels cruel."

"The suffering was cruel. Not the death."

"I have to wash my hands."

"Go ahead. It's just down the hall."

He had to go past an office and then her bedroom. He noticed that she owned few things, but what she had was of good quality: an old chest of drawers, a rolltop desk with a computer, glass-fronted bookshelves and, covering the floor, an oriental rug worn thin in patches. The bed was huge, with a wrought iron head and foot that had been worked into an intricate, almost lacy design. Peter was innocent enough that a woman's bed did not automatically bring sex to his mind. It was heaped with pillows and a multicoloured quilt and looked very inviting—luxurious in a cheerful way.

There were candles on the bookshelves, on the desk and on the bedside table—some large, most of the smaller, devotional size in glass containers. He had never seen a room that communicated so strongly a personality. Even the ambient smells of wax and soap were utterly hers; a trace of myrrh ran through them like a fine gold thread.

He did not take in these details all at once—they came to him one by one over the course of many subsequent visits—but he felt their impact on that first visit with a tumbling sensation.

The shelf above the bathroom sink was cluttered with feminine articles: emery boards, skin lotion, hair dryer, and among them a tiny, ornate bottle labelled *Myrrh*.

"Your place doesn't look anything like mine," he said, when he was back in the kitchen.

"Oh, those cubicles downstairs aren't even legal, I'm sure. The landlord hasn't had a chance to ruin this one yet. Either he chops them up like yours, or rips out everything of value and calls it a 'major renovation' so he can double the rent. Did you meet Ezra?" she asked, introducing a plump tabby.

"Hello, Ezra."

The cat rubbed itself round Lauren's ankles while she poured hot water into a pot. When she set the tea on the table in front of him, he saw again the scar on her wrist. He blushed as if he had seen her breast.

"You're too soft for a New Yorker," she said. "Where are you from?"

"Upstate. Near Corning."

"Corning? I was there not long ago. Life's so peaceful there. Why would you leave?"

You, he nearly said. *Because of you*. It was the only answer that would not be a lie, but it would be too much, too soon; it would frighten her off. Lauren's eyes were full of intense inquiry. He had to turn away.

"I don't mean to interrogate you," she said. "I'm just nervous."

"It's my fault." Peter stood up. "I'll go."

"Don't be silly. I'm always nervous."

He subsided into his chair, and she poured the tea. A silence descended that made the clatter of cup and spoon absurdly loud. Here he was face to face with her at last and he couldn't think of a thing to say; the entire contents of his mind had been erased.

Lauren lit a cigarette and tapped it restlessly against the ashtray while she asked more questions about his move to New York, the problems of adjustment. She asked where he was working.

"I have a job interview tomorrow. At Lyle's Bookstore. My brother knows the owner."

"Lyle's is a good place. Must be one of the last independents still standing."

"They certainly have good taste," Peter said. "I made a reconnoitre of the place yesterday. They stock all four of your books."

"Wait a sec—you know who I am?"

"I thought you looked familiar, and then there was that parcel from the literary agency. I would have thought you got recognized all the time."

"Not very often. And it's always by teenage girls."

"I've read two—the poems, and *Mister Aykroyd*."

"And you still speak to me. Amazing."

Peter smiled. "I did notice the men tend to be pretty brutal."

"Men *are* brutal," she said simply, and poured them each more tea. She took a sip from her cup, regarding him over the rim. "Having a book out is like being the subject of a rumour. People think they know something about you. I hope you aren't making that mistake."

"Too late," he said. "I've already made it."

"Oh, so you think I'm hostile, lesbian, and probably mad."

"No, I think you're hurt and afraid. I think you're in pain."

Lauren put her cup down hard.

"I'm sorry," he said quickly. "That sounded like I was reducing you to a couple of words. I didn't mean to."

She looked at him, measuring. "You remind me of someone... You've never lived with anyone, have you."

"Lived with anyone? How do you mean?"

"With a woman. You've never been married."

"No, that's true. What makes you say so?"

"The way you are. No sense of boundaries." She took a sip of tea. "You hope to get married? Have kids and all that?"

"I don't know," he said. "I thought I'd given all that up." He was still trying to understand what she meant about boundaries.

"Are you gay or something?"

"No, no. I just thought ..."

"You *are* gay, aren't you?"

He stared into his cup. "Nothing like that."

"I've lived alone for a long time," she went on. "People who live alone are considered slightly defective. As if it's completely natural to set up house till death do you part. But I think it's much more natural to be alone."

"You were married to someone?"

"I lived with a man for a couple of years."

"And you left?"

She shook her head. "He did the leaving. I was totally in love."

"He must have been special, for you to be in love."

"To tell you the truth, I don't think it had all that much to do with him."

Peter had no idea what she meant. Lauren Wolfe said peculiar things, but it was an eccentricity he found charming.

Later, he remembered how she had crouched over the injured bird, how she had said, "We have to do something." She had looked at him and used the word *we*. It was an ecstasy to be pierced by this word: for days afterward, it remained embedded in his chest.

EIGHT

THEY WERE SITTING in Bob Lyle's office, a cramped little cubbyhole of a space located in a basement corner of the bookshop. Unlike the store above, which was elegant, Lyle's office was lined with cheap wood panelling, and the only concession to decoration was a set of black-and-white framed photographs of authors standing before microphones in the upstairs room, presumably at readings or signings. There was one of Susan Sontag, and another of Norman Mailer shaking hands with a much younger Bob Lyle, as well as many others Peter didn't recognize.

Lyle himself was a white-haired beanstalk of a man who walked with a pronounced stoop as if in perpetual search for a volume on the bottom shelf. This melancholy appearance was startlingly contradicted by his sudden exclamations and equally sudden gesticulations, which were usually accompanied by sudden wide grins. When Peter got to know him better, he realized that it was not Lyle's mood that changed, but only his expression. His mood was a more or less constant one of benign indignation. But these sudden smiles had the effect of a very bright bulb flashing on and off as if there were a short somewhere in Bob Lyle's emotional circuitry.

"Your brother," Bob Lyle was saying, "did me a great service a few years ago. Did he tell you?"

"No. I assumed he had placed clients with you."

"Mr. Meehan's brother," Lyle said to the round-faced young woman seated near them, on a table covered with boxes, "is an excellent man. Parole officer. He found the perfect job for a young man I'd befriended, in a rare moment of benevolence, through the mails. An incarcerated pen pal."

"Was that the guy who killed his mother?" she asked.

"I didn't realize you were even aware."

"You really should look into Google one of these days. He was still staff gossip when I took this job."

"Peter, this is Molly Safka—been working for me for years. A secretive woman. She keeps things from me." Lyle frowned, and flipped his white forelock out of his eyes, a gesture that Peter later realized was habitual. "He's very good at his job, your brother."

"He actually wanted to be a policeman. But he only did it for a couple of years. I think it got to him. All the violence."

"Good for him. So it should." Lyle pounded his desk, making a spindle of invoices jump. "Where was I, Molly?"

"You were going to tell Peter how lucky we all are to be working here. Your usual line."

"So I was. Your brother has also done *you* a great service by sending you to me."

"I guess it was lucky you had an opening just now."

Lyle waved this aside. "There are always openings. Tell him why, Molly."

Molly's round face and slightly arched eyebrows gave her a look of guilelessness. Seated on the side table, she swung her heels back and forth as she spoke. "There are always openings at the Bob Lyle Booksellers because Bob Lyle pays so little money."

"A *pittance*," said Lyle triumphantly. Smile on, smile off. "And the reason I'm such a *skinflint*"—he emphasized the word as if it were a great compliment—"is because there are hordes of otherwise unemployable English majors willing, indeed eager, to accept my pittance. Hordes. What else are they going to do?"

"Well," Molly put in, "they could go on to graduate school, they could maybe break into journalism . . ."

"Not a hope!" Lyle slapped his thigh. "Journalists come from journalism school. Filmmakers come from film school. There is only one product of instruction in English literature, and that is nincompoops. Nincompoops by the thousands. Nincompoops like our illustrious Miss Molly herself, and . . ." Here he flipped a hand in Molly's direction, as a cue to finish his sentence.

"—and nincompoops like the illustrious Bob Lyle," she said.

"Mr. Meehan here may have effected a narrow escape from nincompoophood by completing only two years of college—I think that's what you said on your application."

"Yes, sir. But I didn't major in English, I—"

"But you *did* take a general survey of the humanities, and that shows distinct nincompoopian tendencies."

"Don't worry," Molly said to Peter. "He actually likes arts and humanities people."

"Love them, my dear. Love them."

"Because they'll work for nothing."

"And they love books, which is what I sell. I am being squeezed, crushed and positively pulverized by Amazon and the rest of them, but I struggle on, sir, I struggle on. The profit margin is slim, even perilous, but Bob Lyle Booksellers has been in business, with dizzying ups and downs, for over twenty years."

"Mostly because he doesn't pay his staff."

"Thank you, Molly. He's an absolute *miser*," Lyle condemned himself gleefully. "He's Molièresque!"

Peter had not endured a job interview since the summer jobs of his college days, and certainly never one like this. He thought he should say something. "I certainly love books ..." he began, but Lyle cut him off.

"Yes, you worked in a library. I have it in writing." He shook Peter's application as if it were an affidavit. The application did not mention that the library was in a monastery.

"Of course, Mr. Lyle, those books were not new."

"Nor for sale, presumably. No, no. I'm far more interested in your work in this—what was it?—this gift shop."

"We did sell a few books there, but mostly it was—"

"It's the cash register that interests me. I trust it was computerized?"

"No. It was an old-fashioned one."

"Still the best, to my mind. Bloody computers, I hate them. I loathe them. I think they should be shot. Nevertheless, if Miss Molly feels up to the challenge of training yet another infant on our perverse and infuriating system ..."

"I think I can manage."

"You won't let Vanessa show him anything, right?"

"Um, no."

"Vanessa is the Princess of Darkness who comes in three or four times a week. An intelligent girl yet strangely ... absent."

"Don't worry," Molly said. "I'll look after him."

"Well, that settles it, Mr. Meehan. Abandon all hope. I'm sorry, but you're hired."

"Oh, this is wonderful, Mr. Lyle. Molly. Thank you so much."

"He's thanking us, Molly. The poor deluded man is thanking us."

"I'm sure he'll learn."

"Yes," Lyle agreed with an exaggerated sigh. "They always do."

Over the next couple of days, Molly Safka showed Peter how everything worked. She took him through the check-in procedure for accepting deliveries, the inventory system, showed him around the office—much bigger than Lyle's—where they did all the ordering. She patiently explained the computerized cash register over and over again. She never complained when he needed rescue from yet another electronic jam.

Molly was one of those rare individuals who, without being sentimental or false, manage to have a kind word for everyone, as if she had learned long ago that life was far too short to behave in any other way. Peter adjusted to employment in record time, largely, he knew, because of her kindness. He had expected to feel like a freak, to be stymied by matters that others from less sheltered backgrounds would handle with ease, but Molly kept a protective eye on him right from the start. Then one day she asked him right out, "Where were you before you came to New York, Peter? I know you said near Corning, but were you in a hospital or something?"

"A hospital. Molly, why would you say that? Do I seem like a lunatic?"

"No. But you're very different. Not in a bad way. It's sort of charming. For instance, when you laugh, there's always this brief pause, like you're trying to decide whether it's all right to go ahead. Like there might be a fine for laughing."

They were stuffing a carousel with Penguin Classics. To avoid her gaze, Peter bent down and slit open another case of books. "It's just shyness, Molly. I'm sorry if I've offended you."

"Don't be silly. You haven't offended anyone. It's just, before you say anything, I have the feeling you've thought about it for a long time. You don't seem spontaneous at all. Ever. So I wondered if maybe you'd been in hospital or something."

"No, no. Not a hospital. Nothing like that."

"Okay. I didn't mean to pry."

Molly knelt to fill the bottom slots and he caught a whiff of her perfume. It was a spicy scent that bore no resemblance to Lauren's and, beyond registering as a pleasant smell, had no effect on him. Molly was one of the nicest people he had ever met, but he knew, even if they were alone together for the rest of their lives, chatting and joking, he would never fall in love with her. Lauren's unhappiness moved into chambers of his heart that Molly's cheerfulness could never reach.

But he wanted to be Molly's friend, and so later, when they were eating lunch in Bob Lyle's dingy little office, he decided to tell her about the monastery. Molly asked a few questions about the monks' daily routine, but mostly she listened in complete stillness, barely touching her food. And then, when he was done, when he had told her about meeting a woman—he didn't mention Lauren's name—and about leaving the monastery in the middle of the night, she said, "My God, what an upheaval. After ten years? It must have been completely traumatic."

"Well, yes, I guess it was. A little."

She looked at him, shaking her head from side to side, as if Peter were an exotic bird suddenly come to roost in her place of employment.

"You're too much," she said in a tone of mild wonder. "Peter Meehan, you are too much."

When he was working the cash that afternoon, a customer asked him what date it was, and it was only in telling him that Peter remembered it was his mother's birthday. He had to take the F train five stops past Dominic's station to get to the cemetery. The New York dead were tucked far away out of sight: thoughts of mortality, not to mention wasted real estate, seemed to be considered out of place in Manhattan.

Snow had not yet come to the small brown hills. The trees struck bare Gothic poses over the gravestones. Ten years had passed since he had last visited, but Peter still knew the way, because he had dreamed about it many times. To get to his mother's grave, he had first to walk past the miniature parthenons and acropolises that housed the bones of the wealthy. Even a cemetery, he reflected, had choice neighbourhoods and better addresses.

The marker over his mother's ashes was a brass rectangle not much bigger than a postcard. Peter knelt on the cold, hard ground and set down the bouquet of daffodils. He prayed that perpetual light would shine upon her, that she would find peace—she who had known little peace in her earthly life, which had ended, suddenly, at the age of thirty.

Peter had been four years old, and Dominic nine. They were playing with a set of plastic cowboys and Indians at the top of the stairs—they could play that way for hours, until finally the cavalry would come riding in at the last moment, trumpets blazing, over the rim of the landing.

Their father, a huge man who ignored his sons except when he was angry, had just gone off to work. He often headed into the precinct on Saturdays. One of his feet, gigantic in police-issue footwear, had come down among the fort and the horses, toppling Davy Crockett and crushing several whooping Indians.

Soon after he was gone, their mother came up the stairs and told them to move into their bedroom. She needed them out of the way so she could vacuum the stairs. They had protested, she had insisted, and finally the boys picked up their troops and braves and took them into the bedroom.

Then their mother did a peculiar thing. Despite the fact that it was March and still cold outside, she raised both their windows wide open. "The windows stay open," she said in answer to their protests. "Put these on." She tossed them each a thick wool sweater. She kissed them each on top of the head.

"Mom, you're being so weird," Dominic had said.

Peter—much to his shame even a quarter century later—had not noticed a thing; he had been too absorbed in setting up the Popsicle-stick palings of his fort.

"Now promise me," their mother said, "you won't close those windows."

They promised.

"And promise me you won't open this door."

Again they promised.

"I'm going to be very busy cleaning all day and I want you to stay in here until your father comes home. I'll bring you your lunch in just a minute."

She returned with a plate of sandwiches and two glasses of milk. Winter was pushing its way into the room, and already it was nearly as cold inside as out. She plunked their winter coats down on the bunk beds, and once again she made them promise to keep the door shut and the windows open.

"I love you both very much," she said, and closed the door.

Did we not think it was terribly strange, Peter thought, her opening windows and closing doors for no apparent reason? Why didn't we say, No, Ma, leave the door open? Why didn't we sense what was going on? We were children, for Christ sake, Dominic had said in later years. We wanted to get on with the fucking game.

They remained deeply absorbed in the Wild West for the next couple of hours, until finally Peter announced that he had to use the bathroom. So did Dominic. They looked at each other, they looked at the closed door, they looked at the opened windows.

Dominic solved the dilemma with characteristic simplicity: he got up, unzipped his fly and calmly peed out the back window. Peter was torn between the promise he had made and the demands of modesty.

"Go ahead," said Dominic. "It's not a mortal sin to pee outside."

"I know that," said Peter, who didn't know any such thing.

"Well, pee or play. Make up your mind."

Peter got up and silently opened the door. He listened for a moment but couldn't hear a thing. He stepped out, and nearly tripped over a wet towel rolled lengthwise along the doorjamb. He thought it was something to do with his mother's cleaning, so he left it there.

He tiptoed into the bathroom and, owing to the need for stealth, did not flush. The air was thick with silence. He stood at the top of the stairs and waved his hand back and forth through the silence as if it were smoke, or a throng of small insects. Why was there no sound of mop and bucket? Why was there no whine of the vacuum cleaner?

He went downstairs on feet that were beginning to feel automatic, as if he were on a down escalator. Before he reached the bottom of the stairs, he could smell a strange, headachey smell, and when he opened the kitchen door it was overpowering.

The oven door was open, and his mother was kneeling with her head inside the oven, her forehead resting on a towel she had folded up neatly for the purpose. In later years, Peter always remembered this detail with a special pang—how she had gone to the trouble of placing the towel beneath her forehead, making herself comfortable while she died. But there were gaps in Peter's memory after this point. Did he touch her? He couldn't remember. Did he yell for Dominic? He might have. His memories of the immediate aftermath were fragments: squatting in a corner crying; Dominic yelling at him; his father whirling into the kitchen; he and Dominic exiled once more to the freezing bedroom, the ambulance arriving with shrieks, departing with shrieks, and afterward, the silence. The heavy, crushing silence.

That night he saw his father cry for the first time, and three days later at the funeral saw him cry for the last time. Mourning did not become him. He took to drinking, took to missing work, took to driving while drunk. He was asked to retire early, which he did, and his half pension kept him half drunk for another fifteen years. He had died just before Peter quit college, the grief of his father's death being lost amid the other anguish of that time. Syracuse had been his father's hometown, and it was in Syracuse, far from his wife's grave, that he was buried.

As for Dominic, well, Dominic took things hard. He had never forgiven their mother for committing what he saw as a crime, an act of hatred, and he never mentioned her without bitterness. The burden of this bitterness, Peter knew, was what caused his brother to drink the way he did. Dominic was tough but brittle, he thought, without a younger brother's resilience.

Peter arranged the daffodils on his mother's grave, and walked with aching heart through the choice neighbourhoods and better addresses toward the wrought iron gates.

There were only a few passengers travelling with him into Manhattan at this hour—among them a well-dressed man who belched and harrumphed continuously—but the trains on the opposite track were jammed with homebound passengers. *Home.* Although he had often visited his grandparents up in Syracuse, Peter had not had a home since he had left the dubious care of his father. The monastery did not really count, because it had an existence independent of any particular monk. A real home was the combined essence of a physical space and the being who inhabited it. Now he had a place of his own, modest though it was, and he looked forward with considerable pleasure to his tiny room, the slumping bed and the knee-high fridge.

He planned to pick up some turnips on the way home and make himself a vegetable stew. Then he would sit at the rickety table with its plastic tablecloth and think about whatever he wanted, about whatever came to mind. Home was the place where your thoughts were most free. He would think about Lauren for an hour, two hours, however long he wanted; no bell would summon him to loftier devotions.

When he got back to Ninety-eighth Street, he found a note stuck to his door. He peered at the yellow square of paper on which the words *Come to dinner* were written in Lauren's neat, tiny script.

NINE

AN HOUR LATER, he presented himself, freshly scrubbed and shaved, at Lauren's door.

"Don't you have a phone?" she said before he had even stepped inside.

"I don't need one," said Peter. "There's nobody who would call."

She hesitated for the briefest part of a second, her gaze one of frank appraisal. "You must be the only man in New York without one—everybody else seems to have half a dozen." Then she added vaguely, "I've been trying to think who you remind me of..."

Peter, nerves aflutter, steered her away from this thought. "Why would you telephone?" he said. "I live right downstairs."

"Oh, but I wouldn't want to interrupt anything."

"There's nothing to interrupt. I don't have visitors. Not that I don't want friends, it's just I haven't been here long enough to have any."

I, I, I, he thought, what a lot of use that pronoun got. Was this what a civilian wore in place of the monk's cowl and tunic? He was almost used to the faded shirts and brown corduroys his brother had given him, but not to this relentless gaudy pronoun.

It used to be *Jesus, Mary* and *Joseph* on his lips, but now it was only *I, I, I.*

"I don't have friends either," she said, "and I've been here for years."

She stood with her back to him, stirring a couple of pots on the stove. He forced his gaze away from the neat arc of her rump and stared into a candle.

He said, "But being alone—that's one of the hardships a writer has to endure, isn't it?"

"Oh, I enjoy it. Living alone is clean and simple. You open the closet and all the clothes are yours—every shirt, every sweater, every single pair of socks is something you've chosen for yourself. There's nothing that doesn't belong. Nothing moves unless you move it. You come home and everything is exactly where you left it—cup, saucer . . . razor blade." She looked at him over her shoulder. "That was a joke."

"Oh."

"Sometimes I think I should have been a nun."

For one horrified moment, Peter had a vision of her going off to join a convent, taking up the life he had just abandoned.

"I visited a monastery last fall," she continued. "Monks, not nuns. It's such a peaceful life they lead. They hardly talk, and pretty much all they do is pray all day. If they'd accept writing books as a form of prayer, I could really go for a life like that."

"It would be quite an adjustment after living alone."

"It might be better, in some ways. Poverty's no problem—I don't care about owning things—but obedience might be a little tough. Depends what they tell you to do."

Peter tried to think of something to get her off the subject of monasteries, but he wasn't quick enough.

"It's the chastity part that would get me," she went on. "Unfortunately, they don't get to have sex. I suppose they just jack off all the time."

Peter looked down at his plate, blushing furiously.

"I hope this isn't overcooked," she said, transporting a wok to the table.

The dinner was excellent, a delicate mixture of shrimp and vegetables, but Peter had trouble eating. Lauren could hardly be called voluptuous—she was almost bony—but he felt every move she made as if it were a caress. She reached for her glass, and a diagonal shadow flickered in the folds of her T-shirt. It did not reveal so much as imply the small breasts beneath, but it left him breathless.

He had lived so long in a community of men, he didn't know where to look. He stared at his shrimp and vegetables for what seemed an eternity before he could look at her again. Lauren's eyes were not eyes he could lie to; he would have to tell her tonight.

But he could not find the words. He looked down at his food and there was a longer, more uncomfortable silence. There was not even the sound of her fork on the plate. Lauren had stopped eating. Peter forced himself to look up at her again and saw that she had turned pale. She was sitting very still, and staring at him with eyes like two zeros.

She accused him hoarsely. "We *have* met before. Your hair is longer. You look different. But you were at the monastery. You were the librarian."

His stomach lurched as if he had been shoved off a cliff.

Lauren's lips were parted slightly; the unbearable eyes still held him.

Peter cleared his throat. "I've left the monastery now. I'm not Brother William anymore. Now, I'm just plain old ordinary Peter Meehan." He laughed—a short, involuntary bark that reverberated around the room.

Lauren laid her fork very precisely across her plate.

Peter began to talk rapidly; he could not have stopped himself now, even if he had wanted to, it was such a relief to confess.

"I had all this happiness, you see, and then you came along. And I knew you were unhappy. Your sadness pierced me—I can't think of any other word for it—it pierced me, and suddenly it didn't seem right that I should be so happy.

"I've never done anything good in my life," he continued, "never made anyone's life the tiniest bit better, never brought joy to anyone. And yet my life *contained* so much joy. And you—you were so sad. So hurt. I was overcome by an urge to help if I could. I know you can't *give* happiness to people, but if I could, I would give you mine. I would take misery in its place."

The candle flames made microscopic highlights in Lauren's eyes, but he could not read the emotion there.

"Have I gone completely round the bend?" he asked. "Do you understand any of what I'm saying?"

Lauren's voice was subdued. "I don't believe this. You're saying you followed me all the way to New York."

"Oh, not immediately. It wasn't an easy decision. To begin with, there's the vow of obedience ..."

"But you had no other reason to come. You followed me."

"Not in any sinister way."

"Really? From my point of view it's *very* fucking sinister."

"But I wouldn't dream of hurting you. I want exactly the opposite. I want to help you."

"How? Like you helped that bird?"

"Dear God. You mustn't think that."

"A man I've hardly met follows me hundreds of miles. He just *happens* to move into an apartment below mine. He just *happens* to keep bumping into me. What am I supposed to think?"

"It's nothing bad, Lauren. I just want to be your friend."

But she was breathing quickly now. He could see she was genuinely frightened; her voice shook.

"If you're so unbelievably harmless, why are you here in disguise? Why aren't you wearing your robe?"

"I'm not in disguise—I'm just—I told you, this is who I am now. At least, I think so."

"Do you have any idea what kind of freaks call me up in the middle of the night? And I don't just mean the disturbed young girls who identify with my characters. It's the same for any woman—you get stared at, whistled at, followed, fondled, cursed—so forgive me if I find your interest less than flattering."

"Please don't be frightened," he said, and reached toward her, but she shrank from him.

She stood up and backed away from the table. "I think you'd better go."

"I was going to tell you tonight."

"Just go. Get out."

"Of course." He stood up, a little unsteadily. "I'm so sorry."

As she closed the door on him, he added inanely, "It was such a lovely dinner."

After that, they no longer bumped into each other in the halls. He knew she was avoiding him. What had he done that was so wrong? He had been on the verge of telling her everything. It seemed unfair of her to assume the worst: that he was a liar or, worse, a pervert. He wished he could make his heart visible to her for just one moment, like Jesus with his Sacred Heart exposed. Then she would see that he wanted nothing for himself, he just wanted her to accept his devotion.

It seemed a paltry thing now, to have his own apartment. One moment it had been a gateway to freedom, and now, if Lauren hated him, it was a condemned man's cell.

Work was no better. He and Molly were side by side at the cash registers. He still had enough of his monk's humility never to ask for a specific assignment or a specific day to work, but Molly was in charge of scheduling and they wound up working together in the same station, whether it was opening deliveries, putting stock on the shelves or, as now, working the cash registers.

"I used to think it would be literary, working in a bookstore," he said. "I've just realized, it's really just so much filing."

"That's not true, Peter. Books are important to people."

"Books about monsters. Books about goblins, vampires—books about things that don't exist. How can that be important?"

"Those aren't the only kind of books we sell. What's wrong with you today?"

"Nothing's wrong."

He didn't feel like telling her what had happened with Lauren; it was too raw. In any case, their conversation was interrupted by a rush of business. The credit card approval system malfunctioned, slowing transactions and fraying customers' tempers. Molly responded to their sharp remarks with tolerance, but Peter felt his blood pressure rise with every complaint.

When one woman raised her voice to him, Molly stepped in

and explained that the problem was not with the staff or the store's computers but was located somewhere in the vast network of electronic communications that made it possible to purchase books without separating oneself from any actual cash.

"If you would like to pay cash, we can have you out of here in no time."

"I didn't bring any cash. I put everything on cards. I always use cards."

"Well, then I'm afraid you'll just have to be patient. I know it's irritating."

"He doesn't know how to use the machine. That's why it didn't go through. Maybe you should hire someone with an IQ above room temperature."

Peter experienced a sudden urge to break the woman's nose. His cheeks felt fiery and he was short of breath. Molly had been sorting the woman's purchases into little bags. She surprised Peter by saying in a cool, even tone, "Ma'am, I think you'd better apologize right now."

"Why should I apologize? He's the one who's holding things up."

The customers in line behind her began to shift uncomfortably. Peter too was intensely uncomfortable. It didn't feel right, being protected by a young woman; it was supposed to work the other way around.

"Ma'am, I think you should apologize right now, or leave the store." Molly took the stack of books from the counter and put them on a shelf behind her.

"That's eighty dollars' worth of books."

"Eighty dollars doesn't buy the right to abuse the staff. Here's your card back."

"You're going to lose your job. I want to speak to the manager."

"There is no manager. I'm the assistant manager. If you want to speak to Bob Lyle, he'll be in this afternoon. Next?"

"This is outrageous. I've been shopping here for years."

"Next? Can I help you, sir?"

The lady did indeed telephone Bob Lyle that afternoon. He came up the stairs from his office, gliding in his stooped, searching way toward the cash registers.

"Molly? Peter? Shall we have a word?"

It was the slowest period, mid-afternoon. The gum-cracking wraith, Vanessa, with very black hair and very pale skin, took over the register while the three of them retired to the basement to discuss the incident.

Lyle tugged at his white forelock while Molly told the story.

"The ignorant cow," he said when Molly was done. "She'll be lucky if I let her in the door again."

Peter was having trouble focusing on the discussion; his mind kept homing in on Lauren. He managed to emit a half-hearted confession. "I may have been a little slow with the machine."

"No, Molly said it was the network, and I've every reason to believe her." Lyle flipped his forelock. "The customer always comes first," he added. "Good service is absolutely critical. But never let them take away your dignity." The smile flashed on. "*I'm the only one who can insult my nincompoops!*" Smile off.

About a week after their unfortunate dinner, Peter sat himself down to compose a note to Lauren. He had bought a box of expensive linen bond paper especially for this purpose. Then, of course, he had to buy the right pen. There seemed no end to material objects once you got started.

But it was difficult to apologize when he wasn't sure exactly what he'd done wrong. The simplest phrase came out in the most tortuous way. What he wanted to say was, *God strike me dead if I should ever harm you*, but no words he came up with seemed to convey his meaning.

One effort began, *If you try to see things from my point of view for a moment*, and another, *They say actions speak louder than words . . .*

It was horrible. He considered himself reasonably intelligent; how could he be so stupid on paper? The expensive stationery was a mockery.

By the time he had discarded several drafts, some of the anger had crept into his note: *just don't assume you know me.* That was what Lauren had said about readers who imagined they knew her. Well, she was making the same mistake about him. Just because she had seen him in a monk's habit, she was assuming he was a fanatic, and it simply wasn't so. Except for the incident with Cathy McCullough—all right, that had ended badly for every-one—but that was years ago and totally uncharacteristic. He just wasn't that person anymore; he was the gentlest man he knew. Sometimes he suspected his gentleness was really only fear of giving offence. But look what happened when you expressed yourself—people became angry and afraid.

He laboured for hours over the wording. When he was certain the note sounded neither timid nor insane, he slipped it under her door.

TEN

HE WASN'T SURE what he expected—perhaps another Post-it stuck to his door, something to tell him she was no longer angry or afraid. But the days went by and nothing of the kind transpired; he did not even catch a glimpse of her.

He thought of Lauren so constantly it was as if she took on physical existence inside his mind, as if she had form and weight and could walk around inside his skull. His pain seemed so pointless. Six months ago he might have offered it up to God, but he had got himself into this trap, and God would not be interested in this kind of pain. Even Jesus, who suffered so horribly, had never suffered the rejection of a woman he loved; he told no parables on that subject.

His apartment had become a cell. To escape it, Peter took long walks through Central Park. Among the trees and birds, you could almost forget you were in a gargantuan city. He discovered a series of winding paths that curled around a lake in the middle of the park. Sometimes it was warm enough to sit on a bench and watch the people go by. New York was full of characters who demanded attention: a man carrying a huge inflatable frog, and another time a woman ambled past, her shoulder adorned with an electric-blue parakeet. At least here in the park there was some relief from the constant wail of sirens and car alarms, the unexplained detonations—firecrackers or gunshots, he never knew which—that interrupted his sleep.

He was so lonely that one day he called Dominic from the bookstore and—possibly because he heard the loneliness in Peter's voice—Dominic invited him to spend Christmas Eve at his place. "Do *not* bring presents," he warned him. "If you show up at my door bearing gifts of any kind, I will dump you at the Lost and Found, got it?"

By the time Peter showed up on his doorstep a few days later, Dominic was already well into the Scotch.

"You sure you won't have some?" he offered when Peter was settled in the living room. "Eighteen-year-old single malt. Thing of beauty."

"No, thanks. Just a Coke is fine."

"You know how to live, Pete. Gotta say."

The whisky served to make Dominic chatty—a good thing, since Peter himself was not up to much conversation. As they sat under the glassy gaze of the moose, the bear and the fish, his mind kept veering off on different tangents—to Lauren, of course, but also to the Christmases of his childhood, and the more recent ones at the monastery. How he missed Brother André and the others! They would be exchanging their gifts of sturdy socks and cheap aftershave, and they would sit up late in the kitchen alcove, allowed to talk on this holiday, laughing at silly jokes over fragrant cups of hot cider.

He saw himself beside the wet, black highway, the trucks flashing by. He could be back at Our Lady of Peace: confession and penance, a few weeks of regrets, and he would again be Brother William. A different Brother William, to be sure—a Brother William devoted to Our Lady of Winter, Our Lady of Ice, so pure, so cold, so numb. It was said that over millions of years a lump of coal could turn to diamond. Perhaps numbness, in time, would become serenity.

"You got this," Dominic said, handing him a square envelope.

There was only one place it could be from, and indeed the postmark was Corning, NY. Peter opened it, and pulled out the card. It showed a picture of the monastery barn and its white cross, the fields blanketed in snow.

> *Dear Brother William,*
>
> *We all miss you and pray for your return. You would be welcomed back with open arms. Please know also that, above all, we wish for your happiness, wherever you may find it.*
>
> *Father Michael.*

He handed it to Dominic, who perused it with a scowl before handing it back. "He's called here several times asking for your address."

"And you didn't tell me?"

Dominic took a sip of his Scotch. "Nope. Figured if you wanted to be in touch with those guys, you'd be in touch with them."

"What did you tell him?"

"Nothing. That's the magic of caller ID. Why—you going back?"

"Well . . ."

"Didn't think so. Let's eat."

Dominic had ordered in Chinese food, which he warmed up in the microwave. They sat at the kitchen table and had their

Christmas dinner of spring rolls and General Tso's chicken. Every now and again Dominic made an effort at conversation. He asked Peter about the bookstore.

"It's been busy. Quite hectic, in fact."

"I'm surprised. Thought bookstores were dead."

"Bob has an online business in New Jersey. I think that's what's saved him."

"You oughta find yourself something with a future, Pete. You ever think about going back to school? Finishing your degree?"

"I can't say I've thought about school. College was—college was not a happy time for me."

Dominic scooped some more chicken onto his plate. "You never did tell me why you quit."

"I told you, I had a vocation."

"Yeah, but you never told me what led up to this sudden vocation. One minute you're studying—history, wasn't it?—next minute you're in a goddam monastery. Obviously there's some missing pieces there, Pete."

"Things weren't going well, and— I really don't want to talk about it. I was extremely unhappy."

"Maybe you *should* talk about it. You're not exactly Mister Sunshine now, are you."

The urge to spill it all out was nearly overwhelming, but he would not, could not, allow himself. Dominic knew nothing of Cathy McCullough, nothing of the darkness Peter had entered, nothing of how it ended. To talk about it now, ten years later, could do no good and might do harm. Dominic was in law enforcement, after all, even if he was no longer a police officer.

"Are you okay?" Dominic said. "You're not gonna throw up, are you?"

"No, no. But what about you? Why did you suddenly quit the police to become a parole officer?"

"I told you. Couldn't take the goddam violence."

"It must've been terrifying, being liable to get killed any minute."

Dominic shook his head. "I wasn't scared of them. I was scared of me."

"What do you mean?"

"I caught some jerk-off with a pound of cocaine in open view. I put him in the back of the car. All the way back to HQ he's screaming and yelling and calling me faggot this and faggot that. I pulled over and told him to shut the fuck up, and that's when he spit right in my face."

"Oh, God."

"I broke his nose, dislocated his shoulder, broke a couple of ribs."

"Oh, Dom, how awful."

"The worst thing was, the whole time I was doing it, I gotta say, it felt fucking tremendous. I loved it. It was like sex almost—you wouldn't know about that—but it felt fucking great. And I knew I would do it again and again, if I had the chance, and I'd never stop doing it until I killed someone, and maybe not even then."

Peter shook his head. "This is not the Dominic I know."

"Put me in the right situation and I'm fine, but trust me—I'm not someone should be walking around with a gun in my belt."

"Were you forced to leave the department?"

"Not at all. My loo made a deal with the creep—basically told him, you don't mention your broken ribs, we don't mention your coke. Nice little fairy tale, huh? Everyone lives happily ever after. You up for more chicken?"

"No, thanks. That was good, though. Thank you so much for having me over."

Dominic pulled a toothpick from a plastic container and started working it between his teeth. He paused, then said, "What's going on with you, Pete? You seem pretty wound up these days."

"Must be the city getting to me."

"Really. The city?" Dominic gave him a sly glance. "Or that girl? What was her name?"

"Lauren. Lauren's fine. In fact, we've become friends. I had dinner at her place."

"You're kidding me. You and the writer?"

"Me and the writer."

"Hey, that's great, Pete." Dominic seemed honestly pleased for him, because the next thing he said was, "You're gonna have to bring her out here. I wanna meet this person."

"Oh, I don't know if she'd do that. She's shy. And it was just the one dinner."

"You bring her out here. I'll be your charming older brother. Seriously."

Dominic's enthusiasm made it seem for a few moments as though such a thing was possible, and Peter went to sleep that night with just the tiniest bit of hope.

One Saturday, as the store was closing, Molly invited him (he supposed out of pity) to come skating with her and her fiancé, Roger. Peter was in so abject a state by then that even pity was welcome.

He met them at the Sixty-third Street entrance to Central Park. Roger, gangly and laconic, led the way. He was apparently the sort of logical young man who never needs to ask directions, and soon they were following the sound of music over the crest of a hill. It was like a scene from a painting; Peter had seen such images in books of medieval art, a happy crowd rendered in primary colours.

Boys lunged at each other, girls screamed, smaller children clung with both hands to the boards and stepped around the edges like tiny drunkards. Everyone travelled in the same counterclockwise direction, but pockets of chaos contracted and expanded, colliding and re-forming into new constellations.

"I used to play hockey when I was little," Peter said, struggling for conversation. "But I was never very good. I used the stick to hold myself up."

"Don't worry," Molly assured him. "Roger uses *me* to hold himself up, right, Roger?"

Roger was opening the door of the pavilion and said dryly, "You're the right height, that's all."

"He says the most romantic things."

The skate shack was full of smells—coffee and popcorn and leather and wet concrete. They rented skates at a long counter where boys were chucking skates back into their shelves as fast as the departing skaters returned them. Peter rented a pair of size nines that were still warm from someone else's feet.

He was still fiddling with his laces long after Molly and Roger had ventured onto the ice. Finally he stood up with the odd sensation of being two inches taller and wobbled outside, past a high chain-link fence, to the edge of the rink. He stood for a while gripping the boards, waiting for a break in the traffic. When there was finally enough space, Peter eased himself into the turning wheel of skaters, keeping close to the boards.

His entire concentration was absorbed in the effort to stay upright. Each stride kept going long after he stopped putting any effort into it. The moment you tried to move the other leg, you were pulled in two directions at once. He felt ungainly and foolish.

"You okay?" Roger said as he and Molly came up behind him.

Peter waved a hand and nearly upended himself.

His ankles were in torture, but slowly he began to find his balance. A member of the rink staff whooshed past, leaving him tottering in his wake. They wore blue nylon jackets with STAFF stencilled on the back, and they went hurtling by with muscular, self-important strides.

A short while later, Peter caught sight of Roger towering over the other skaters on the opposite side of the rink. In a burst of confidence, he cut across the empty centre of the ice. A hard grip on his arm nearly toppled him.

"Outta here," said a thick youth in a staff jacket. "Keep to the sides."

Peter staggered a little, his face hot with anger.

"Power corrupts," Roger observed. "They think it's their rink."

Still, Peter managed to have a good time. Lauren's skating poem came into his mind a couple of times, but the effort of avoiding collisions kept recalling him to the here and now.

Eventually, the music stopped and a voice announced over the public address system that the rink was closing. They left the ice and took off their skates at the nearest bench. Peter rubbed his feet. They seemed to expand like balloons. Roger and Molly, pink-cheeked from the exercise, invited him to join them for a cup of hot chocolate, but Peter declined, feeling he had imposed enough.

He thanked them and said goodbye, then walked up the outside stairs to a nearby observation pavilion. A light snow was falling, and the park looked beautiful. He stood for a long time watching tired skaters crowd against each other on benches, bending to remove their skates, wiggling their ankles and groaning dramatically.

A Zamboni bobbed onto the corner of the rink and steamed around and around in narrowing circles, leaving in its wake a smooth, creaseless surface. The floodlights were very bright, and when the tractor was finished, the ice shone like a silver plate.

It was pleasant standing there, watching the thinning crowd, the skaters straggling up the hill, like being inside the painting he had imagined. Contentment lapped around him, but it was spoiled a little by his own awareness of it: he had sketched himself into his painting, a lonely figure on the edge of the crowd, observing happiness but not sharing it. A staff member locked the chain-link gate and the floodlights went out. Lamps lit the paths over the hills, and the tall buildings stood shoulder to shoulder round the park, a million bright windows looking down. There were only a few people left, and one of them, he saw with a jolt, was Lauren Wolfe.

She was leaning against the fence, a still figure where the last of the departing couples flowed by. A pair of skates hung over her shoulders, vivid white against the black of her jacket. She remained in profile, staring at the clean, fresh surface of the ice.

The rink was deserted, but still she stood by the fence. Peter went quietly down the stairs and was stepping into a patch of shadow when Lauren suddenly tossed her skates over the fence, grabbed hold of the chain-link and, with the ease of a street urchin, climbed over it. The metal clanked and rattled when she jumped down on the other side, and then it was quiet again. She remained crouched in the shadows, tying her skates. Headlights flashed through the trees; distant horns honked.

Peter looked nervously at the darkened skate shack, where a single light burned. Lauren stood up and approached the rink with an elegant skater's strut. She opened the wooden gate and skated out to the middle of the ice as if she owned it. Such nerve, Peter thought: when she wants something, she just takes it.

The only sound was the skirring of Lauren's blades on the ice. She seemed to prefer skating backwards, bending at the waist as if some invisible partner pulled her backwards by the hip bones. She made a couple of circuits of the ice, the *whick, whick, whick* of her blades louder as she picked up speed. Then, as she reached the far side of the ice, she lifted off and spun in the air, coming down on the blades with only the slightest uncertainty. One hand shot out for balance.

She did a figure eight, then lifted off again. Peter sent his mind out to hers, flew with her, turning at the peak of her flight, spinning and coming down beside her. Lauren made skating look like pure freedom.

She stopped in the centre of the ice and spun faster and faster on a single point, as if she would drill her way into the earth. She came out of the spin, making a star shape with arms and legs, and then went round again. Peter felt mucilaginous by comparison—a snail, a blob, a lump of speaking mud.

The scrape of metal on ice continued *whick, whick, whick,* a razor on a strop. Peter was reminded of her poem and was touched by a sadness. He tried to think of something brilliant to say to her when she came off the ice. Something that would give her an undeniable insight into the purity of his intentions.

A shadow caught his eye. Someone had come out of the skate shack and was standing just outside the door.

Lauren came wafting round and spun into the air, but she landed at a bad angle and fell. She sat back on her wrists, her legs spread out in a black V.

The dark figure went sloping down toward the rink and stopped in the shadows. It was the youth who had snarled at Peter earlier. If he wanted her to leave, why didn't he just yell at her?

Lauren got to her feet, brushing snow from her behind. Peter's mouth formed her name, but no sound came out. She skated slowly toward the gate, head tucked down, contemplative now. There was a double thud as her skates made contact with wood.

As she opened the gate, Peter wanted to cry out, but he was trapped in a space between breaths.

The youth stepped out of the shadows and grabbed Lauren by the wrists, yanking her forward so that she staggered off the ice. He pinioned her against the boards.

Peter ran down to the iron gate and shook it, making a tremendous rattle. The boy turned and looked.

Lauren jerked an arm free. Her wrist flashed in the light, wafer pale, and she gave the youth a backhand that caught him in the side of the face.

The answering blow was reflexive as a tennis player's. The boy hit her across the face—a tremendous slap that echoed around the rink. Lauren cried out.

The boy grabbed her wrists and bent them back, forcing her into a genuflection.

Peter was yelling—he didn't know what—loud enough to hurt his vocal cords. His fists hammered at the fence.

The youth flung Lauren aside. He cursed them both and stalked back up the stairs toward the shack.

"Are you all right?" Peter called through the fence. "Can you get up?"

Lauren was on her hands and knees in the snow. She got to her feet unsteadily and leaned against the rink boards.

"Fuck. He really smacked me."

"Can you climb back over? Or should I come and get you?"

"I'm all right."

It took her a while to get her skates off and then to get back into her shoes. She stood up, suddenly tiny, and tossed her skates over the fence, one after the other. Her feet were so small, the fence might as well have been a ladder.

After she had climbed over the top, Peter helped her down. She stepped into his cupped hands, her fingertips brushing his shoulders. Peter swayed a little. She could not have weighed more than ninety pounds. Her thigh brushed his cheek; her legs smelled of damp denim. The fence clattered and then her weight left his hands.

"Thank God you're all right," Peter said. "You could have got into real trouble."

"Nobody's going to arrest me for illegal skating."

"That's not what I meant," he said, glancing at the skate shack. "I'd like to break that bastard's neck."

"Really? I thought monks weren't supposed to get angry."

"Who on earth told you that?" he said, then quickly added, "Of course, you have to forgive people."

"Not me, baby. I don't forgive anybody."

His heart sank at the words.

Her hair was still standing up from her forehead where the wind of her skating had blown it back. She looked up at him, dark-eyed and serious. "Please tell me you didn't follow me here."

"No. No, I swear. I went skating with a friend from work."

She took his hands with icy wet fingers. "If you hadn't shouted, I think that guy would have done some damage."

"I didn't really do anything."

"You're my first white knight," she said, releasing him.

He looked to see if she was making fun of him, but he couldn't tell. Was he forgiven? As they made their way out of the park and into the lights of Central Park West, he fell into a thoughtful silence. He had only cried out in fear; there was no pleasure in undeserved praise.

She turned and gave him one of those direct stares, accompanied by an unexpected remark. "You're a virgin, right?"

He stammered over an answer. "Um, well, I— Not all monks are virgins, you know."

"But you are, right?"

"Yes, well. I am. Yes."

"Me too," she said. "The only difference is I've slept around a lot."

Peter wasn't sure what she meant, but he wished that he had known her since childhood, so he could have protected her even back then.

They had to wait for a traffic light at Broadway. Cars honked and spun their wheels in the slush. Passing couples glanced at them, and Peter knew that he and Lauren must look like a couple too. He was starting to shiver, but he hugged himself tightly to hide it.

Lauren seemed oblivious. "Shall we walk all the way?"

"Sure. If you like."

"You're not too cold?"

"No, no. Not at all."

They walked a few blocks without speaking. Then Lauren said, "You know what's really great? What's really great is that once in a while—just often enough to keep you alive—it's actually possible to get what you want."

"How do you mean?"

"Skating. I've always wanted to skate on an empty rink. I've *dreamed* of it. It's an actual dream come true."

He looked at her closely. "But your lip. You're bleeding."

She touched a knuckle to the corner of her mouth and looked at the blood. It glistened blackly in the street light. "Well," she said. "A dream come true—it's worth a little blood." She held her hand to his face. "Want some?"

He jerked his head back, and she grinned.

When they were in the front hall, she paused at the foot of the stairs and thanked him again.

"I guess you're not really the monster I thought you were," she said. "Will you come to dinner again? I promise I won't kick you out this time."

"I would love to."

Lauren smiled, and lifted a skate in farewell. Then she was gone.

Later, as he lay in bed listening to her footsteps overhead, images tumbled around in his head: Lauren spinning into the air, the boy in the shadows, and the way she had held out her knuckle, slick with blood—the strange, urgent glee in her voice. *Want some?*

ELEVEN

EVIDENTLY, LAUREN HAD decided Peter was not a man to fear. When he went to her place for dinner the following week, she questioned him endlessly about the monastery. He enjoyed pleasing her by answering questions, even though it was painful to talk about Our Lady. But it was just as well that she was full of questions, because he was tongue-tied in her presence, and would have been unable, unassisted, to come up with a single thing to say.

Lauren was full of questions two weeks later as well, when she travelled with Peter out to Queens to have dinner with Dominic. The first time Peter had suggested she meet his brother, she said, "Absolutely not. I don't have the slightest interest in meeting anyone's family." But when Peter told her Dominic had been a parole officer for eight years, she changed her mind. Suddenly she couldn't wait to meet him.

Dominic cooked them a surprisingly good meal, and Lauren interrogated him all through dinner about his work with ex-cons and about his single year as a cop. The conversation never lagged, and Peter considered the evening a great success. He took pride in being with Lauren (for once, pride did not feel like a sin) and she was so pretty, so sharp and so curious, he had no doubt that Dominic would be impressed, even envious.

But the following Friday, Peter sat glumly in the dim cave of McCauley's Irish Bar as his brother explained exactly why—far from envious, far from impressed—he was in fact alarmed. He had been laying it out in detail for twenty minutes now. Peter's initial shock had turned to pain, and now the pain was turning to resentment.

"You're just off the fucking farm, Pete. Someone's got to straighten you out. You don't know what's what."

And you do, I suppose, thought Peter, looking around at the cardboard shamrocks, the peeling letters of ERIN GO BRAGH scrawled across the mirror, the bleary television behind the bar. Dominic had insisted on this dingy uptown dive—Dominic Meehan, the great expert on women.

"If you seriously think this woman is interested in you—if you even imagine she will *ever* be interested in you—then you are out of your screaming mind. You don't even exist for her."

"That's not true. Lauren has had me over for dinner twice, and I'm going there again tonight."

"Then she wants something from you."

"She doesn't. She came all the way out to Queens with me, didn't she? And that's saying something, because Lauren never goes anywhere. She just works all the time."

"That I believe. She was sure working overtime the other night. Questions, questions, all night long. What is that shit? Am I supposed to be flattered by that?"

Three men entered the bar, cops by the look of them, greeting Dominic noisily as they commandeered a table. When his brother turned to him again, Peter said, "She's curious, Dom. That's why she asks questions. She likes to know things."

"She *has* to know things. She writes books. You were a monk, I work with scum. She'll probably stick us in a book someday. That's her interest. She didn't so much as look at you—God forbid she should speak to you—the whole time you were at my place."

"Because she was fascinated with your work. She was so nice to you, Dom. Why are you being so mean?"

"She was *not* nice to me. She used me. She got a lot of information, and that's what she came for. She's a ball-buster. I'm telling you for your own good."

Someone had carved the name *Rose* into the bar in square letters. Peter traced them over with his finger as Dominic went on. Rose would likely be an old woman now, her admirer dead of cirrhosis.

When Dominic stopped for breath, Peter said, "I don't have to defend her to you. She's not like that at all."

"She used me, she'll use you. This city is crawling with women like her. All looking out for Number One."

Peter shook his head. "You're wrong. She's not like that. Nervous, yes. Suspicious, yes—afraid, even. I realize she's high-strung."

"High-strung!"

Responding to some unheard argument, the obese bartender pulled out an immense baseball fact book and slammed it onto the bar.

"Can't you see the gentle person she is, under all that? Lauren would never hurt anyone. She was practically in tears over a, over a— Never mind. You don't want to see it. But she's so soft underneath."

"*Way* underneath. *Nautical miles* underneath. Listen to me, sweetheart. That little piece of work is going to eat you for breakfast."

"You're just jealous. You don't have anyone or anything and you're jealous that I do. It must be pretty lonely without your wife."

Dominic let out a sigh rich with the fumes of Scotch.

"Jesus. Is that what they teach you in the monkey shop? What happened to Christian kindness all of a sudden?"

"Dom, I'm sorry. You just keep—"

"What's wrong with you, Pete? Are you defective in some way?" He squinted at his brother as if he would smack him into shape. "You can't see what's in front of your face."

In response to a remark from a table across the room, Dominic swivelled on his stool and bellowed a jovial insult into the shadows. The insult was returned with refinements by its recipients, and they all laughed.

Peter took this opportunity to change the subject. He pulled a cheque from his wallet and slid it over to Dominic.

"The money I owe you. It was really good of you to set up that account. Grampa's house must've been worth quite a bit."

Dominic placed the cheque next to his glass of Scotch. "I'll put it toward a good cause. The Scotch widows and orphans fund." He ordered a fresh whisky and another ginger ale for Peter, and slid a twenty to the bartender, who examined it against the small bulb over his cash register.

When Dominic had contemplated his new Scotch for a while, he said, "So tell me, Pete: this harmless little waif, this Mary Magdalene of literature—did you fuck her yet?"

The word fell between them like an axe. Peter pressed his forefinger into a drop of moisture on the bar and rubbed it into the surface. His cheeks were burning. He stood up so fast his chair nearly toppled.

"Don't be such a repressed little sap," Dominic said. "Some artsy little twat from Barnard or somewhere. Sit down, for Christ sake."

"Lauren is— I don't have words for what Lauren is ..."

"You're gonna have to learn to take a joke, Pete. You can't take everything so seriously."

"I don't have words for what Lauren is," Peter said again. "But she's worth ten of you, I know that. Ten of you or anyone like you, Dominic, and you can't talk about her that way."

Faces glanced up in the dim light as Peter made for the exit. He heard Dominic call after him, "Come back, for Christ sake. I'm just trying to—" but Peter did not wait to hear what his brother was trying to do.

He walked down the winding paths of Riverside Park until his anger began to ebb. Thin webs of cloud hung motionless in the last of the light above the New Jersey hills. It was dark when he stopped off at the Korean grocer's and bought a pint of raspberries. They were expensive, but he thought Lauren might like them.

When he stood in front of her door, raspberries in hand, he had to knock again and again before she finally responded. The locks shot back, but the door stayed closed. He pushed it open and stepped inside.

"Lauren?"

The place was dark.

"Where are you? I can't see a thing."

He felt for the kitchen table and put down the raspberries.

The place was so dark he had to inch his way toward the living room, saying Lauren's name. He stubbed his toe on a chair and pain travelled in a slow blade up his shin.

Lauren was seated on the floor by the bookcase, knees drawn into her chest. Thin lengths of street light framed the window blinds behind her.

"Why are you sitting in the dark?"

There was a sudden flare, a glowing hand, a pale curve of cheek as she lit a cigarette. Peter sat on the edge of the couch.

He asked her again, "Why are you sitting in the dark?"

The red tip of her cigarette throbbed brighter, and he heard her exhale.

"I'm sick."

"Sick? Have you caught a cold?"

"Not like that."

"Do you want me to go? Should you be in bed?"

A car passed in the street. A fan of light opened across the ceiling, then folded shut.

"I like sitting in the dark. I hate the sun. It's a fucking search-light. I can't stand it sometimes."

Peter watched the firefly glow of her cigarette. "Did something happen to you?"

"No, nothing *happened* to me. It's just the way I *am*."

"Why are you crying?" he asked after a while.

Her only answer was to sniffle louder. Despair pressed in on the room as if the entire house had sunk to the ocean floor.

"I'd do anything, Lauren. Anything to make you happy."

She stubbed out her cigarette.

She crawled to him across the carpet on all fours and reached up blindly for his hand. Her palm was hot and moist. She climbed up onto his lap and clung to him, her face hot and wet against his neck. Sobs racked the small body. Her tears flowed into his collar and cooled as they rolled down his chest. This was what Dominic could not see, and perhaps what Lauren herself could not see: how she needed him.

Peter made soothing noises in his throat. Lauren's hip bone was digging into him, and her hair was tickling his nose, but nothing could have made him change position. He held her with one arm around her shoulders, his other hand holding her wrist. He felt the scar and beneath it the beating pulse.

The smell of her hair intoxicated him. A breast pressed into him, and the heat of her breath came through his shirt. He developed a fierce erection and began sweating with embarrassment. He tried to think of something else. He thought about her pain, about her poems, about the fish with the hook in its mouth.

Was she asleep? His left leg began to go numb, but he wasn't going to move. A white ribbon of street light lay across her face, the glistening streaks of her tears. Peter gently inclined his head until the tip of his tongue touched her cheek and he assumed a salt tear into his mouth. It had been weeks now since he had taken the body and blood of his Lord into his mouth; this intimate theft was his Communion.

She stirred, and looked at him with puffy eyes.

"I want to be asleep," she said. Her breath smelled of cigarettes. "If I get into bed, will you stay with me till I fall asleep?"

He followed her into the bedroom, where she sat on the bed and pulled off her T-shirt and jeans. The small breasts made his heart pound. Longing flowed into him, and beneath this longing flowed fear—fear in a thin, dark stream.

"Will you pull the chair up?"

The armchair was so small his hands trailed over the ends of the arms. Lauren curled up under the quilt in her underwear and turned her back to him. He had thought she would talk for a while, now that her tears were done, but she lay completely still.

He retrieved the raspberries from the kitchen and sat in the chair eating them, watching Lauren sleep. If he lived to be a hundred, he knew that for the rest of his life the taste of raspberries would remind him of her tears, the small breasts, the triumph of winning her trust. He was her guardian angel; he would sit here forever, watching over her.

He dozed off and woke to her saying his name.

"I'm so cold it woke me up," she said. "I thought you'd left me."

"I'm not going anywhere. Do you need another blanket?"

"Another blanket isn't going to help. There aren't enough blankets in the world." Panic shook her voice. "There should be a novocaine that would numb you from head to foot. Sometimes I can go numb, but I can't tonight. Peter?"

"I'm here."

"Peter?"

"I'm right here."

"I have to keep saying your name. So I can believe you're real."

"I'm real. I'm here."

"Hold me."

"Would you like to sit in my lap again?"

"Get into bed and hold me. I need to be held."

He sat tremblingly on the edge of the bed and swung his legs up.

"No, you have to get under the covers. I'm freezing to death."

He got under the quilt.

"You still have your clothes on. It doesn't matter. Just hold me." She lay across his chest and he slipped one arm around her.

"You're so warm," she said. Her hand travelled along his ribs and came to rest over his heart. His nerves were a network of fear and desire. He pledged himself to lie beside her in utter purity, a knight on a monument.

"I can't sleep."

"Think about something peaceful. A wide green field."

"I can't control my thoughts." She sat upright, the panic rising again in her voice. "I'm never going to sleep. I'll go mad if I don't."

"I'm right here."

She swung a leg over him, her weight on his stomach. She leaned forward, and suddenly her tongue was in his mouth. He tried to turn aside, but she grabbed hold of his ears to hold him still. Again the small hot tongue darted into his mouth. She turned a little and bit his cheek. He gasped in pain and surprise.

"What's wrong, Peter? Do I have to seduce you?"

His words came out in a stammer. "I just want to hold you. I just—"

"It's not enough. I want more."

"Lauren, please. You're the most beautiful woman I've ever seen. But I just want to hold you."

"It's like you're the woman. You want me to seduce you."

"I don't. I adore you, Lauren. But sex is the least of it."

"Not for long, sweetheart." She reached down and squeezed him. "You said you'd do anything, right? Well, this is what I need. Fuck me, Peter."

"Don't say that, Lauren."

"Fuck me, fuck me." She was rubbing from side to side on his chest.

"Lauren, you'll ruin everything."

"This *is* everything. Nothing else exists. Just this. Just this."

She dropped a knee on either side of his head and knelt over his face. "Just this. Just this. Just this," she said, bumping herself against his chin. The smell of hot female mixed with scents of soap and myrrh. "Just this, just this."

"Please," he begged. "Won't you lie down again?"

"Just this, just this, just this."

He took hold of her wrists, but she turned her face up to the ceiling, chanting like someone in a drugged reverie, "Just this, just this, just this."

"Lauren, please. It's not right."

"Just this, just this, just this."

"Lauren, stop!"

She climbed off him and turned her back.

"Lauren?"

He touched her shoulder, but she jerked it away.

"Just leave me alone. What good are you?"

"Let me hold you again."

"If you want to stay a virgin, stay a virgin. But not in my bed." She kicked him with her heel.

"What did I do? Why are you so mad?"

She spun around to face him. "Peter, I have my work and nothing else. Nothing. I'm not what you think, or need, or want. I'm just a selfish bitch, you see?" The hysteria that had been climbing in her voice finally broke. "Why are you still here?" she wailed. "Why won't you leave me alone?"

Peter undressed as fast as he could—belt, pants, socks, every article of clothing fought him. He gave up on buttons altogether: he yanked his shirt off over his head and tore his arms out of the inverted sleeves. Lauren lay mute, watching. He hadn't seen her pull them off, but her underpants were gone. He knelt between her legs. She guided him inside her and he had less than a second to be amazed at the heat of her body, barely enough time for one ragged cry, before he came.

Afterward, Lauren rested her head on his chest, silent.

Peter lay still, stunned with grief. The firestorm was over; the defences of ten years lay in ashes.

Long, silent minutes passed.

"Well," he said hoarsely. "That's three."

"I'm your third? I thought you were a virgin."

"Third vow. That's all three vows I've broken. Obedience when I left the monastery. Poverty when I rented my place. And now chastity."

"I suppose I should feel like a whore. It wouldn't be the first time."

"It's my fault. All my fault. That's what's so terrible." He flung aside the covers and searched for his clothes. He felt a sudden desperate need to be alone. Tears spilled from his eyes, and he kept his back to Lauren so she would not see.

"Don't worry," said Lauren from behind him. "The second time is easier."

Peter was not ready to believe that. He stayed away for three terrible nights. Half waking, half dreaming, his vows loomed in his mind like three great locks, three great bolts that he had slammed back, one by one. Now he had let something dreadful into his home; some terrible, nameless thing was crouched beside him in the room. But when he turned to look, the thing was gone, and he woke, yearning to hold Lauren again. He just wanted to hold her, to comfort her; sex had nothing to do with it.

But then he had to see her, and the next time he was in her apartment, Lauren climbed on top of him and he found that his body was ready. She licked his ear and whispered, "My virgin."

"Ex-virgin, you mean."

"My little monk."

"Ex-monk."

I am wreckage, he thought, a heap of things that *used* to be.

Lauren's hair fell over his face as she kissed him. "I am going to teach you such things," she whispered. "Such terrible, terrible things."

The guilt was not nearly so bad this second time; it turned out she was right about that. And by the third time, he was beginning to feel something like confidence. Confidence that drove him to a fourth and fifth time in the very same night. Guilt—guilt and those other black, nameless things—became more and more obscure. Pure white happiness tumbled over them, a snowfall on an eyesore.

Later, they were both ravenous. They went into the kitchen, where Lauren put together a plate of bread and fruit and cheese. Over the past few weeks Peter had imagined a wide variety of settings for his great declaration of love—a boat ride in Central Park, the top of the Empire State Building, a magnificent thunderstorm—but it was in her kitchen, clutching a prosaic hunk of cheddar, that Peter first told Lauren Wolfe that he loved her. That he had never loved anyone like this. That this love would never change, never dim, never stop.

Lauren was eating from a bowl of grapes the entire time, her orphan eyes locked on his. He tried to explain his love in several different ways, but it came out sounding the same each time.

"And what," he asked with a nervous laugh, "do you think of all that?"

Lauren shrugged. "It's okay by me."

She got up and opened the fridge, leaning into the white glare. Her hair hung down over one eye as she looked back at him over her shoulder.

"Just don't blame me if you get hurt."

LEG-HOLD TRAP

Hold *is a kind word for it*
As if he said caress
When what he meant was
I'm going to break your leg
Into a red unholy mess

No need to shriek
No need to beg
He's only holding *your leg*
This isn't hell you're in
He doesn't hate you, after all
He only wants your skin

Don't panic

You have a choice
You have teeth
You know exactly what to do
Just chew your way
Through bone and sinew
Tendons, veins, and nerves

No one's forcing you to stay
Run away
Run away

—Lauren Wolfe

TWELVE

AFTER THAT, it seemed to him that the city changed. New York was no longer the dirty, noisy place that scraped at his senses. Now it was the place where his *girlfriend* lived. It seemed to him a fine place now, the obvious place to be, full of possible futures. The steam billowing from the streets, the exotic smells of the restaurants seemed rich with potential. The tense rush everybody was in—all the hurry he had previously thought extreme, even fake—now seemed natural. The career women with their serious, lovely faces, the businessmen gripping their briefcases, the truck drivers shouting at one another: it all made sense. Everyone had this tremendous, important thing in their lives. He was not a failed monk—he was that most normal of beings, a man in love. He was in on the secret; he *knew*.

And yet these epiphanies took place in an existence that, to an impartial observer, might appear dreary. The bookstore took up most of his time. Bob Lyle had taken a liking to Peter, and after only a few months trusted him with some of the managerial tasks, so that he found himself going to work long before the store opened to help with ordering and returns.

When Peter had worked three twelve-hour days in a row and Lyle then asked him to stay another half shift, Peter had considered objecting. But Lyle raised his white eyebrows and looked at him over the top of his glasses, and Peter agreed. Molly was taking more days off at this time, no doubt planning for her wedding.

So Peter put in long hours standing at the cash register, or in the basement checking deliveries, or in the office placing orders. It was the stock work he enjoyed most; he had always taken pleasure in putting books into their proper places. It appealed to the part of him that appreciated order.

Underneath this surface calm, however, he felt like two people: one, the man in love, happy and self-confident, above all *optimistic*; and the other, a man full of guilt. Which was why, when Bob Lyle finally relented and gave him a day off, Peter crossed the park to Fifth Avenue and stepped into the cool, dark immensity of St. Patrick's Cathedral. St. Patrick's was the biggest Catholic church in the country, serving a huge parish; there would be no chance of his knowing the priest. As a monk, Peter had striven to become nothing, but he sought a different kind of anonymity now, the kind you could vanish inside, a place where you could get away with things.

The confessional grate slid open, and Peter bowed his head. The smell of cough drops came through the grille. He recited the list of his sins, sins more numerous, more serious, than at any time in his life—well, except for Cathy, but that was different; he hadn't been himself. The priest listened silently until Peter was telling him about breaking his vow of chastity, when he cut loose with a tremendous sneeze.

"I'm sorry. Excuse me." The priest blew his nose loudly. "Please continue."

"That's it, Father. Those are my sins." He was supposed to say, *For these and for all my past sins I am truly sorry.*

There was a crackle of paper, another cough drop. "You haven't said you're sorry."

"I know, Father."

"*Are* you sorry? You know the drill. I can't give absolution unless you express remorse."

"I'm not sure what I feel."

"Leaving the monastery is a major spiritual and emotional upheaval. Confusion is only to be expected." The priest sounded no older than Peter; his self-assurance was irritating. "I'll be finished here in half an hour," he went on. "Why don't you wait for me in the back?"

The holes in the grille were like a hundred blind eyes. There might as well have been no one at all on the other side.

"I talked to my prior before I left. It doesn't help."

"A Benedictine prior would not have experience with these matters. I can help you. We'll have a coffee, talk it out."

"I didn't leave the order without thought, you know."

"A huge decision like this, and you won't even discuss it? You're that afraid of the truth?"

"I am facing the truth. Courage can look like fear, can't it? A man running to save someone looks the same as a man running away."

"You're twisting things around. Saying black is white. You're heading straight for disaster. Don't turn your back on God."

"I'm not confusing you with God."

"Listen to yourself." The priest leaned close, hissing menthol through the grille. "That's a terrible thing to say."

"I'm sorry, Father. I only meant I should have given the matter more thought before I came to confession."

"Some quick advice, then. Avoid this woman. She may be the finest person on earth, I'm not saying she isn't, but for you this woman is death. Do you hear? Death."

"I can't avoid her. I love her."

"You call it love? You mean lust. If you die without absolution, you will be permanently severed from God. An eternity of torment. What is your love worth compared to that?"

"But she brings me such joy," Peter said. "Why would God make her so beautiful, so talented? Is He just baiting a hook?"

The priest blew his nose. "Obviously, this woman was not put on earth for you to break your vows over. You're simply being tested."

"You pretend to know everything, but you don't know anything," Peter burst out. "I'm talking about love. *Real* love. Love you feel in your heart, in your bones, in your veins. Not some abstract idea. This is *real*."

"I'll tell you what's real: you don't want to be saved. You've fallen in love with your own damnation."

"It doesn't feel like damnation."

"No," the priest said, "I'm sure it never does."

How could one honour the faith that could condemn such joy? He was not turning his back on God; God beckoned to him now in a different form: He existed in a scarred wrist, a bitter poem, in the beating of a sad, sad heart.

Peter walked out into the glare of Fifth Avenue, no longer two people. Brother William was quite dead.

Dominic, by contrast, did seem capable of remorse. He asked Peter to join him on a trip up to his hunting cabin near Fire Mountain, and managed to make the invitation without his usual crabby tone. He was clearly trying to make up for insulting his younger brother, and Peter was grateful. Luckily, Lauren herself was going away with her agent and close friend Naomi—otherwise, Peter would not have known what to say.

It was pleasant to be cruising up the highway on a crisp, sunny morning. It was worldly, in an innocent way, and you could make a case that it gave glory to God, taking joy in the hills, the spiky trees, the flashes of sun on the passing cars. After the greyness of the city, the light seemed full of diamonds. Peter was glad that he had come.

"Jesus, Pete, don't you ever say anything?"

Peter had not noticed the silence, but now he cast about for a topic of conversation. Cars were good: men would relax into a knowing, manly attitude when they talked about their cars. Peter pointed at the dashboard.

"How's the mileage? She do okay?"

He had heard men use the feminine pronoun in reference to their automobiles, as if they were discussing a wife, or a private nation.

"Mileage is fine. Only thing I don't like is no ventilation. Buy American, you always get some dumb-ass problem with the interior."

"Yes, that's what I hear."

Dominic gave a skeptical snort, and drove on in silence. The woods closed in, and yellow signs warned of stray deer.

Dominic's hunting cabin consisted of one dim room. Light squeezed through two small windows in tiny sips. The pine walls were decorated with a collection of traps—all shapes and sizes of traps—vicious contraptions that made Peter's flesh crawl. They were arranged around the top of the walls, out of reach, spread open like iron flowers.

"Not mine," Dominic said. "Belonged to the previous owner."

"What happened to him?"

"Colleague of mine named Lopez. Came out here one night and ate his shotgun."

"How horrible. He must have been in such pain."

"Nothing unusual. We got more suicides than the cops or the fire department. Everybody we see is severely fucked up. They get out of prison and think they're free. It's a joke. These people have got prison written in their blood—nothing they can say or do is going to change it."

"Men change all the time, Dom."

"Oh, sure. They take up an instrument. They quit smoking, maybe. But they don't quit rape. They don't quit robbery, sodomy, aggravated assault. It's in their blood."

"You can't help people if you despise them."

"I told you, I like my clients. I just don't pretend they're going anywhere." Dominic opened a can of beer and sipped at the foam. "I'm telling you, sometimes I feel like God in that office, not because I have any power, but because I can see a con's fate in his eyes. Eight years a parole officer, I can count on one hand the number of guys that got out and stayed out."

He poured the beer into a glass mug and crushed the empty can in his fist. He tossed it, and it hit the garbage can with a loud clang.

"You think I'm cynical," he went on, "I say I'm realistic. Lopez was a friend of mine: he was not cynical. He thought he could help people, and it killed him. Anyway ..." He swung an expansive arm at the murky cabin, the rifles and traps. "I bought this place off his widow for a song. No way she was gonna use it after what happened. Guy's brains all over the walls."

Peter crossed himself and said a prayer for the dead man.

Dominic shrugged. "Guy just decides, I've had enough, I can't take any more, I'm out of the game. Frankly, I don't see the problem. But it's not enough the guy suffers in life, right? He's got to go to hell for eternity. The one unforgivable sin, right? According to Mother Church."

Peter had divested himself of cowl and tunic; he could not divest himself of the teachings so easily. He found himself sounding like the priest he'd just scorned. "You can't presume to know what God has in store for you. And you're not allowed to kill anyone. Not even yourself."

"Such kindness. Such compassion. I'm overwhelmed. You're worse than me, if you think our dear departed mother is actually in hell."

"That was different. Ma was clearly not in her right mind. She was always such a cheerful person—she was always crooning those Irish songs, remember? She had to be terribly disturbed to do what she did."

"Cheerful is not the same as happy, in case you don't know."

"Yes, it is. What are you saying?"

"She was miserable and she put on this disguise, this *front*. I can't believe you haven't figured this out, Pete. News flash: happy people don't kill themselves."

"I didn't say she was happy at the *time*."

"She was *never* happy. Why the fuck else do you think I'm a drunk and you're a—whatever the fuck you are?"

"Don't you blame her for your drinking. Dad was the drinker in our house, not Ma."

"Jesus, what's the point?" Dom got up and picked up his shotgun.

"*You're* the one who won't forgive her, Dom. Not me. You're so easy on your suicidal colleague, but you can't forgive your own mother."

Dominic didn't reply. He just shrugged on his coat and went outside.

Peter sat in a damp armchair that smelled of mildew. The pot-bellied stove was smoking so badly that his eyes stung and his throat felt raw. He pulled the Lauren Wolfe novel out of his bag and started reading it for the second time. The narrative concerned a young girl who shows up in a small town in Iowa. She has a strange personality, alternating between fits of anger and generosity. The Iowa girls love her at first, but slowly they turn against her—as do their parents, as does the local sheriff—and eventually she is driven from town in handcuffs and dropped at the side of an endless highway.

Peter was trying to understand it, but the meaning eluded him. At first he liked the heroine, and then he didn't. He could see why young women readers might like her. But was it a good book? He decided he was not qualified to say, and he didn't care; the book called to him with its sadness.

He should have refused to come out here. He hated the grimy log cabin with its smelly furniture and its smoky stove.

Dominic came back just before dark, empty-handed. "You should have come," he said as he propped his rifle in a corner. "Out in the fresh air. No noise except the leaves. The odd chipmunk. I didn't think of work even once."

"Good for you, Dom. I'm sure you needed it."

Dominic poured himself a Scotch. "I hope you didn't just sit in here all day."

"Oh, I was fine. I was reading."

Dominic came over and plucked the book from the arm of the chair. "Your sweetheart. I should have known." Dominic examined the jacket photo. "Christ, she looks like a stray." He put on a pathetic little voice. "'Take me home? Please, mister? Take me home, huh?'"

Peter snatched the book from him. "You only met her once. You don't even know her."

"Uh-huh. I bet she always wears black, though."

"What difference does that make?"

"In my experience, women who only wear black are either extremely pretentious or extremely depressed."

"You mean they wouldn't sleep with you."

Dominic laughed. "Exactly. Cold bitches."

"Good," Peter said, opening his book. "Good for them."

After they had gone to bed, Peter lay awake for a long time. The cabin was so tiny, he could hear the air that whistled round some obstruction in his brother's nose. A light rain pattered on the roof, and the smell of mildew became the smell of wet pine. Peter propped himself up on one elbow and stared into impenetrable dark; the room was filled to the rim with it. Even without closing his eyes, he could see Lauren's orphan face. But she was not always sad; he had made her laugh just before she went away.

"Peter," she had said in response to some monkish remark of his. "You're being very obtuse. I thought Catholics were supposed to be subtle."

"Only Jesuits. The rest of us are literal-minded."

"Oh, that's right—you think we killed your Messiah."

"No, no. Not since Vatican II. The Romans killed Him."

To an Irish Catholic, her being Jewish seemed deliciously exotic, as if she were a native of Borneo.

"But you guys think we're awful, right?"

"Well, we pray for you all the time. We keep hoping you'll come round."

"You keep hoping the *Jews* will come round?"

"Very much so."

"Oh," she said in delight, "I can't wait to tell Naomi." And then she laughed—a throaty staccato sound that thrilled him to the core.

Rain pattered on the roof; a small animal scrabbled under the cabin. Peter knew he was no comedian, but he fell asleep hoping he could make Lauren laugh again soon.

He was first up in the morning. He no longer woke at a quarter to five every morning, but it was still dark and he had to fumble around the stove with a flashlight. Dominic groaned and rolled over without waking up. By the time he roused himself at six-thirty, a pot of coffee was steaming on the stove. He leaned his elbows on the table and moaned after each sip.

Peter opened the door and ate his toast on the front stoop, breathing in smells of mulch and pine and, from somewhere not far off, an intense odour of skunk. Beads of water glittered on the car. The rain was long over. Toward the west, the sky was still milky, but over the eastern hills it was deep blue.

He was about to go back inside when a deer walked into the clearing, picking its way through the twigs and rocks like a girl in high heels. It stopped near a jagged stump, nostrils twitching. Its ears flicked and swivelled, scanning the air for the slightest sound. It stared directly at Peter, then dipped its head to nibble on a plant.

It straightened up, chewing ruminatively, as if listening to Brother Conrad read.

Peter stepped softly, slowly, down from the stoop. The bony brown head swung up, the long lips curling round some vegetation. The black, glistening eyes showed no fear.

He took a step closer. Another. The deer stopped chewing, and batted its long lashes. Peter still held a remnant of toast. He lifted his hand slowly, proffering it, and took another step closer. The deer sprang into the air. There was a flicker of white tail, and then the clearing was empty.

Peter turned toward the cabin and caught his breath. Dominic stood in the doorway, his face in shadow. He was holding a rifle, still aiming at the spot where the deer had been.

There was a silence, through which Peter thought he could hear his heart pound. Eventually he said, "You could have killed her. Why didn't you?"

"Out of season," Dominic said, lowering his rifle. "Not because I didn't want to. She'd have kept me in venison for a year."

"How could you possibly kill something so beautiful? So innocent?"

"Saint Francis here. As if you live off roots and berries. All those cute little sheep prancing on the hills. But we all know they end up so many sheepskin rugs and slippers."

"The monastery has to support itself, Dom. It's how they make a living. It's not like killing a deer."

"So morally superior, you are. At least shooting the thing is merciful. You think she'll enjoy being ripped apart by wolves? Dying of disease?"

"Let's just forget it." Peter pushed his way past him into the cabin.

"I don't want to be polite about this," Lauren said when he was back in her bed. He was curled up behind her, kissing her neck. "You're a novice and I'm not, so let's just consider you're my pupil, all right?"

"Have I been doing everything wrong?"

"Yes."

Peter was stung. He had assumed she must be feeling the same rapture he was.

"You make love like a teenager," she went on, "and it's really very sweet. But if you want to get any good at this, why don't you pretend you've hired me as your teacher?"

"I don't like the sound of that."

Lauren sighed. "Otherwise I have to pretend I'm having a wonderful time when I'm not. You don't want that, do you?"

"No."

"Good." She took his hand and pressed it between her small palms. "The first thing you have to understand is that people *do* what they like to have *done*. Know what I mean?"

Peter's murmur of assent was unconvincing, even to him.

"If I kiss you a certain way, that's the way I like to be kissed. If I touch you a certain way, that's the way I like to be touched."

"But we don't have the same equipment."

"Obviously you can't do *exactly* the same things. I mean, you can hardly take hold of my balls, for example."

"Well, um, no."

She threw off the covers. Peter took no pride in his body, and covered himself instinctively. "Such a child," she said, pulling his hand away. She took hold of his middle finger.

"Feel this," she said, pressing his finger, not exactly into her, but onto a soft, buttony thing and moving it around.

"That part of me," she said in the tone of a mathematics professor, "equals this part of you." She took hold of him with one hand and pulled the skin taut and moved her thumb over the most sensitive spot. Peter gasped.

"How do you know they're the same? They certainly don't look the same."

"Take my word for it, sweetie. See what happens. And this," she continued, "is roughly equal to this." She guided his finger a little way into her. "Look at it, Peter. You have to look or you won't know what you're doing."

She moved his finger up and down. Her strict tone was exciting him: it was like being a child again; he was not responsible. "It feels very good around there—not way inside, but right near here—and from what I've gathered over the years, the feelings roughly—now don't be too literal—the feelings *roughly* equal what you feel around here." She touched his balls lightly. It was like being trained how to operate an automobile: these are the pedals, this is the wheel, this works the lights.

She gripped the hooded piece of flesh and said, "Speaking of monks..." and knelt over him in an attitude of prayer. And when it was his turn, he kept in mind her instructions and could feel the waves of pleasure roll through her.

He lifted his face and said with wonder, "The Golden Rule. That's what you meant. Do unto others..."

"For God's sake, Peter. Don't stop."

Moments later she arched her back with ragged cries of *God, God, God.* And then she shook and shook and went still.

"Thus endeth," she gasped a little later, "the first lesson."

Peter became an avid pupil. Lauren gave him books full of explicit pictures, cheerful suggestions. He had never considered that sex might be *fun.* He studied closely, and each time they went to bed he hoped to thrill her with some new grace note—a way of gripping her wrists, a straying finger.

The weeks went by and Lauren taught him more and more. She was a sexual virtuoso; she could do things with her teeth and fingertips, things that drove him wild. As the lessons proceeded, his body became more and more responsive: it got so she had only to lightly brush a hand over his chest and he would be ready to leap into bed. And afterward, when they lay drowsily in each other's arms, he would swim slowly back to consciousness, and wonder how so much time—two hours, three hours, an entire afternoon—could have passed. Oblivion in her arms was so complete, it was like dropping out of existence.

He came to know every freckle, every crease of her body— the knobs of bone inside her elbows, the backs of her knees with their pale blue tracery, the ridge of callus on the soles of her feet.

She slept with one hand thrown back against the pillow. Peter would lie beside her, looking at the scar on her wrist, death's jagged initial across the delicate veins. He knew that she must feel more deeply than he, must have travelled through dark regions he could only guess at. But it also told him that he was the stronger, and sometimes—gently, so as not to wake her—he would give the scar a surreptitious kiss.

As the weeks turned to months, he found himself travelling through a series of fixations. At first he was fascinated by her breasts: Lauren's breasts were small and fit perfectly in the palms of his hands. Sometimes he would fasten on them like a newborn, until she pushed his head lower. And for a time he developed a fascination with her behind, and found himself turning her over more and more often. Eventually he became utterly fixated on the dark thatch between her legs, revelling in its exotic flavours of sea water and musk.

From a purely objective point of view, he considered genitals the most unprepossessing of organs. Legs had grace and power, hair changed with every nuance of light, and eyes had eloquence beyond speech. The female organs, seen objectively, well, even the arch of Lauren's foot was more beautiful. And yet, aroused, he could stare into that unprepossessing organ as if the universe unfolded before his eyes. *Vagina, penis*, the words were hopelessly inadequate, and the four-letter variety even worse. There was no vocabulary of endearment for these regions—no *sweetheart*, no *beloved*, no *dear.*

One night, jaw aching, wrist stiff, Peter propped himself up on one elbow and looked at Lauren's face. A damp strand of hair lay across her eyes. He pulled it away.

She groaned. "Don't look at me."

He lay back against the pillows, holding her hand, and spoke toward the ceiling. He spoke quietly, seriously, telling her how he loved her, how nothing mattered more to him than her happiness. "I just love you," he said in wonder. "I just love you."

"That's nice," she said, her voice sleepy.

"You've never really said how you feel about me," he went on. "I can't help but notice that you never use that word, *love.*"

Lauren's voice was suddenly clear and serious. "I'm not in love, Peter. I don't fall in love. I'm done with that."

"Nobody's ever done with love."

She sat up and gripped his elbow. "I'm fond of you, Peter. You understand? I'm fond of you, but I'm not in love. And I'm not *going* to be in love. Don't bother waiting for anything like love from me. It won't happen."

"You're so adamant," he said miserably.

"I know myself. About this one thing, at least."

"I thought I knew myself once. I thought I was a monk. Now look at me."

"You wanted to know, so I'm telling you. It's better than lying, don't you think?"

"I suppose I should be grateful you don't hate me."

"Of course I don't hate you," she said, fondling his ear. "You're gentle and naive. You're very sweet, and I'm really very fond of you."

Lauren got up and pulled on a football jersey with the number twelve on the front and back, her writing sweater. "I have to kick you out now. I have work to do."

Their lovemaking always ended like that, with her announcement that she had to work. He had been hurt the first few times—he had suspected it was just an excuse to get him to leave—but he was used to it now, and he knew she wasn't making it up. The stacks of manuscript pages grew higher and higher on her desk. She really did work all the time.

While Lauren was in the shower, he pulled the dictionary from her shelf and looked up *fond*. "Tender and affectionate," it said, "loving; sometimes, affectionate in a foolish or overly indulgent way; doting."

He put the book back on the shelf and went back down the cold stairs to his own apartment. What did he have to be upset about? Lauren was a writer; she chose her words with care. *Tender and affectionate; loving*: exactly what he felt about her. She did love him, after all. She just wasn't ready to admit it.

THIRTEEN

AS SUMMER APPROACHED, Lauren discovered that she liked having Peter around. He was always gentle, and he was getting to be pretty good in bed. By becoming his sexual tutor—teaching him everything from how to kiss to how to hold her afterward—she escaped the clutches of a far darker suitor.

She did not know why suicide stalked her so relentlessly. There was so much about life that she enjoyed, why did she so frequently want to end it? Her one attempt at therapy had not got her anywhere. "Look," she'd said to her therapist, "I wasn't molested, I wasn't beaten, I had an easy life. Why am I such a fucking misery?" Her therapist pointed out that not being beaten or molested hardly put one at the peak of the happiness graph, and it would take some time to figure out what was behind her depressions. Her philandering father had caused the family to split up when she was eight years old, but lots of kids go through such trauma without turning into sluts or resorting to razor blades. "Let's see if we can figure it out together," her therapist suggested, but it wasn't long before he was comforting her on his couch and Lauren had quit. Whatever the reason, if there was one, behind her unhappiness, over these last few months with Peter, Death had retreated to a more manageable distance and no longer whispered gorgeous syllables in her ear.

One day she asked Peter if he would like to have his own set of keys; she liked his being there—guarding the place, she called it—while she was out. And she couldn't bear the idea of his being cooped up in that horrid little cell downstairs. She had certainly made the poor guy work for it, this privileged position in her life, not out of any desire to be difficult, but only out of her natural sense of self-preservation. At first she wouldn't let him use his key when she was working; he could only come in when she was done. And it wasn't that often; he didn't have many days off. Eventually she let him drop by even while she was tapping away on the keyboard.

She would not permit him to talk when she was writing—that was out of the question. But he seemed content just sitting by the window reading a book. And Lauren could work for nine hours straight. Once in a while, feeling his eyes on her back, she would have to tell him not to stare; it made her nervous.

Peter was the most undemanding person she had ever met; he never asked for anything, was always content to do whatever she wanted—watch television, go to a movie, go for a walk. He took pleasure in doing the smallest things for her—feeding Ezra, cleaning her windows. Sometimes she had to ask him to stop. It reminded her of Hilda, the housekeeper they'd had at home when she was growing up. She had never found a way to be comfortable around Hilda, the class aspect was just too confusing.

A couple of times Peter had expressed interest in Lauren's background, and she told him the truth, up to a point. But she also told him that her parents were dead. She often told people her parents were dead. Nothing on earth could make her discuss her father—he could rot in his stinking research lab—and as for her mother, who had lately taken up with a Parisian gigolo (as Lauren thought of him), the occasional e-mail to France kept her quiet. From the moment she had left home, Lauren had refused to accept a dime of their money, the smallest drop of their love.

But that was not the only reason she had cut off Peter's questions about her past. He would try to seem merely curious, but she could detect a tremor in his voice—when she spoke of Naomi, for example, who had known her longer than anyone. He seemed jealous of people who had known her before he had. He had asked about old boyfriends, and when she mentioned one or two from her college days, he feigned (badly) a cool disinterest, but he was clearly upset. She never mentioned Mick.

At first she felt guilty about seducing a monk, even if he *had* come after her. But as time went on, it seemed to her that in some ways a monk, trained over the years to selflessness, was exactly the kind of person she could get along with. Lauren was quite aware that she was selfish, but Peter seemed to demand so little that she didn't see how she could hurt him. Or, if she sensed the possibility, she chose to ignore it.

One Sunday when her work was going badly, she went into the living room and found him sitting by the window, reading as usual. A light drizzle had been falling all morning, and mournful grey light oozed through the windows. They hadn't exchanged a word for hours.

A strange noise filtered into the room, a low, rough-edged growl. Lauren went to the window and looked out. In the air shaft below, a cat grey as smoke was stalking another cat.

Peter said, "Sounds like there's going to be a cat fight."

"They aren't fighting, Peter."

The female cat was crouched down, and the grey cat was sinking his claws into her back as he mounted her. Unearthly sounds rose up. Peter joined her at the window; she knew he'd be shocked.

"Lauren, how can you watch?"

"*Look* at them."

"For God's sake. If anything in this world was meant to be private ..." He backed away a little.

"Peter, they're *cats.*"

She dug her nails into his wrist and pulled him back to the window. The grey cat was screwing the other one now.

A few minutes later, she took him to bed and lost herself in a perfect orgy of biting and licking. Lauren had small, sharp teeth that she knew could really hurt. She used her nails, she pulled his hair; she whispered wicked things to him and went down on her forearms, her rump in the air. He dug his nails into her hips, and she gasped. He slid into her from behind, and she felt the world dropping away, all fear receding, until nothing existed but pure sensation. He thrust harder into her than ever before.

And then, to her exquisite dismay, he went still.

She groaned. "Why did you stop?"

He was arched over her, dripping sweat onto her back. "Something doesn't feel right."

"Don't stop like that. You'll kill me."

He pulled out of her, and she gave a small cry.

"Lauren, you're bleeding."

She turned to see. He was still hard, glistening with blood.

"Wow," she said. "Look at that. It's like the sword of Achilles."

"I was going too hard. I didn't mean to hurt you."

"You didn't hurt me, silly. It's my period."

"Oh, thank God." Peter was totally agitated, voice quavery. "I'm going to wash off."

"No, wait." She leaned closer, examining the weapon, hearing wonder in her own voice. "It's like you murdered me."

"Don't say that, Lauren. I'd never hurt you."

She ducked down and the taste of her own blood on him thrilled her. Before he could even protest, she came up again and kissed him.

"God, Lauren." He rubbed the back of his hand across his mouth and left a red streak. "You frighten me sometimes. You really do."

She pulled him back to the pillows and told him a story—partly to shock him, perhaps, but also simply because it was true. Peter was very selective in the things he wanted to know about her.

"I have this friend," she told him. "She lives in New Jersey now. But a couple of years ago, she was raped."

Peter fingered a corner of the sheet nervously.

Lauren told him how the guy had punched her friend in the face. Kicked her. How he'd had a knife and had made her do everything to him. "I mean *everything*. Came in her mouth, her ass. Everything."

"Well," Peter said. "Well, I hope he's in prison now."

"They never caught him. Anyway," she said, "when he was done, my friend was hysterical—just kept shrieking over and over, 'Why don't you kill me? Why don't you kill me?' And the guy just leaned over real slow, and spit in her face. And then he said in this dead quiet voice, "Cause, honey, you ain't *worth* killing.'"

"That's just . . . I never heard of such evil."

"But you know what's really weird? I think I kind of envy her."

"Lauren, don't say that."

"It's true." She had known this would really get to him. It *was* true, too—a little bit true, anyway. "Part of me envies her. Such an extraordinary experience, don't you think? Like she was murdered and lived to tell the tale."

"You don't really envy her," Peter said. He was usually so gentle, but now his face was flushed, and he almost yelled. "You don't envy her, Lauren. If you did, you could just go and hang around some dangerous corner until it happened to you."

"Maybe I will," she said. Then, tracing a cross with her fingernail over his heart: "Some Catholic you are. Haven't you ever envied the martyrs?"

"Not their suffering. Only their closeness to God."

Lauren couldn't make him understand: it wasn't the pain she envied; it was the experience. Having *had* the experience.

"No, no, no," was all he could say. "No, no, no."

She left him curled up on the bed and went into the bathroom to shower.

Despite such moments where she deliberately tormented Peter, it was mostly a cheerful time for Lauren. Somehow she had managed to kick Mick out of her bloodstream. As the days became sunny and warm, she took to wearing brighter colours—blues and whites, the occasional flash of red—as if she too had left the cloister.

Sometimes she worried that Peter's life was becoming too intertwined with her own. When he was not working at the bookstore, he spent nearly every waking hour in her apartment. Most nights she made him go back to his own bed to sleep; otherwise he was liable to start thinking they were married or something.

One evening, he came up when she didn't really feel like seeing him. Earlier, a young fan had shown up at her door, a small, nervous girl dressed in black leather pants. She had dark brown hair cut exactly like Lauren's, and a wonderful curve to her lower lip. Lauren did not normally approve of surprise visits from fans, but the girl had such a passionate interest in her work, and, really, Lauren thought she had the most beautiful mouth she had ever seen. She smelled of patchouli.

"We just have so much in common," the girl was saying as Peter unlocked the door. "I couldn't believe you wouldn't see it too. I've read all of your books at least five times."

"Goodness. Poor you," Lauren said, then introduced her. "Peter, this is Sandra. She's come all the way from Minneapolis to say hello."

The girl indicated her leather jacket on the chair. "You can just toss that anywhere," she said, then turned her attention back to Lauren. "It's like you've felt everything I've ever felt. Thought everything I've ever thought."

"You're a writer too, aren't you?"

"Well, you know. Not published or anything."

"I thought you were a writer. You have that desperate look."

The girl managed a shy smile.

Peter picked up Sandra's jacket and hung it in the closet. He seemed to take his time about it, as if hoping the girl would decide to leave before he finished.

"What are you working on these days?" Lauren asked Sandra. She really didn't want Peter's company right now; he wouldn't know what to say to this girl.

"I'm working on a short story. About a cat."

"What happens to the cat?"

"She gets electrocuted."

"Another light-hearted cat story."

"Right." The girl gave a low laugh. "Exactly."

Lauren could sense Peter's tension. It was the first time he had seen her show any interest in someone else. He had overheard her long telephone conversations with Naomi, their schoolgirlish giggling fits. But he had never seen another person in the apartment.

"People say I even look like you," Sandra said.

Lauren poured the girl some tea, offered her cigarettes and took an inventory of her background: Where do you go to school? What do you study? Is your creative writing class worthwhile? The girl blossomed in her regard like a time-lapse rose. People often mistook Lauren's questions for personal interest, when it was really just a way to prevent them asking about her. She knew they sometimes mistook it for something else, but there was nothing she could do about that. She was a writer; questions were part of the discipline.

Taking a sip of her tea with that beautiful mouth, the girl asked Lauren if she'd ever been obsessed with another writer.

Lauren managed to turn this too into another question. "Maybe one or two—but I wanted to sleep with them. That's different, right?"

"Right."

Lauren had to admit she was enjoying the worship of this pretty young fan. It was not that she was excluding Peter on purpose—she just found herself asking more and more questions of the girl, watching with fascination the full lower lip—but when he suddenly stood up to leave, she did not try to dissuade him.

"I think I'll go downstairs," he said. "I'm very tired. Nice to meet you, Sandra."

When he was gone, Sandra asked timidly, "Boyfriend?"

Lauren shook her head. "Friend."

The next night, Peter sat reading while Lauren worked. He had brought home a stack of books from the library, all of them about love, all of them disappointing. None of them dealt with the kind of tender care he offered Lauren. His mind kept drifting.

That horrible story Lauren had told him kept invading his thoughts, about her friend who had been raped. The brutality of it disturbed him; so did Lauren's reaction.

From her office came the intermittent clicking of her keyboard.

He would have to explain to her that he did not share her fascination with violence, with blood. Oh, the taste of her blood when she had kissed him—rusty, earthlike, as if he had licked an open grave.

He was still annoyed about that pouty girl too, that Sandra person. Especially the way Lauren had seemed to look right through him, which was exactly what Dominic had said.

Finally, she switched off her computer and stood in the doorway, stretching. She leaned far back, exposing her navel, the small waist. Peter returned his eyes to the page as he spoke, as if the book claimed his total interest. "How late did your devotee keep you up?"

"Sandra? We didn't talk much longer after you left. I thought she was sweet, didn't you?"

"I suppose."

"You didn't like her?"

"I don't know. She made me feel redundant. It's *my* job to worship you."

"But she's a writer. It's totally different." Lauren headed toward the bathroom, peeling off her T-shirt. "Why don't you get into bed? I'll be right back."

Peter undressed and got between the sheets. Something made him uneasy; he could smell the faint trace of something that did not belong here. He sniffed the edge of the sheet.

A moment later, Lauren climbed in beside him and tucked her face into his shoulder. Peter lay rigid. Lauren moved her hand up and down his chest, but he didn't respond. Finally she asked, "What's wrong?"

Peter found he could not reply; his throat was constricted. Lauren raised herself on one elbow and peered at him, asking with more concern this time, "What's wrong, Peter?"

His voice was a foreign instrument; he could hardly make it say the words. "That girl. Was she in this bed?"

There was the slightest of pauses. Lauren turned away. "Yes. She was. How did you know?"

"I can smell her. That oil she wore. I smelled it on her jacket. It's on the sheet, the pillow." His voice shook. In fact, he was shaking all over. "And did you . . ."

"Did we what? Did we have sex?" Lauren turned on her back and sighed heavily. "Yes. We had sex."

"Oh."

"I'm sorry, Peter. I didn't realize it would hurt you."

"How could you not realize? I couldn't dream of touching another person."

"It isn't that way for me. That's just not the way I feel. It isn't exclusive with me."

"Obviously."

"Please don't get worked up. I told her I didn't want to start any-thing with her. She's just a girl. I didn't think it would bother you."

"Another woman? It might even be worse."

"Oh, please. Don't go all Catholic on me. If it's okay for you to lick me, it's okay for me to lick her. Let's not pretend God cares where we stick our tongues."

Peter sat up. His eyes were filling, but he didn't want to cry. "How could you do this, Lauren? Doesn't it mean anything to you, what we do? I don't do it with anyone else, and I never have."

"I can't become a virgin in retrospect, even if I wanted to. Love is one thing, sex is another. If you don't learn that, you'll never understand anything."

"It means nothing to you, what we do together."

"In my time I've been licked by old men, teenage boys, and even a dog I once owned, named Lou-lou."

Peter pressed his hands over his ears. She pulled them away, relentless.

"It's the truth, Peter. You hate the truth. You don't even *like* the real me. It's just your fantasy you like—some fluffy little doll you've created in your head."

"I don't want to know."

"It was a hot day, and I was lying on the roof and the sun was on my legs and I was horny and the dog was right there ..."

"Lauren, I don't want to know."

"—and he started to lick me and I didn't stop him. That's what sex is to me, Peter. A bodily function. It's better with some people than with others, and yes, when you are in love, there is nothing in the universe that compares, but I'm not in love. I've told you—I'm not in love."

He sat on the edge of the bed, his back to her. For a moment he felt a strange sensation, as if the bed were drifting through interstellar space. They were the last two human beings in the universe. Nothing existed but the two of them, and he was nothing to her. His heart withered in his chest.

"I've never told that to anyone, Peter. Please look at me."

He faced her bitterly.

"You were a monk. Can't it be like confession? Can't you forgive me? You have to, don't you?"

He heard the note of panic in her voice. She climbed out of bed and knelt before him, resting her forehead on his knees, arms clasping his legs. *One minute she's pushing me away, the next minute she's on her knees.*

He pushed her away and dressed himself in a hard silence. Lauren crawled up and lay curled on the bed with tears on her face. His heart was a cinder. And yet he couldn't help noticing that, with tears sparkling on her lashes, she was beautiful.

He went downstairs to sleep in his own bed.

Later, he dreamed of Brother Raphael. He lay beside the old monk on some kind of pallet, drifting through outer space. The icy, shrivelled fingers clutched his hand as the two of them floated across a night of black velvet, and all around them the cold stars throbbed.

FOURTEEN

PETER STAYED AWAY for a week. Lauren's small fists pounded on his door, she called his name, but he would not answer. "I'm sorry," she would call through the door, but he did not so much as move.

Lauren cornered him one evening outside the bookstore. He set off briskly down Broadway, and she trotted along at his side.

"How long are you going to be mad at me?"

He walked faster, not looking at her.

"Just tell me how long I have to be punished."

"I'm not punishing you, Lauren. You hurt me, and I'm still in pain. I would have thought that was obvious."

"Well, aren't you ever going to forgive me? I thought you were supposed to forgive even your enemies."

She was right, of course; if he truly loved her, he must forgive her. He began to realize, now that she was beside him, how much he *wanted* to forgive her. But just at that moment, she gave up. She left the intersection and darted through the traffic. He ran after her and caught hold of her elbow, spinning her round to face him.

"You don't give me a chance," she said. "You're like a brick wall. A Sherman tank. You think because you were a monk, you're harmless. But monks do other things besides preach to the sparrows."

"Oh, I suppose you're going to bring up the Inquisition now? That's fair, Lauren. That's rational, that's female."

"You think I'm mean, but you're the one with ice in the heart. It's like you've turned into a different person."

"Fine. You're a saint, and I'm the big bad monk. But it's your bed that's Grand Central. Not mine."

"*I'm* horrible. I don't have words for how disgusting *I* am. But I thought you were different."

They walked side by side, snapping at each other like any quarrelling couple. We could be married, Peter thought. And then suddenly Lauren abandoned the game. She stopped in front of a pizzeria and said, "Let's order pizza and watch television all night."

It caught Peter off guard, and as they waited for their food in the tiny pizzeria, a calm front of forgiveness crossed into his heart. The hurricane had at last blown over; all loved ones were present and accounted for.

They took the pizza to her place and watched a series of fatuous comedies. Peter's own mind was on the bedroom the entire time. How could he touch her? He half expected to see sores where she had been touched by another's hands, another's mouth.

When finally they did go to bed, the sight of Lauren's small, pretty body, his violated paradise, broke his heart. He cried a little, and Lauren waited with her arms looped round his neck, kissing the top of his head. Then, when he was ready, she made love to him not with her usual abandon but with tenderness, so that the memory of Sandra began to recede, like a last faint wisp of patchouli.

Peter had always assumed writers spent their time reading great literature, and it surprised him how much television Lauren watched. Television seemed to bring out a playful side of her character that was otherwise hidden. Her taste was almost indiscriminate. She laughed at the most tiresome jokes and knew the characters on her favourite shows by name. He supposed it was an escape from writing.

Sometimes, when her work went well, she would stand up from her desk and give a clap of satisfaction. And once, when a chapter had turned out better than anticipated, she spun round her office doing a silly little dance—*completely* out of character, Peter thought. Most days, however, Lauren's writing left her sombre and dejected.

"Why can't I write a happy book for once?" she would wail. "Why do I write about such sick characters?"

At such times she would curl up on Peter's lap, fretful and sad, while he stroked her hair.

Lauren did not talk much about her manuscript, but Peter knew it concerned two desperate teenagers. He knew also that it involved a lot of highly charged sexual material, including scenes of incest. She threw a lot of pages out. The girl's father, apparently, was a complete monster. Peter asked once if this was based on Lauren's own childhood, but she refused to answer.

As to the teenage sex, he gathered there was a certain wildness in those chapters. More than once she had cried, "Research time!" and hauled him over to the bed in the middle of the afternoon. Another day, she came over to the armchair and commanded him to sit absolutely still. "I mean it," she said, kneeling to unzip his pants. "You stay like the Lincoln Memorial." Ten minutes later Peter was left shaking and weak. Lauren sat back on the floor with a thoughtful expression. "Clorox," she decided. "Oysters and Clorox."

Such was Peter's contribution to literature.

He wanted to make a different sort of contribution. He knew he did not really understand Lauren's work; some of it he found, frankly, weird. But his love, now that he had forgiven her, had grown deeper, and he wanted to show this by helping Lauren with what was most important in her life. He wanted to make himself necessary to her. Indispensable.

He had seen the photographs in Bob Lyle's office showing various authors behind a microphone in the upstairs room. But when he broached the subject of starting a series of readings, Lyle winced and stooped even lower, as if the idea gave him backache.

"I've done it before, Peter. You have to do it all the time—I mean, virtually seven days a week—or it doesn't pay. Just costs you in staff time and electricity. And the chains get all the big names."

Lyle was in his pure melancholy mode that day, and the smile did not flash on even once. Peter trapped him in his office later in the week.

"Peter, I'm a bookseller, not a publicity agent. If people want to meet authors, they should hang around in bars."

"But it's hearing an author read new work that's exciting. And the upstairs room is perfect."

"People don't want to hear authors read. Not really. Because when you read a book, you hear a very specific voice in your head. She shall ever remain nameless, but I went to see a favourite author of mine *centuries* ago and my God what a mistake *that* was. She was an absolute heroine of mine—stood for everything freewheeling and unconventional and romantic. Unfortunately, she sounded like Audrey Hepburn on speed. Couldn't read her after that."

"Still, you did have readings at the store. And for quite a long stretch, to judge by ..." He gestured at the photographs in their uneven row around the walls.

"One lives in a community, my boy. One tries to do one's part. You're being remarkably insistent. Have you enrolled in assertiveness training?"

Peter wasn't sure what that was; he only pressed the issue because of Lauren. In some ways Bob Lyle was now his prior. Obedience laid its claw on his sleeve. He shook it off.

"I think it would get people into the store. I think it would sell books."

Lyle regarded him for a long moment from under his forelock before flipping it back.

"I would want nothing to do with the enterprise. It would fall on your shoulders, the entire proceeding."

"Of course. That's the whole idea."

"He's having visions of a salon," Lyle said, calling on the photographs for sympathy. He got up and unhooked his umbrella from the door. "Just make sure you get authors with sex appeal. *Downtown* people."

"I had someone pretty good in mind. But she doesn't live downtown."

"Peter, really." The smile flashed on. "Sometimes your ignorance is positively radiant."

All the way home, Peter anticipated Lauren's arguments against doing a reading. He waited until late in the evening when she was feeling happy with her day's work. They were sitting in her living room; *Ray Donovan*, a favourite programme of hers, had just finished.

Peter told her in general terms about his idea.

"Bob said if I could get *you* to read, he'd go for it. Let me finish. The more I thought about it, the more sense it made. You have such a beautiful voice."

"I have a froggy voice."

"You don't. It's very compelling."

"I've heard it on radio. I sound like a thirteen-year-old boy."

Lauren was zapping the television with the remote as they talked, flipping from one disconnected image to another.

"All I'm asking is that you don't rule it out right away. Look at the things I've let you talk *me* into."

"A willing victim, if you ask me."

"I admit it. But think: novels take so long to write, a reading would be a good way to keep your name out there between books. People will know you're still around."

She switched off the television and turned to face him. "Okay. I'll do it."

"You'll consider it?"

"No, no, I'll do it. I'll do the reading."

"It can't hurt sales, you know."

"Peter, stop trying to persuade me. I've already agreed."

"Lauren, this is wonderful."

Lauren shrugged. "It's just lucky. We want the same thing at the same time."

"I know," he said. "I think that's wonderful."

•

"Lauren Wolfe," said Bob Lyle, sifting through the clutter on his desk for a pen. "Lauren Wolfe doesn't do readings. Lauren Wolfe is that truly American phenomenon, the well-known recluse. How did you pull it off?"

"Lauren and I live in the same building. We've become pretty good friends."

Molly was on the telephone. She looked up sharply.

Peter went on. "I thought Lauren would fight the idea tooth and nail, but we seem to have caught her at the right moment."

"What luck," Bob Lyle said, and, having now found the pen, resumed sifting through the clutter in search of the letter that had prompted his search for the pen in the first place. "And how can Peter Meehan, grossly underpaid retail clerk, afford to live in the same building as Lauren Wolfe?"

"You should see my cell—you wouldn't ask. The landlord cut the place up illegally."

"A *very* downtown writer—that species you affected not to know." Lyle discovered the letter, signed it with a flourish and looked up at Peter, smile on high beam. "My boy, thou hast committed a coup."

Over the next two weeks, Peter put up signs at the store announcing the reading, and Lyle arranged with Lauren's publisher to have boxes of books sent over. Molly borrowed a coffee urn from a friend who ran a catering business, and they ordered plates of biscuits and bottles of apple cider.

When the night of the reading arrived, Peter had worked himself up into a state. "I just want everything to go well. I just don't want any disasters," he said to Molly, but what he really wanted—a last trace of a monk's aspiration to sainthood—was perfection.

Peter welcomed people as they came upstairs to the second floor. Lauren had not yet arrived, and he was already suffering stage fright for her. His stomach was fluttery, his throat dry. He poured some cider into a Styrofoam cup. One sip brought the whole monastery to mind—the creak of the cider press, clusters of monks at work in the rainy orchards, the fragrant bushels of Cortlands and McIntosh. He did not take another.

Half an hour before the scheduled start of the reading, they ran short of chairs. "Quick, Molly. Where can we find more?"

"People can stand, or they can sit on the floor. It's carpeted."

"We need more chairs."

"Peter, calm down. It's not an international crisis."

"Why are you in such a bad mood?"

"I'm not in a bad mood," said Molly, as she arranged a stack of Lauren's books into an elegant spiral. "I just think you're getting too worked up."

The room continued to fill and people stood along the front row of windows; they didn't leave as he had feared. Lauren's name had drawn quite a few young couples and some older people, but the room was lined mostly with pale college girls, clutching notebooks that Peter suspected contained their own compositions. A ripple went through them when Lauren at last arrived, but none pushed forward to speak to her.

Peter was surprised at how differently Lauren behaved in this context. Anxiety was like a robe she kept at home; out here in the world she wore cool professionalism, her manner brisk and pleasant.

Despite his announced lack of interest, Bob Lyle had propped himself against a wall of poetry, thoughtfully turning the pages of *The Hesitation Cut*. Peter took Lauren straight over to him, and the two of them immediately launched into chatter about the publishing world.

A few minutes later, Lauren made her way back through the crowd toward Peter.

"You look wonderful," he said. "You certainly made a hit with Bob."

She looked around. "So many *people*."

A young executive woman pushed her way toward them. "My, my, my, look at *you*," she cried at Lauren. "What happened to the Hamlet look?"

"Naomi, don't make a fuss. How did you hear about this?"

"Somebody from the store called. Look at you. White jeans, print shirt—I haven't seen you wear anything but black for at least ten years."

"Shush. This is my friend Peter. He's responsible for all this."

"Naomi Black," she said, shaking Peter's hand. "Are you the one that called?"

"That was me."

"Thank you. Slypuss here would never have mentioned it." She turned back to Lauren. "Such a fashion plate tonight. I thought your idea of dressing up was that number-twelve jersey."

"That's my work shirt. I don't wear it outside." She turned to Peter. "Naomi's my Jewish mother."

"You need a *platoon* of Jewish mothers. Don't you agree, Peter?"

"He's Catholic, Naomi. He doesn't know what you mean."

"I love Catholics. They're the only people who feel more guilty than Jews. Mind you"—here she narrowed her eyes at Lauren—"you should feel guilty. Holding a reading and you don't call me? What kind of bullshit is that?"

"I just *forgot*, for God's sake."

"It's passive-aggressive. You didn't forget."

"Such a *noodge* you are. Really, Naomi, you should move south of Delancey."

"Honey, I don't go south of Fifty-seventh Street. But I love this." She fingered the material of Lauren's shirt. "For once you don't look like you're at a funeral."

"How long have you two known each other?" Peter asked.

"Too long," Naomi said. "Lauren came to my fifth birthday party and sat on my head."

"She took my sparkler," Lauren explained, and the two of them began to argue about this decades-old incident. He envied Naomi for having known Lauren when she was a child.

Then Molly came over, and Peter introduced everyone. Molly greeted Lauren briefly, and after a moment Peter took her aside. It was hard to keep the anger out of his voice.

"Why were you so cool to Lauren, Molly? You were almost rude."

"I was not rude," she said, "and I wish you'd stop misreading me. I'm frankly a little concerned about you."

"Why?"

"You seem a little odd, that's all. A little worked up."

"I just want this to be a success. What's odd about that?"

"Forget it. Are you going to do an introduction?"

An introduction. There was no time to worry about Molly's mood now. Peter left her at the top of the stairs and, on an inspiration, asked Bob Lyle if he'd like to make the introduction. Despite his earlier reservations, Lyle was acting more and more the happy host, shaking hands with old customers, smile flashing on, smile flashing off. The stooped shoulders straightened, the white forelock flicked back.

"My boy," he said, smile definitely on, "I'd be delighted."

Peter stood nervously off to one side when, a moment later, Lyle coughed primly into the microphone until the room quieted. His introduction was complimentary without being fulsome, and he displayed a good knowledge of Lauren's work, mentioning each of her books with a few apt phrases.

There was a flurry of amusement when Lauren stepped up to the microphone; it towered over her head. Lyle lowered it, and she began to read.

She read a half-dozen new poems in a kind of breathy, hypnotic monotone. Peter had trouble concentrating on the words, he was so on edge. Every time an audience member made the slightest noise—a clearing of the throat, the rustle of a candy wrapper—he wanted to scream.

Lauren switched to a short story about a little girl who is terrified of a large dark thing that lives behind her bedroom door. Sometimes she is sure it is a bear, other times a shape-shifting blot of travelling darkness. Nothing her mother says will calm her down. The little girl becomes convinced it is her father behind the door, and the story ended with the introduction of a psychiatrist with "large, clean hands as pale as cottage cheese."

Peter could see the college girls were impressed.

Then Lauren finished with a poem built on the phrase, *Nothing exists, just this, just this.* The night she had chanted it to him came vividly to mind, the way she had rubbed herself in his face. To hear her say it again in public sent a shock through him.

After the applause, Bob Lyle guided Lauren downstairs to the counter, where she spent nearly an hour accepting compliments and signing books, while Molly and Peter rang up the sales. Then

Lauren sat on the staircase talking with Lyle, while they closed their registers.

Peter was still annoyed with Molly, but he couldn't help himself, he had to ask, "How do you think it went?"

"I'd say you had an unqualified success," she said. "Come on. I'll help you clean up."

Lauren was excited and uncharacteristically chatty on the way home, jumping from one thing to another. "Wasn't Bob Lyle sweet to me? It was so nice to see some older couples. People my own age. Sometimes I think I'm just a phase girls go through, like horses and Nancy Drew. They actually seemed to like me."

"Of course they liked you. They loved you."

"I know people buy my books, but I never imagine people *enjoying* them. My books are—well, they don't seem very enjoyable to me."

"That last poem you read. What was the name of it?"

"'Nothing Exists.' You didn't like it?"

"I was distracted by the, uh, refrain."

Lauren stopped in the middle of the sidewalk. People had to walk around her. "You're not angry, are you?"

"Angry? No. Kind of proud, I think."

They walked a few blocks in a lovely silence. Lauren slipped her small hand into his, and his blood leapt. Holding hands was for someone special. Holding hands was not about sex, holding hands was about love. She would not have held hands with Sandra.

"Sometimes I worry about you," Lauren said out of the blue. "I worry that you're too fragile."

"No, no, no," he said happily. "It's *my* job to worry about *you*."

"You know I love you," she said matter-of-factly, "but some- times it's like you're made of glass."

Love. Without even realizing it, she had said she loved him. He did not dare call attention to it, lest she take it back.

"I'm not glass," he said lightly. "I'm not glass. I'm made of . . ." He thumped his chest with the flat of his hand. "Pewter. That's what I'm made of."

Lauren laughed. It thrilled him to bring forth from her throat that low, stuttering sound.

"Mr. Pewter. Solid, dull, dependable. That's me."

A police car prowled the block, its searchlight flowing over the buildings like a white sheet. *Love.* Lauren squeezed his fin- gers, and his veins flowed with silk.

They went upstairs and Lauren put the kettle on for tea. They sat in the kitchen at the rim of a pool of light cast by the table lamp. An afterglow settled around them; there was no need to speak. Five minutes would go by, they would trade a comment or two, then another five or ten minutes would pass. *Happiness,* Peter thought, that's what this is called. I've made her *happy.*

"I thought your short story went over well."

"Mm. They did seem to like it."

Lauren poured the hot water into the pot, sat back down again. Ezra strolled in, yawning, and hopped onto her lap. Another silence.

"It had a disturbing quality. A strange edge to it."

"Do you think?"

She poured them each a cup of tea. They sat sipping in silence.

"Lauren, I'm so happy. I've never *been* so happy. I never want this night to end. I don't want anything to change. Not the slight- est, smallest thing." He tapped his cup. "I want the tea to be hot forever. I want there always to be more in the pot."

She smiled at him over the rim of her cup. "Your friend Molly seems quite attached to you."

"Molly? She was in such a strange mood tonight."

"I missed it. Bob Lyle was regaling me with stories about Susan Sontag."

Their cups clacked on their saucers. A jangle of guitars drifted in through the air shaft window. Someone on another floor was playing rock music.

Lauren reached into her shoulder bag and pulled out her cigarettes.

"I'll find you an ashtray," said Peter, getting up. He went into the office, but everything seemed to be buried in paper. The computer screen flickered in the darkness. *Coral uncoiled the rope and—* Lauren had broken off in mid-sentence. Peter never did learn what Coral was about to do with that rope. He went into the bedroom and retrieved an ashtray from the dresser.

The ashtray was in his hand, and he was turning back toward the kitchen, when he saw a man on Lauren's bed. Peter did not wonder even for a split second if he was imagining it. A man lay on Lauren's bed, and this fact hit Peter with the impact of a large solid object.

Several physical reactions took hold. His tongue dried in his mouth, and he couldn't get enough air; only the top part of his lungs seemed to work. His heart hurled itself against his chest.

He could not make out details. It was dark, and the man was curled up almost fetally. He must be drunk. A thief, perhaps worse.

Peter turned toward the kitchen, moving in slow motion, a diver on the ocean floor.

Lauren had lit her cigarette and exhaled a stream of smoke toward the ceiling. Her face had a thoughtful expression. She looked separate and unreachable—not just in another room; he was seeing her across a terrible divide. He yearned to be where she was: to not know there was an intruder on her bed.

"What are you doing?" Lauren said as he approached. It sounded like a shout. He jerked a finger to his lips.

She gave him a quizzical look.

He crossed the space between them and moved toward the apartment's front door, beckoning her.

"Peter, why are you being so weird?"

He opened the door and beckoned again. Her expression said, *I'm not moving.* He shut the door and gripped her shoulders. He put his lips to her ear and whispered, "Don't say anything. Come outside."

"Peter, stop this. You're making me angry."

There was no point whispering now. "There's someone on your bed."

Lauren's face went white. He gripped her arm and pulled her up. He had nearly pulled her outside when she yanked her wrist free.

"Lauren, no!"

But she was across the kitchen in a flash. She went straight for the bedroom.

He found her staring down at the bed, her mouth open a little. He reached out, about to clasp her forearm and urge her away, when, to his astonishment, Lauren fell to her knees and clutched the man's arm, crying, "Mick, Mick, Mick! Oh, Mick!"

FIFTEEN

"THERE'S SOMETHING WRONG with him. He won't wake up." Lauren looked up, her eyes shining with panic.

"Maybe he's drunk."

She shook the man again. "Mick, wake up. It's me."

"You've never mentioned anyone named Mick. What's he doing in your apartment? How did he get in?"

Lauren switched on the bedside lamp and sat on the edge of the bed. She pushed against Mick's shoulder until he lay back with a deep groan against the pillow. His shirt was soaked with blood.

For a long moment, neither of them moved.

"I'll call a doctor," Peter said. "The emergency number."

"We better not."

"Lauren, he's bleeding."

"It may not be serious. We should look first." She made no move to do it.

The last thing Peter wanted to do was touch this stranger, but he forced himself to sit on the edge of the bed and tried to undo the man's shirt. The buttons were sticky with blood.

Finally, he took hold of the two sides and yanked the shirt open. Something heavy fell to the floor. The flesh at the side of the man's abdomen had a small black hole.

"Bullet wound, it looks like."

"Is it still bleeding?"

"I can't tell. Get a cold cloth for his head. I'll get some paper towels."

Lauren ran water in the bathroom, while he soaked some paper towels under the kitchen tap. When he came back, he saw what had fallen from the man's shirt. It was almost hidden in the shadow just under the bed.

Lauren placed the cold cloth on the man's forehead, and he began to respond. His groans sounded closer to the surface, closer to speech. Peter wiped at his stomach with the wet towels.

"You see what he was carrying? You see what's on the floor?"

"Don't worry about it. Mick, are you all right?"

"Don't worry about it?"

Mick rubbed a hand over his face in a strange circular movement, as if clearing webs from his cheeks.

Peter whispered harshly, "He has a gun. We should call the police."

Mick gripped Peter's hair with a sticky hand, his voice a croak. "No police."

"Let go of my hair."

"No police. Kill you."

"You're not going to kill anyone. Let go of my hair."

Lauren touched the offending arm. "Mick, it's all right. We're not going to call the police."

Mick screwed up his face, trying to see.

"It's me. Lauren. You're safe now."

"Tell him to let go of my hair," Peter said.

"Mick, honey. You can let go now. Peter's okay."

Mick's arm fell back in surrender. Peter picked up the gun by a corner of the grip and carried it like a bomb to the kitchen. Lauren followed him and filled a glass at the sink.

"He's very thirsty."

"He's lost a lot of blood. We have to get him to a hospital."

The croak came from the bedroom. "No hospital. No doctors."

"Lauren, this is ridiculous. Do you want him to die in your bed?"

"He's not bleeding that much that I can see."

"If he matters to you, why are you refusing to help him?"

"I just don't want him in jail," she said. "Doctors have to report gunshot wounds."

The ragged voice came again: "No doctors. No police."

"Lauren, you know what's right. You know what has to be done."

"I really don't think he's dying."

"What if the bullet's still inside him? He'll get infection and fever."

"He's trying to say something."

Peter followed her back into the bedroom. She slipped an arm under Mick's neck, and tilted the glass to his lips. Peter thought of Brother Raphael dying in the infirmary, a lifetime ago.

"Come on, Mick. Drink some."

Water ran down his chin.

"You have to prop him up more. Put another pillow under him."

"Well, give me a hand, then."

Peter hoisted him forward, yanking the other pillow into place.

"Sorry, man," Mick said. "Sorry, man."

Peter took the glass from Lauren and gave him some water. "He'll need more."

"Sorry, man." Mick had a foolish grin on his face, a patient coming out of anaesthetic. "Don't be pissed off."

"You need medical care."

"No fuckin' doctors, man. Seriously."

"You have a hole in your back too. A bigger one."

"Same bullet. Means it went right through."

He seemed much stronger than even moments ago. Lauren brought him more water, and he drank half a glass unaided.

"I have some disinfectant." Lauren lifted a bottle of hydrogen peroxide.

When they had finished cleaning the wound, Lauren taped gauze over it. Her pale hands on the man's hairy stomach made Peter want to retch.

"I think he could take some soup," Lauren said. "I'm going to make some."

Peter followed her out to the kitchen. "I'm going to call an ambulance. I'll do it from a pay phone."

Lauren slammed the soup tin on the counter. "Peter, if you call an ambulance, I will never speak to you again."

"I want to do what's right."

"No, you don't. You want to get rid of him."

"He's clearly a criminal. He's putting you in danger."

"You don't know that."

"I've seen enough to know he's putting you in danger."

"Peter, listen to me—these are not just words—if you call an ambulance, I will never speak to you again. Do you understand?"

"You can't mean that."

"I might even hurt you. I might do something horrible."

"Lauren, you've never even mentioned this man to me. How can he be so important?"

"He just is, Peter. You're not calling anyone."

"This stranger appears, and suddenly you're a different person."

"He's not a stranger to me. If you don't like it, leave."

Peter lowered himself onto a kitchen chair. He watched her open the soup and pour it into a pan. His skull was ringing, as if someone had tapped it with a small hammer.

Lauren finished heating the soup and took it into the other room. The only sound for the next few minutes was an intermittent slurp.

"Have a little more," he heard her say. "You're looking much better."

"Yes, ma."

More slurps.

Peter looked at the gun. He wanted to eject the man from existence as suddenly as he had dropped in.

"I got a problem, Laur."

Laur?

"That's obvious."

"Nothing I can't handle. Fucking moolies. I got nothing against people of a different colour, but you can't do business with those guys."

"Is this the one from before?"

"Cat's Eye, yeah. Can't even have normal names. Gotta do everything black."

"You invaded his turf."

"Shit, no. I'm not *crazy*. I had a beef with one of his guys. Guy ends up in Rikers Island next day, not my fault. I got nothing to do with that. Cat's Eye begs to differ."

Rikus. Diffuh. Where had Lauren found this person?

"I told you it was stupid to stay in that business."

"Yeah, yeah. So you said."

"You promised me you were getting out."

"I *am* getting out."

"You're so believable."

"I *am* getting out. Soon as I can afford to. It okay if I stay here?"

"Of course."

So easily she admitted this criminal into her home. Lauren might be calm, but Peter knew that catastrophe had struck.

"Only a few days," Mick said. "The moolies aren't gonna show. They don't know nothing about this place."

"It's okay."

Mick lowered his voice. "You fucking this guy?"

"Shhh."

"No problem. I just wanna know."

If she answered, Peter didn't hear it. A moment later the bedroom went dark, and Lauren came into the kitchen.

"He's sleeping."

"I'm so glad."

"Peter, I know I should have told you about him, but I just couldn't. I thought he was out of my life for good, but the truth is, Mick is very special to me."

"So I see."

"You sound like a jealous wife."

"Maybe I should go."

Lauren didn't try to stop him, so he felt he had to stand up. His stomach was turbulent. He said, "Do you want to sleep at my place?"

"No, I'll sleep on the couch."

"You could have my bed. I'd sleep on the floor."

"Peter, it's really not necessary."

"I don't like to leave you with him. He's dangerous."

"Not to me. He just doesn't live like we do. Go on, now. I'll see you tomorrow."

He lay on his bed, staring at the ceiling. Directly overhead, that criminal was defiling her bed, *their* bed—that sacred place where she had taught him the geography of her body, the hills and plains of rapture.

That Lauren and Mick had been lovers at some point, he knew with a certainty that would have been beyond him even two months ago, a lover's certainty. Mick was an alien species; Lauren must be attracted to some quality Peter had never possessed and never would. He felt the dread of one facing a fight in which he is horribly overmatched.

He lay on the bed as if nailed to it. For some moments he had the sensation that he was looking down at himself, observing a martyr on the rack. But he refused to be a martyr. He would figure a way out of this predicament, he would work out a strategy. But for now he just glared at the ceiling, willing Mick out of existence.

He was still awake when birds began to chatter in the air shaft. Grey light seeped from the walls, traffic noises started, and it was time to get ready for work. He showered and shaved and examined himself in the mirror with disgust.

He knocked on Lauren's door. She opened it a few inches, and said in a whisper, "Mick's sleeping."

"How is he?"

"He's okay, but he's sleeping. I'm working."

"Oh. Oh, all right."

"What happened to you?" Molly asked when he was opening up the cash register.

"I'm not feeling too well."

"You look terrible. It better not be contagious."

"I'm just tired. Damn this thing." He slammed a fist against the register.

"Take it easy, now. Let me." She reached over and adjusted the key in the register so that the drawer sprang open. "The reading went so well last night, and I think Bob was really pleased. Did something happen afterward?"

"Molly, can you mind your own business for once?"

She stared at him, her features slack with disbelief. Then she turned and fled. He found her later in the office and apologized, and she accepted coolly. He had damaged something between them, but just now, with the fear of losing Lauren feeding on his heart, he hadn't the strength to repair it. He could not face customers. He asked Vanessa to take the cash register for him.

It was late afternoon when Bob Lyle came gliding upstairs and found him stocking Self-Help. "Peter, can you tell me why the counter is manned by the ghostly Vanessa? Unless I'm mistaken, you yourself are scheduled to do cash."

"Vanessa needs the practice."

"Vanessa needs many things—more iron in her diet for a start. She is certainly not ready to handle the cash register for more than ten minutes by herself."

"We all have to learn sometime."

"She won't pick it up by magic. Someone has to help her."

"Bob . . ." Peter controlled his voice, but anger pounded at the place where his vow of obedience used to be. "I'd really rather not handle the cash today, if you don't mind."

"I do mind. There are exactly three customers in the store, and Vanessa has managed to form them into a disgruntled lineup. Molly was very patient with you when you first started. I know Vanessa's been here longer, but I don't see why you can't extend the same courtesy to her."

When he got home, he went straight up to Lauren's. She opened the door only two inches, and he stood there helplessly, hoping to be invited in.

"I thought I'd stop by. See how things are going."

"He's going to be fine," she said, as if Mick's health were of national importance.

"It's you I'm worried about. How was the couch? Did you sleep all right?"

"What?" Confusion crossed her face. "Oh, yes—no problem."

"Laur?" Mick's voice came from beyond the kitchen. *Laur.* As if they'd grown up together.

"I'd better get back."

He ransacked his mind for a way to gain admittance. "Do you need anything? Can I get you anything from the store?"

"Thanks. I got groceries earlier this afternoon."

"Really? You went to the Korean?"

"I have to go, Peter."

He went slowly downstairs to his apartment. Something evil crackled in the air, a malign electricity. A spell had been cast, history was wiped out: he and Lauren Wolfe had never been lovers. He—the man who for her sake had destroyed everything he held dear, who had in effect ended his life—had been transformed into nothing more than the guy downstairs.

SIXTEEN

THE FOLLOWING NIGHT, after another bad day at work, Lauren knocked on his door. "We want you to come for dinner," she said. "If you don't have plans, of course. It's nothing special, just pasta and salad."

That *we* travelled through him like a spear. But as he stood under the thin drizzle of his shower, he began to see his predicament almost as a mathematical problem; there must be a right way to solve it. A hard stand wouldn't work. He could not simply say, "Either he goes or I go"; she would choose Mick. He knew this from the way she had changed when Mick appeared, the taut, tightrope way she had begun to move. It was how he himself had to move in *her* presence.

He developed a strategy as he shaved: he would show them both what a broad-minded, tolerant person he was. Above all, he would display confidence. He was not the kind of man who had to fear that some two-bit thug would steal his lover away. He could afford to be expansive and generous, and most important (in contrast to Mick) he would be gentle. Lauren must be in no doubt as to which man was better able to look after her.

•

"Hey, Pete," Mick greeted him at the door, hand extended. "Thanks for coming." Big in the shoulders, lean of face, Mick was an imposing presence. The bullet seemed to have had little effect. It was easy to see how Lauren could be attracted; Peter's confidence faltered, but he maintained a mask of good cheer.

"You're the chef, I see," he said.

Mick chopped at a lettuce. "Oh, hey—in the kitchen? I'm a wonder."

Wondah. He may be handsome, Peter thought, but he talks like an imbecile. He asked Mick how long he and Lauren had known each other.

"Laur and me? I don't know—two years maybe. Listen, Pete." Mick dumped shredded lettuce into a bowl. "I gotta thank you for the other night. Seriously."

"Please. Forget it."

"That," Mick said, pointing the knife at his chest, "is exactly what I *won't* do."

Two *years.* And she had not even mentioned this person.

"I see the guest of honour has arrived," Lauren said. She came into the kitchen carrying a slim candle in either hand. "Maybe you could light these. My lighter's on the table."

Peter set the candles into holders and lit them, the smell of hot wax bringing back memories of chapel, of prayer, of a calmer heart. Lauren was stirring something on the stove and spoke with her back to him.

"How's life at the bookstore?"

"Busy. You know—not too bad."

"And how's your friend Molly? That was her name, wasn't it?"

"Molly's fine. Molly's always fine. That's the kind of person she is."

Mick opened a drawer and found a vegetable peeler; he certainly seemed to know his way around Lauren's kitchen. "Molly your babe, Pete?"

"Uh, no. Molly is just a friend. We work together."

Mick broke into a country-and-western song as he sliced cucumbers. When he got to the melancholy refrain, he crooned it over Lauren's shoulder, and she squirmed like a child. They had the easy familiarity of a married couple.

Mick tossed the salad in a flamboyant, showy way, clowning as the chef. Every third toss or so, he would nudge Lauren with his hip and make her laugh. Everything he did made her laugh. Peter had had to work hard for every smile he got from Lauren, and yet this clown, this criminal, had her in the palm of his hand.

"Why don't you open the wine, Mick? We'll have the salad first."

"As you wish, my dear," Mick said in a silly British accent. He carried on with it while he worked the corkscrew. "An unassuming vintage, a sporty little wine with an impudent finish."

"You didn't make that up," said Lauren. "You must have memorized it."

Mick winked at Peter with horrifying camaraderie. "She don't let nothing by, this girl. Gotta watch my every move. Gotta watch my p's and q's, right, Laur?"

Lauren set three salad bowls on the table. "I'm trying to teach him to be a human being. But it may be hopeless."

"Nothing is ever hopeless." Mick raised a pedagogic finger for emphasis. "We always got hope. Even in our darkest hour. What do you say, Pete?

"Oh, I agree. There's always hope."

"See, Laur? You gotta never despair."

"I always despair," Lauren said, taking her place at the table and pouring wine into Peter's glass. "I should get a tattoo: *born to despair.*"

"I'll give you a tattoo."

"I bet you would."

"You know where, too."

"Mick."

Mick passed the salad bowl to Peter. "Help yourself, guy. Laur makes great dressing. How many people you know make their own dressing?"

Brother Damian had made a very plain dressing, but Peter was not about to mention the monastery; that would be entirely the wrong tack. He tried to think of something else to talk about, but Mick threw him again by saying, "Lauren told me you were a monk, is that true?"

"Yes, I—yes, a small monastery upstate."

"You had to get up in the middle of the night to pray?"

"Five in the morning."

"Musta been pretty quiet. Even Manhattan's quiet then."

"Yes."

"You don't talk to each other?"

"Not at mealtimes, but we could talk at other times. I wasn't a Trappist."

"That's cool, not talking. I often thought about being a monk."

"That's a laugh," Lauren commented. "Some monk you'd make."

"These Jewish girls"—Mick jerked his thumb at Lauren—"don't understand nothing. I was raised Catholic. I don't go to church too much, but I still got the feeling for it."

"Oh, please." Lauren rolled her eyes.

"The way I look at Jews, it's like they haven't been to high school, you know? The Old Testament is fine and good. We got the Old Testament too. Adam and Eve and all that. The Flood. But Jews don't get the New Testament. It's like they're still in grade school." He turned to Lauren. "See, to a Catholic, no matter how far away from it you get, you never lose that feeling for it. I got a lot of respect for monks. Takes discipline to do what they do."

"Which is exactly why you'd be a terrible monk."

Mick shrugged. He picked up his fork and assaulted a tomato.

"People from all sorts of backgrounds find they have a vocation," Peter said. "It's surprising who turns up in a monastery."

"Sex could be a problem, though."

"A minor concern," said Lauren. "A trifle."

"*Laur.* I'm trying to have a serious discussion here."

Lauren lowered her head in mock contrition.

"There aren't many temptations," said Peter. "You don't even dream about it after a while."

"That's pretty hard to believe," Lauren said.

"I can't speak for anyone else. But it's true in my case. Even the dreams stopped." Not now they wouldn't; he would dream about Lauren for the rest of his life, *Just this, just this.*

Mick said, "Guess I'll stick to welding."

"Welding? Is that what you do?"

"Welders get shot all the time," said Lauren. "Didn't you know that?"

"You'll get a smack, little girl. Don't say I didn't warn you."

Peter hoped this was only a manner of speaking. Mick was twice his size, a criminal used to violence. If Peter had to protect

Lauren—which he would certainly do unto the death—he would be badly beaten. But Mick had warmed to his theme.

"My father's got a small shop down Red Hook. I help him out sometimes. I've had jobs with the water department, Con Edison... you name it."

"Like Vulcan," Lauren put in.

"What's that?" Mick asked.

"He was welder to the gods. And the other gods looked down on him. He had a limp, and he wasn't too handsome, but he had the best-looking wife of them all. He was married to Venus."

"How come he got the babe?"

"I forget. Anyway, she was having an affair with Mars, and he rigged up the bed with a steel net. Next time Mars and Venus went at it, this net fell on them and the roof opened, and all the gods looked down at them and laughed."

"Beautiful," said Mick, ambushing a slice of cucumber. "I love that story."

"It's the only welding story I know."

"I got one for you: My father. One day these guys came in to knock him over. Figured he had a lot of cash or something. He got rid of them with the blowtorch."

"How resourceful," Peter said.

"You can turn those things into flame-throwers practically. These guys had some kind of polyester pants on that didn't burn, they just melted. Made it easy for the cops, two guys limping along the street in melted pants."

"Do you wear one of those medieval helmets?"

Mick shook his head. "Those are for arc welding. Different thing." He turned to Lauren with a big grin. "See? We can talk. I don't know what you was so worried about."

"Oh," said Lauren, "I can't imagine."

Mick gave her a playful cuff on the back of the head. In spite of himself, Peter was almost beginning to like Mick—at least, he could see why one *could* like him. He was a big bear: you didn't want to get him riled, but there was something cuddly about him, with his big muscles and his beautiful eyes.

"Welding seems like good work," Peter said, as if this were foremost in his mind. "Why would you stop?"

"That's a very good question, Pete. I wonder that myself."

They ate in silence for a while. Still chewing, Mick pointed his fork at Peter. "You ever ridden a hog, Pete?"

"Ridden one? You mean like in a rodeo?"

Mick and Lauren burst into laughter. Peter felt the blood rise up his neck and into his face.

"Sorry," said Lauren. "But it *is* pretty funny. A hog is a motorcycle."

"Correction." Mick raised his pedagogic finger again. "A hog is a Harley-Davidson."

"Oh," said Peter. "Those are good ones, aren't they?"

"I think I'm beginning to like this guy," Mick said to Lauren. Then he winked at Peter. "I'll take you for a ride sometime."

"I've never been on a motorcycle."

"Oh," said Lauren, "there's nothing like it."

Mick said quietly, the matter settled, "We'll go for a ride."

When they were having coffee, Peter asked Mick how long he would be staying—asked casually, a matter of mild interest. "Oh, another couple of days," Mick said, putting something back in the fridge. "Soon as things cool down."

"You mean with your Cat's Eye friend?"

Mick's face changed. "Who told you about him? You don't

know nothing about that. You understand me? You never heard of me, you never heard of him. You understand me?"

"Of course. I was just—"

Mick smacked the fridge, and it sounded like a steak hitting a counter. "I'm not playing with you."

"I understand that, Mick. Consider it forgotten."

Mick's hard stare remained on him a few moments longer. Then, as if he had been the frightened one, he said, "You gave me a turn there, Pete. You really did."

"You're the one who mentioned the guy's name," Lauren said. "It's not Peter's fault you were delirious."

"Nobody's talking to you."

"No, we just happen to be in my apartment."

"Nobody's talking to you."

Lauren went off to the living room by herself. Peter was surprised at her lack of tact in dealing with Mick.

Mick shrugged. "We'll go for a ride sometime."

Even though Lauren had snapped at Mick a couple of times, Peter could sense the power of his attraction for her; she seemed helpless before it. He thought about it all through work the next day. When he got home, he made himself a supper of tinned stew and then couldn't eat it. He sat on the edge of his bed, listening to the noises overhead: the clonk of Mick's boots, the boom of his voice.

He was putting his garbage in the can under the stairs when he heard Mick and Lauren coming out of her apartment. He waited for them to appear on the stairs. Lauren was carrying a black helmet by the strap.

"Just the man we're looking for," said Mick. He shook Peter's hand as if they were meeting for the first time. "We're going out on the town and we want you to come."

"And you thought I was a bookworm," said Lauren. She was all dressed up: black jeans, black blouse, big silver earrings.

"Where are you off to?"

"Place downtown. Come on, guy. You'll have fun."

He said okay. At least then he could keep an eye on them. He gave them what he hoped was an engaging grin.

"What should I wear?"

Lauren reached out and squeezed his hand. "You're perfect just as you are."

"I'll take Laur," Mick said. "Then I'll come back for you."

Peter followed them outside. Mick mounted the motorcycle like a graceful cowboy. Lauren climbed on behind him, opening her knees and hitching up close behind him. Jealousy bit Peter's heart. The helmet covered her hair now, and made her look like someone he didn't know. She put her arms around Mick and they took off down the street with a noise like ragged thunder.

It was a warm night, and Peter sat on the stoop to wait. If Lauren was so crazy about Mick, why was she including Peter in this outing—or, for that matter, in last night's dinner? Was she trying to tell him not to worry? Or was she trying to tell him to get used to his new status as third wheel? It mystified him that he could be so in love with someone he did not begin to understand.

Mick came back for him half an hour later and handed him the helmet. Peter straddled the seat behind him.

"What do I hold on to?" Peter yelled over the noise.

"You hold on to me!"

He gripped the leather of Mick's jacket with a feeling of

repulsion, two magnets end to end. As they zoomed up the street, the force of acceleration nearly yanked him off the back end.

Mick swerved this way and that through the traffic, a native manning the tiller through rocky shoals.

Vibrations sent a sawtooth buzz up Peter's spine and shook his thighs. An old man in a homburg stopped in the middle of the street, and Mick swooped around him. The wind gave Peter goosebumps, chilled his cheeks and blew into his nose. Under different circumstances it might have been exhilarating.

Lights, trucks and pedestrians whooshed by; the air seemed full of missiles. At Columbus Circle, Mick opened the throttle and they shot down Ninth Avenue. The buildings seemed to step back out of their way.

They reached the Village a few minutes later. Peter climbed off the bike, and his legs felt like water.

"Like it?" Mick was securing a heavy chain around the front wheel, each link thick as a finger.

"I'm not sure," Peter said. "It's a long way from sheep farming, I'll say that."

He took off the helmet and saw with shock that they had come to a church. Red light poured like blood down the limestone exterior, and Peter felt as if he were committing a sin just by looking at it.

"It's not Roman Catholic, is it?"

"Not anymore."

A small crowd clustered around the bouncer at the wooden doors, their faces red with reflected light. A young woman in a tight dress demanded to know when she was going to be let in.

The bouncer didn't even look at her. "You get in when I say you get in, Sweetpea."

"We been here an hour, for Christ sake." She gestured with her cigarette at the woman beside her—a mass of blond hair above two muscular buttocks.

"There's other people ahead of you."

"You're a pig, Bernie."

"That's what they pay me for. Hey, Mickey."

Mick and the bouncer slapped palms. Mick jerked his head at Peter. "Good people. With me and Laur."

"Have a good time, bro."

"Did we just jump the line?" Peter said.

"Democracy at work, Pete. Don't sweat it."

He followed Mick through the crowd into a vast cavern. Synthesizers shrieked, bass notes kicked him in the belly. The floor quaked underfoot. A long serpent of a bar coiled along one side. Behind it, Gothic windows, once stained glass, had been blinded with black board and foil. Lights burst overhead like mortar fire.

Lauren was sitting at the end of the bar, sipping a large drink. Peter had never seen her like this—perhaps it was the unsettling context, but he almost wouldn't have recognized her. At this moment she looked anything but fragile. She saw them and smiled; the black light turned her teeth pale violet. She kissed Mick on the cheek and said something Peter couldn't hear. He asked her to repeat it, but she had turned away.

Her small foot was tapping in time to the music. Lauren was a literary person; could she really be enjoying that jet-engine blast? Behind the bar, three bartenders were raking in money like croupiers. Mick leaned over the bar with a fifty-dollar bill in his hand and got some attention. He gestured at Peter to order.

"Ginger ale," Peter shouted. The bartender cupped a palm to his ear. Peter had to shout it again.

When the drinks came, Mick made a face of disgust at Peter's ginger ale. All gestures were exaggerated here, all faces demonic. Mick drank his beer straight from the bottle. Peter stood with his back to the bar, the curved edge digging into his back. A blond man with a ponytail squeezed between them to order drinks. Faces ballooned out of the darkness and gleamed for an instant, then submerged again.

Mick led Lauren out onto the dance floor, a shifting pandemonium where men pumped their hips back and forth like rutting dogs, and women slid fingers down their bellies. Lauren was reserved by comparison, but she danced well. Mick was quite stiff, Peter was glad to notice.

Then Lauren came over and took Peter by the hand, ignoring his protests. Well, he would take it like a good sport. Awash in the shifting, bobbing crowd, he lifted first one foot, then the other, put one in front, then behind, lurching this way and that like a tin man. All his senses were overwhelmed. Lauren was laughing, but he could not hear her; she could not see his blush.

Peter watched a girl dancing next to them and tried to memorize the way her feet skidded about, the scribbling motion they made all over the floor. He flung himself into the spirit. He flapped his hands and sent his feet skipping one after the other. He shook his head from side to side, let the music yank him left and right.

Lauren stopped dancing and leaned against him, laughing. Then they threaded their way back to the bar. Mick had vanished.

"Probably in the men's room," Peter said. "I have to go myself."

He had to join a line behind a bodybuilder in a net undershirt. A woman was on her knees in the middle stall, throwing up. The first stall banged open and two young men with very short hair staggered out, wiping white powder from their noses. A barrel-shaped man in a pastel shirt yanked a paper towel from the dispenser near Peter's shoulder. He dried his hands carefully, then pressed Peter against the wall and kissed him on the mouth. Then he vanished out the door, leaving Peter wiping his mouth in disgust.

"Did you see that?" he asked the bodybuilder.

He shrugged. "Guess he thought you were cute."

"This place is weird," Peter shouted to Lauren when he found her at the bar. "A man kissed me in there."

Lauren was staring fiercely into the milling dancers. He followed her gaze and saw Mick dancing with a doll-faced Asian girl. She couldn't have been more than eighteen.

Lauren slammed her drink down on the bar.

The girl spun. Mick stepped up behind her and took hold of her hips. Moving together, they slithered down toward the floor and back up again.

Lauren jumped down from the bar stool, and Peter followed her outside.

"You saw him," she said as they crossed the parking lot. "He's doing it on purpose."

"I don't understand why you go out with him. Why keep him in your apartment?"

"Torturing me—that's how he has fun. He likes to put the knife in. He likes to twist it, too. He'd fuck her right in front of me if he could."

"He probably doesn't even know you're upset."

"Of course he knows. Why do you think he does it? He wants

to hurt me as much as possible. And it works. Believe me, it works."

It frightened him how much pain Mick was able to cause her. If only *he* could cause her such pain.

"Can we walk a little slower?"

"No." She was stalking ahead of him, arms swinging.

"Lauren, what can you expect from a person like that? In a place like that?"

"Really, Peter. You don't understand anything."

The angrier Mick made her, as far as Peter was concerned, the better. They walked several blocks in silence, until Lauren flagged a cab. She sulked in the back seat all the way uptown. The moment they entered the building, Lauren said a curt good night and headed for the stairs.

"Wait, Lauren. I want to say something."

She paused on the bottom step. "Mick's my problem, Peter, not yours."

"He's very much my problem. The way you feel when Mick is dancing with someone else—that's how I feel when you're with Mick. As you say, it's like a knife."

"Except I'm not doing it on purpose."

"I certainly hope not. Maybe it's my fault for not making my feelings clearer. I'm selfish, Lauren. I want you all to myself. I want you all the time. When I'm with you, I'm happy. When I'm not, I want to die."

"Jesus, Peter." She leaned wearily against the wall. "Can't we just be friends?"

"Didn't you hear what I just said?"

Lauren sighed in exasperation and stared up at the ceiling. "I'm being tested. I'm going to lose you *and* my boyfriend in the same night."

"I thought *I* was your boyfriend. We slept together. You said you loved me. I didn't imagine it."

"Friendship love—not *lover* love."

"Then why was I in your bed?"

"Sex is not love, Peter. I didn't lie to you. I told you I wasn't in love right from the start. I warned you."

"I thought your feelings were changing. We have such good times together. I make you happy."

"Nobody makes me happy."

"Not even the other night? The night of your reading?"

"It was a good night. Nothing more."

The wrong things were being said. He wanted to unsay them, to have things back the way they were, but Lauren gave the blade another twist.

"I don't love you, Peter. Not in the way you want. That will never happen with you and me."

"Oh."

"You said it yourself—I'm as crazy about Mick as you are about me."

"But Mick hurts you. He makes you miserable."

"That's life, Peter. I'm going to bed."

He stood in the hallway, listening to her trudge up the stairs. He stayed there for quite a while after her door closed.

It was later, much later, when he sat up in bed. Shouts echoed in the hall. Mick was banging on Lauren's door, demanding entry. Lauren yelled for him to go away. Cries and curses flew back and forth. Then it went quiet. Peter got out of bed and silently opened his door. Mick's voice, a prayer-like mutter, drifted down the stairs. Lauren's door clicked open, then shut.

Peter slept late into the morning, dreaming that Lauren came to apologize. She knelt in his doorway and begged him to forgive her. His heart broke on waking. He had no stomach for breakfast. He looked at himself with loathing as he shaved. As he was pulling on his trousers, someone knocked at the door. Lauren was coming to say she loved him after all. He would forgive her instantly.

He threw his shirt on and called out, "Be right there!"

Then a man cleared his throat in the hall, and hope left him. He did not want to see Mick.

But it was not Mick.

"Hello, Brother William."

"Oh, dear," said Peter, clutching his shirt together at the throat. "Father Michael."

SEVENTEEN

THE PRIEST WAS a strange figure, standing there in a check shirt and blue denims. He had a solemn, permanent look, as if a tree had taken root in the hallway. He gestured at his civilian clothes.

"Thought I'd better come incognito. Priests coming and going, it might upset neighbours. May I come in?"

Peter stood aside to let him in and saw his room with new eyes: the cheap wooden panelling, the narrow bed, the remains of his stew congealing on a plate; it did not look the home of a happy man.

"I wanted to come much sooner, but you're very difficult to find. I tried your brother. Eventually I hit upon the idea of trying to find Miss Wolfe instead. We missed you at Christmas."

"I thought of Our Lady as well."

"Easily big enough for a monk," said Father Michael, gesturing at the tiny apartment. "Is the living room through there?"

"There is no living room. This is the entire place."

"Very compact. Very efficient."

"It's all I can afford. I don't want to waste money on rent."

"Of course. I wasn't criticizing."

"Who in their right mind would break a vow of poverty for a broken hot plate and a stained floor? That's what you're thinking, right?"

"Oh, no. I don't confuse happiness with a physical location— not that I'm a scholar on the subject. Let's leave all that to the Jesuits."

"Will you have some tea? Or there's seltzer."

"You're very kind. Seltzer."

Peter poured two glasses and handed one to Father Michael.

"Have you come to talk me into coming back?"

Father Michael took a sip. "Mandarin orange, isn't it? Very nice."

"There's no chance of my coming back. I've realized I have no vocation."

"You must know that many of the greatest saints suffered the torments of doubt."

"It's not even a torment anymore. I just don't think about it. Apparently God can vanish from one's life just as suddenly as He can enter it."

"That's a kind of torment, don't you think?"

Peter looked at the floor. "Anyway, my life is here now."

"You're so eager to throw away ten years at Our Lady for this place?"

"Not the place."

"For Miss Wolfe, you mean."

"She and I have become very close."

He arranged his face to conceal this lie, but it was like trying to hide the blood from a grievous wound.

"She loves you? Are you engaged?"

"What's important is that I love her."

"No plans for marriage, though."

"Not immediately. I'm happy with things the way they are."

"You don't look happy, William."

"My name is Peter now, and I'm not worried about how I look."

"I didn't mean it unkindly." Father Michael stared thoughtfully into his glass. "You seem to find it impossible to believe that I really care about your happiness, but I do. What the Church may say about broken vows is one thing; what I feel is another. If Our Lady of Peace was not the right place for you, if you have truly found your niche in the world, no one would be happier for you than I."

"But you'd probably prefer it if everything went wrong for me," Peter said. "If I were utterly miserable. It would mean you were right. You and the brothers. The Church."

"I'm older than you ... Peter. Being right doesn't seem as important as it used to."

It was like trying to hit a moving target; nothing Peter said struck home. After a pause, he asked, "How is Brother André?"

"Brother André left Our Lady shortly after you did."

"Oh, Father. I'm sorry to hear that."

"Didn't surprise me, really. Not like your own departure."

"But André was everything a monk should be—simple, humble, kind ..."

"André learned his part very well. But even a seasoned actor gets tired of playing the same role night after night. We miss him, of course. Any more losses and we won't even be able to tend the sheep."

"Do you blame me for his leaving?"

"No doubt it was an influence. Nothing more. You were much more the monk than André ever was. André will get along anywhere."

"And you think I won't?"

"When you came to us, you were a very young man, hardly more than a boy, in considerable—how to put this—emotional turmoil. You had done something terrible."

"And I've prayed for forgiveness ever since. I don't want to talk about that now."

"Let's discuss it calmly for a moment."

"There was nothing I could do that would have helped."

"Perhaps nothing that would have helped *her*. But facing the consequences might have cleared your own mind and heart in a way that even taking holy orders could not do. The secrets of the confessional are absolute, but in the face of what's happened now, I have to question my own judgment. I should have insisted that you face the legal consequences, but I was swayed by your sincerity and all your other good qualities. I came to believe that you were fully healed, but frankly, I tremble now to think that I was wrong."

"Just because I left the monastery doesn't make me a terrible person."

"No, but it seems to me you *needed* the monastery—more than André ever did—to reach your full potential. Just look at the gentle, productive man you became in our fellowship."

"Well, now I have Lauren." The claim sounded hollow even as he made it.

"What about God? Does He not figure anywhere in your life?"

"I was in church last night, as a matter of fact."

The ballooning faces, the blinded Gothic windows swirled into his mind. Surely this blasphemy must be visible on his face? But Father Michael looked at him without passing judgment. Peter added, in a feeble attempt at honesty, "I don't actually think about God much anymore."

"Don't try to live without Him, Peter. Even the most remarkable woman is no substitute for God."

Peter turned his gaze to the windowsill, where a pigeon hurried pointlessly back and forth. The sound of a newscast echoed dimly from a higher floor.

"Some prior I'm turning out to be," Father Michael said after a moment. "We're barely able to support ourselves, these days. Did you know Clement Smith died?"

"No. I'm sorry to hear that." Peter hadn't known the lay brother very well. "Clement was a good man."

"He was only thirty-two. Asked to be buried at Our Lady. You wouldn't believe the paperwork that involved. The Smith family was not entirely in favour." Father Michael shook his head. "What will become of the older monks if Our Lady has to close?"

"I'm sorry, Father. There's nothing I can do."

"Come back with me. You're not the first person to have a crisis of faith. Go through the motions, live as if nothing had happened. Faith may well come back to you."

"I'm in love, Father. I plan to spend the rest of my life with Lauren. I could never go back to Our Lady."

Father Michael bowed his head for a moment. When he looked up again, he said, "Whatever you do, I hope that you will find happiness. But if you should not find it here in the city, I hope you will come back to us—at least for a visit. You will always be welcome."

"Thank you."

Father Michael handed him a card. "Your bridges are not burned. Call this number if you feel like talking. I'm there till Sunday night. After that, you can always reach me at the monastery."

As Peter held the door open for him, Father Michael tried to end their meeting on a lighter note. "I noticed a motorcycle out front. You haven't taken up with the Hells Angels, I hope."

"Not yet, Father."

"Still," said the priest, looking around, "it's a long way from sheep farming."

To the lonely man, the world is composed of couples. Everywhere Peter looked, men and women travelled two by two as if they had just stepped ashore from Noah's ark. And Lauren was not the only woman with peculiar taste: suddenly it seemed the most fern-like girls clutched the paws of bearded oafs; ballerinas strolled arm in arm with teamsters. Peter still thought that sooner or later she would come knocking on his door, disgusted with herself for her behaviour with Mick.

One day he telephoned her from the store. When she answered, he was on the verge of screaming, *Choose me! Choose me!* but he hung up before his throat could even open to make a sound. What he needed was for Lauren to *want* him; it was no good if he had to convince her.

Sometimes his immediate surroundings disappeared—the cash register, the customers—obscured by images of Lauren: the scarred wrist, the groove of her spine, the smallness of her fingers. He remembered the tilt of her neck when she was working, her bony shoulders, the way she licked his ear.

He did not pray; he *willed* her to come to him. Listening to her light tread on his ceiling, he would *will* her to open the door, to skip downstairs, to invite him up. He frowned until his head ached, trying to transmit his will to her apartment.

But she did not come.

A month went by. He wrote letters and tore them up.

On the pretext of borrowing a wrench, a screwdriver, he would chat with the landlord in the hall, across from Lauren's apartment, in hopes of seeing her. Peter was always uncomfortable with Zaleski, who was prone to making negative observations on his other tenants, and the tactic was only once rewarded: Lauren and Mick were coming home from somewhere, tired and happy. Mick greeted Peter in a friendly way, and asked after business at the bookstore.

"I've been meaning to read more, lately. Laur, you know, she's read every book ever written, I think."

Lauren had opened her door and was going inside. Mick touched her shoulder and said, "I'll be right in," then turned back to Peter. "Not that I have to keep up or nothing. But maybe you could point out some excellent books for me."

"Of course. Come by the store sometime."

"Nothing too fat, you know. Short is good. Like Laur and me been reading *Gawain and the Green Knight*. Great story. Exactly about the right length."

"We have quite a few thin books. Come and see."

"I'll do that, Pete. Something a little more up to date, maybe. Good talking to you."

When Lauren's door was closed, Zaleski handed Peter a wrench. It took Peter a moment to remember it was for the leaky faucet he had invented.

Zaleski leaned toward Lauren's door and made a silent spitting gesture. "Anything with a motorcycle," he said hoarsely, "no good."

•

Peter thought he had kept his heartbreak well hidden from his co-workers, but Molly knew he was not himself and one day, after they had closed the store, she asked him a few gentle questions. Sitting on a box of books in the stockroom, he told her everything—from Lauren's initial warning that she would not fall in love to her sudden devotion to Mick. Tears burst from Peter's eyes in a hot flood, unstoppable. Molly's warm hand touched his shoulder.

"I hate to see you hurting this way," she said. "I don't care how well she writes—you deserve someone better."

"No, I don't. I don't deserve anything. I just *want* her." He blew his nose and began to feel a little better. "She doesn't have to *do* anything. I just want her to love me."

Molly took hold of his hand and uttered softly one very simple word. A simple word, but it shook him nonetheless. What Molly said was, "Why?"

"*Why?*"

"Yes, Peter. Why?"

He sputtered a little. "Because I love her, and I want—I want her love. I don't understand how you can even ask."

"Why would you want someone who makes you feel so awful? It's pretty obvious she doesn't love you."

"It's not obvious at all. And anyway, how would you know? You barely spoke to her." Despite his bluster, the tears burst forth once more. "Anyway," he added, when he was able to breathe again, "she said she loved me."

"Not in a romantic way, I bet. From what I saw, she thinks of you as a friend."

"Not just a friend. You don't sleep with a friend. You don't hold hands with a friend." He came down very hard on *friend*, as if a friend were a contemptible thing.

"But she told you she wasn't in love, Peter." Molly spoke so softly he had to lean forward to hear her. "She said she wasn't *going* to fall in love. Why would she lie about that?"

"Lauren doesn't know herself."

"It sounds like she knows herself very well. It's probably the most important thing she ever told you, and you chose not to hear it."

"That was just her tough exterior talking. It's the person underneath that matters. That's who I love. And I know she could love me."

"Don't take this the wrong way, Peter—but don't you think it's just a little arrogant to decide you know someone better than they know themselves? What difference does it make who she is underneath? You have to live with the whole person. You have to live with what they do. You can't invent them to suit your own wishes."

"I'm not inventing Lauren. I adore her the way she is. I'd do anything for her."

Molly gave him a searching look. Peter was grateful for her sympathy—he thanked her several times—but she didn't seem to have a clue about Lauren.

That Sunday, he took another trip out to the cemetery and knelt before his mother's grave. The first yellow leaves of autumn skittered around the little brass plaque. He thought about the scar on Lauren's wrist. He imagined Lauren dying: she lay back against him, and he held her in his arms, stroking her brow, while she drifted off to death. He shook off the image with a shudder.

On the way home, he stopped to buy groceries. Thunderclouds

grey as tanks were stationed over the rooftops. He remembered how they would assemble over the hills around Our Lady, how the walls of rain could be seen advancing for miles, how the lightning forked over the cemetery. He thought of Clement Smith, the lay brother newly buried there.

The sky opened before he was even halfway down the block, releasing a downpour. His cheap umbrella was just big enough to keep his head dry, but provided no shelter whatever for the rest of him. He was about to burst into a sprint when another hand, a brown hand, closed over the umbrella handle.

"You live at 362, right?"

A boy was walking beside him, clutching his umbrella.

"You live at 362?"

Peter was too startled to reply.

"Your *address*, man. You live at 362, right?"

"Yes, I do."

Wind yanked the umbrella.

"Yo, man. You got to tip it."

The boy forced the umbrella down so they could not see anything but the wet sidewalk turning like a treadmill under their feet.

"Who else live in that place? That 362 place. I'm just asking. I'm looking for someone. Friend of mine I owe some money to."

Peter could barely understand the boy's accent, but he sensed that every word was a lie.

The boy had a gap in his teeth. He made a prim sound with it, a sort of *tsk*.

"Guy I'm looking for's a big guy," he went on. "I seen his bike on this street. Rides a Harley."

"A motorcycle? Doesn't sound familiar."

"Gimme some of that 'brella, man. I'll take it if I want to."

The umbrella struggled in their grasp like an animal.

"I'm sorry," Peter said. "I've only just moved in. I don't know anybody."

The boy stopped, keeping the umbrella over his own head. Peter received a quick baptism before he could duck back under. Beads of water glinted like rhinestones on the boy's hair. His breath smelled of chewing gum. Peter guessed he was about fourteen. A plain gold cross hung from a chain around his throat and glowed dully against his brown skin.

"Guy's name is Mick. I'm a friend of his. I got to find him."

"Have you tried his relatives? Or perhaps the police could help you."

The boy winced as if the words caused him physical pain. "I told you, I got something of his. Some money I got to pay him. *Tsk.*"

Peter wasn't sure if he was expected to believe this. His confusion displayed itself in a silly smile.

"You think I'm playing wit' you?"

"No. No, of course not. It's just that I don't know this person you're trying to find, that's all."

The boy shook his head sadly and looked off into the distance. He made the *tsk* sound again. His fingers released the umbrella handle and he loped off into the rain, hands jammed into his pockets.

"What did he look like?" Mick wanted to know. "How old was he?"

"I think about fourteen. Quite well-dressed."

They were alone in Lauren's kitchen; Lauren was not home. Mick was wearing only jeans and an undershirt that showed off his muscles.

"He looked dangerous, Mick. I don't care what you do with your own life, but you have no right to put Lauren in danger."

"He have any gold teeth?"

"I didn't notice any. He did have a gold cross, though." Peter suddenly couldn't bear Mick's cool response. "What does it matter what he was wearing? For God's sake, the point is you're putting her at risk. And you should just go away."

"He said he saw the hog outside?"

"On the street. I don't think he was sure of the address."

"He knows the street, though. Damn."

"You should go away and take your drug business with you. It's the only thing to do. If you care about Lauren, you should go away."

"I appreciate your concern, Pete. But maybe you should let me worry about her."

"Frankly," Peter said, "I wish you would vanish from the face of the earth."

"Because of Laur." Mick's fine eyes, with their long, almost feminine lashes, looked him up and down. "Sorry, bro. She's taken."

"I didn't even know you existed until you showed up here that night."

"That don't make no difference, Pete. Laur and me, we're together, and that's just how it is. She's sticking with me."

"Be honest, Mick. Can you really give her what she needs? I mean, with the way you live? You're a danger to her. She's not as tough as she makes out."

"Laur's a little high-strung. So what?"

"Someone has to take care of her. It's not as if you plan to marry her, is it."

"What are you, her father? We don't discuss marriage in this house."

"You would if you loved her."

"Pete, listen to me." Mick leaned across the table and took hold of Peter's wrist with a light grip. "I can understand you got a crush on Laur, I really can. And you did me a favour telling me about the mooly. Truth is, you probably just saved my life. But I don't want to discuss me and Laur with you, all right? It's for your own good, Pete. You're getting too wound up about this. It's in your face, bro. Your voice, even. Your voice gets real tight when you talk about her."

"But if you don't really want her—if you're not going to marry her..."

"Shut up now," Mick said gently. "I'm going to lose my temper, and I don't want to do that with my friend." He clapped a hand on Peter's bicep and gave it a squeeze.

It was all so confusing: Peter liked Mick; he was not immune to his rough charm, and he could see why Lauren liked him. But he also wanted to bash Mick over the head with a crowbar, to smash his skull with some implacable object that would finish him off at a blow.

A week went by, during which Peter did not spot Lauren even once. One evening Mr. Zaleski was standing at the alert on the front stoop, keeping his eye on the neighbours walking by. He watched with the unimpressed eyes of a border guard, as if he might demand at any moment to see passports. The evening was still warm—it had been a fiercely hot, Indian summer day—and Zaleski had just finished sweeping leaves from the steps. He pulled out a handkerchief and dabbed at his brow.

Peter was coming home from work, and the two of them

exchanged greetings. After sharing some observations about the unusual heat, Peter added, in what he hoped was a casual tone, "I haven't seen Miss Wolfe around lately."

"Miss Wolfe?" Zaleski waved his hand absently; he had his eye on a police car at the end of the street. "So pretty," he said. "And so sick."

"She's not sick," Peter snapped. "She's an artist."

Zaleski looked around at him, surprised. "You don't know. With her, everything is problem—rent, hot water, name it. Crisis, crisis, everything is crisis. Push, push, push. Is big nerve she got. Big, big nerve."

"Did she say she was going away?"

"How would I know? I'm not spy. Just landlord."

Another police car turned onto the street, and when it passed the house, Zaleski's head swivelled slowly as if on a turret.

The next morning was a Friday. Fridays were easier because Molly worked the second cash register beside him.

"Thank God you're here," Bob Lyle said when Peter came in the door. "This machine is being recalcitrant." He was stooped over the cash register, trying to decipher its obscure electronic heart. "I want to void a transaction and it won't let me. It's being coy."

"You have to insert the card. Is Molly in yet?"

"The software company gave me a free course of instruction. Obfuscation is more like it. Nothing has made sense to me since."

Peter hung up his coat and went behind the counter to help. "Molly's not in yet?"

"Miss Molly? No," Lyle said. "Miss Molly is not in."

"Bob, are you angry with me? Did I leave the register unlocked again?"

"No, I'm not angry with *you*. I'm irritated. *Vexed.* I'm *vexed* with Miss Molly, who by now ..." He consulted his watch. "Who by now is probably no longer Miss Molly."

"What do you mean?"

"The crazy kid has run off and got herself married, my boy. Suddenly decided she didn't want a big wedding, didn't want all the fuss, so she and Roger have just run off. *Poof!*" He snapped his fingers. "Like that. Getting hitched in Woodstock or some other godforsaken hamlet. And then off to Europe and connubial bliss."

"But—well—she's coming back, isn't she?"

"No, the little minx has also given her notice, I'm afraid. Which is why I am *vexed*."

He abandoned the register to Peter and piloted his way through Non-Fiction and Biography, his stoop more severe than usual, as if the volume he had for so long sought along the bottom shelves had dropped altogether out of print.

Without Molly behind the counter, work at the cash desk was frenetic, and the pace was not at all eased by the assistance of the iron-deficient Vanessa. Peter had to keep helping her out of computer jams and customers tended to avoid her, meaning he was under pressure the entire day. The only consolation was that it gave him little time to worry about Lauren, whom he had neither seen nor heard for a week. But then, as soon as he was off work, all the pain came flooding back. If he could just *see* her, he told himself, if he could just be *with* her, surely they could resume the happy life they had before Mick.

He wandered home in a daze. He stepped into oncoming traffic at one intersection, provoking a hysterical outburst of horns and nearly causing an accident. This time it was Molly who was distracting him. It occurred to him that he must not have been a very good friend if she could suddenly take off like that without a word to him. He had thought they understood each other, but apparently not. Being so absorbed in his love for Lauren, he had neglected to give his co-worker the affection she deserved. Molly had always been a cheerful presence. After a day with her, he never came away feeling bad, whereas with Lauren he felt bad pretty much all the time. It was a bewildering fact that he was so drawn to the one who hurt him, but there was no arguing himself out of the attraction; you might as well fight gravity.

He stopped into a stationer's to find a card for Molly. He'd write her a cheery letter as well, wishing her and Roger all happiness, and he would buy them a present. Perhaps Bob would have some ideas about what might be suitable. The newspaper stand at the checkout caught his eye, a photo on the front page of the *New York Post*. He picked up the paper for a closer look. The picture was of a smiling black youth. Peter would never have recognized him had it not been for the plain gold cross.

EIGHTEEN

PETER SPREAD THE newspaper across his wobbly table.

The boy's smile was very different from the sullen demeanour he remembered. But the grin showed a slight gap in the front teeth, and Peter recalled the prim little *tsk* sound the boy had made between his lies. The body had been dumped in Riverside Park not far from Ninety-eighth Street. A Detective Rossi admitted that as yet they had no suspects and no motive.

Peter could think of a suspect *and* a motive. But the newspaper said the body had only been dumped in Riverside Park; the boy had been killed somewhere else.

Someone rapped sharply on the door. He opened it, and Lauren pushed by him, wailing something about Mick. A solid week Peter hadn't seen her and the first word out of her mouth was *Mick*. He couldn't make out what she was saying; was Mick in jail?

"No, he's not in *jail*," she said. "He's just vanished again, the bastard." Tears rolled down her face. "He knows it kills me. It's like he's ripping out my heart, and he always does this to me."

Peter pulled a chair out for her and put the kettle on for tea.

"I can't *think* when he's gone—I can't *read*, let alone *write*—I open a book, but I can't even read to the end of a sentence. I can't even have a complete *thought*. He's a drug. He's slamming around in my veins."

Peter fixed the tea and set out two chipped mugs.

"I know how you feel," he said. "It's how I feel about you."

"No it isn't. You'd be dead if you felt like this."

"The only difference is I'm more optimistic. I keep hoping you'll change. That your heart will come round to me."

Lauren sniffed. Her face was white as a mime's, with dull black streaks where her eye makeup had run. "He's got to be some kind of sadist, taking off like this. He knows it'll kill me and he doesn't care."

"Maybe he isn't away by choice."

"What are you talking about? He called me. He said he was going away for a few weeks, some place upstate, and he wouldn't even tell me where."

Peter poured the tea. He was on the verge of telling her about the dead boy, but he hesitated. He was afraid it would evoke her sympathy, not for the boy but for Mick.

Lauren got up and went to the window. "I keep looking out the window," she said, "hoping his bike will be there. Hoping this is all a nightmare."

She sat down for a second, but got right back up and paced back and forth from the table to the window in a perfect replication of Peter's own restless agony.

"But I'm not dreaming," she went on. "I know this is going to go on and on and on and it's going to kill me." She bent her head and cried into her fist, the bony shoulders quivering under her T-shirt.

"I saw the police here the other day ..." Peter began, but she didn't hear a word.

She sat at the table, puffing fiercely on a knuckle and talking into her hand.

"I know who he's with. I can see them," she said, staring red-eyed over her fist, "right in front of my eyes. It's that bitch from the club. He's probably fucking her up the ass."

She folded her arms and put her head down. Her hair parted, exposing the pale neck, a girl about to be guillotined.

"I noticed a lot of police," Peter began again. "I was wondering ..."

"You mean that murder?" Her voice was muffled by her arms. "That's got nothing to do with him. I told you, he's *away*." She sat up again, her makeup a mask of Tragedy. "He's too busy fucking. He's too busy eating that bitch."

"Lauren, stop."

He said it for his own protection, not hers; he could not hear her jealous ravings without imagining her doing those things with Mick. He pushed her mug toward her.

"Now, listen to what I have to say. I've got something to tell you." He cleared his throat. "Something about Mick."

"Don't start running him down. I've heard it all before."

"Just listen, for God's sake."

She had never heard him speak sharply; she looked at him now, waiting. He told her quickly and without embellishment about the boy who had come looking for Mick. How he had informed Mick. How Mick had said he would "take care of it."

Lauren looked at him with a blank expression, as if he were reporting trades on the stock exchange.

"Lauren, I was afraid you might be in danger. That's why I

told him about the boy. I mean, he *did* have a bullet hole in him the night we met."

"So you told Mick about this kid and you think that's why he disappeared. You saw for yourself: Mick gets shot in the stomach and he couldn't care less. And now you're trying to tell me he's in hiding because he's scared? Is this some weird idea of how to make me feel better? Some story about him being scared of a boy?"

Peter still had the newspaper. He drew it now from beneath the stacks of want ads. He set it before her on the table, open to the photograph.

"I wish there were a better way to tell you. But that boy there, that's the boy who came looking for Mick."

Lauren stared down at the paper, at the boy's grinning face. She folded her hands in her lap.

"Lauren, Mick asked me over and over again what the boy looked like. What he'd said. How he was dressed."

"Mick wouldn't do this." Lauren's voice was barely a whisper. "Mick would not do this. He's never done anything violent."

"Really? Then who was it who shattered your closet door?"

"A door is a piece of wood—which he has now fixed, by the way. Mick would never hurt a person, not seriously. I know he has a temper, I know he gets in fights. But not this. He's not like this." She nodded at the photograph. "Never."

"Why do you think he carries a gun?"

"He's not a monk, Peter. He's a drug dealer. He carries a gun for protection."

"Maybe he's used it."

"You're just jealous. You're making this up because you're jealous. I don't believe you ever met this kid. I don't believe he came looking for Mick. And I certainly don't believe Mick killed him. You're just trying to get him put away, that's all. You know I love him and you want to take him away from me. Everything that matters to me, people always try and take away."

By now she was on her feet, shouting. She made a sudden movement and her teacup shattered against the fridge. She turned away and wept.

"You shouldn't be alone tonight," he said gently. "Why don't you sleep here? I'll sleep on the floor."

She shook her head. "I want to be by the phone in case he calls."

"You shouldn't be alone. Let me come up with you."

"You've done quite enough, thanks."

"Lauren, I only want to help."

"Yeah. A shrink said that to me once," she muttered, moving toward the door. "He had his finger halfway up my vagina at the time."

All that night, he listened to her pacing back and forth in her apartment. He wanted desperately to comfort her, but how could he, if she would not let him?

At lunchtime the next day, he called his brother from a pay phone and asked him if he knew anything about the murder. "You still have friends on the force, right? Do you know if they have any suspects?"

"That's Rossi's turf—but he has no reason to talk to me about it unless it involves a client of mine. Why're you so interested?"

"The body was found just a couple of blocks from here."

"So Manhattan's not a monastery. Big surprise. How's life at the bookstore?"

Peter told him about Molly's elopement. "I hope she comes back to the store. She's so warm, she makes people feel good without even trying."

"So why don't you try a little Internet dating and find yourself someone like that instead of Suicide Sally."

"Don't call Lauren names, Dom."

"She writes about suicide, you're attracted to suicide."

"Dom, I'm the least suicidal person I know."

"Uh-huh. What do you call joining a monastery?"

"It's not even remotely the same."

Peter was saved from further discussion by a synthesized voice that demanded he deposit more money. "I'm out of change, Dom. I have to hang up now."

"Fine. I'll let you know if Rossi knows anything. In the meantime, let me give you a couple of good dating sites to—"

Dominic's words were obliterated by a recurrence of the automated operator, and Peter hung up.

The afternoon dragged. Only a handful of customers showed up in the store, so there were long hours of doing nothing. Bob was doing something in New Jersey, and Vanessa spent the entire time staring into her phone.

He stopped off at the Korean's on the way home and bought some fresh fish and vegetables. His plan was to cheer Lauren up by making dinner for her. Mick's disappearance could only work in his favour. Lauren would have spent the day brooding. He decided the best way to bring her round would be to adopt an attitude both jovial and forceful—a little cheerful bullying was in order.

He bashed on her door until it rattled. An odd sound issued from the other side of the door, a long, low moan, as if the wind were blowing through a confined space. He bashed the door again.

"Room service!" he yelled. "Room service, miss!"

The moaning came again, and he put his ear to the door. "Lauren?" He tried the handle, but it was locked. He put down his groceries and peered through the keyhole. Light gleamed off the kitchen stove.

He called out, "Lauren, are you there?"

He ran downstairs and fetched the keys she had given him, then opened her door and stumbled over his bag of groceries. Two oranges wobbled across the kitchen into a pool of blood. Lauren was lying on the floor, half turned on her side. Peter's first thought was rage at Mick: the thug must have beaten her savagely. But then he saw her wrist.

He pulled her into a sitting position, leaning her against the stove, but she sagged to one side, barely even groaning now. Blood pulsed from her wounded wrist. He ransacked her bathroom cupboard, sending brushes, jars and makeup clattering to the floor; there were no bandages. He had always prided himself on his competence in emergencies; part of him stood aside now and observed that he was behaving in a remarkably calm, efficient manner. He found a T-shirt in her dresser and tore it into strips.

He pressed the folded cloth against the cut. Blood soaked it through instantly. He pressed on another and bound it with another strip, turning it several times around the child-sized wrist. Ezra gave a forlorn meow, eyeing him from under the kitchen table.

Peter noticed with alarm that there were three empty pill bottles on the floor. He shifted Lauren to one side and pushed a finger into her throat. Vomit, scalding hot, rushed over his fingers. Pills and capsules, half dissolved, stuck to her shirt.

"Again," he said firmly. He waggled his finger in her throat and she gagged and coughed horribly, but nothing came up.

"What, is she drunk?" Zaleski's voice came from the open door.

"Call an ambulance," Peter said. "She's taken an overdose."

"My God. All this blood."

"Call an ambulance. Don't just stand there."

He soaked a face cloth in warm water and wiped Lauren's face.

"Help me get her onto the couch," he said when Zaleski returned.

"Move her? I don't think is good idea."

Peter picked Lauren up himself. She was so light it broke his heart.

"You can get lawsuits," Zaleski observed. Peter suppressed an urge to beat him senseless. He lowered Lauren to the couch.

"They'll want the pill bottles at the hospital," he said. "Put them in a plastic bag."

"I will not touch this bottles. They are covered with blood."

"Oh, for God's sake." Peter went back to the kitchen and collected the containers. His hands looked as though he had just performed surgery. There came the wail of approaching sirens. "Go downstairs and open the door for them."

"Is no good blaming me," Zaleski went on. "Blood is poison this days. You know poison? Especially someone like her."

"Get downstairs and open the door," Peter said. He felt eerily calm.

He rode with Lauren in the back of the ambulance, the plastic bag of saline swinging from a pole beside his head. The attendant congratulated him on his handling of the situation.

"Small person like her hasn't got a lot of blood volume. If she makes it, it'll be thanks to you."

"If? You don't think she'll ..."

"Hard to say. Depends on the pills."

"I thought you called them in to Emergency."

"We don't know how many. We don't know if the bottles were full. We don't even know for sure if they contained what the labels say. People keep old bottles."

The ambulance swayed, and they both grabbed poles for support. Peter placed a hand on Lauren's brow and tried to transmit life through his palm. "She's so cold."

The attendant nodded. "Effect of narcotics. Small person, doesn't take too many."

My small person, Peter thought. And then, for the first time in months, he was praying.

"Talk to me, Lauren. Talk to me."

The physician's voice echoed through the emergency room. Peter was sitting in the corridor just outside, but if Lauren made any response, he didn't hear it.

"Talk to me, Lauren. Can you talk to me?"

He had been listening ever since the ambulance attendant had wheeled her through the double doors and told him to wait outside. Voices traded information in terse phrases.

"Maintain that airway. Keep the oxygen coming."

"Lauren, can you hear me?"

"Cut her out of those jeans. I want her crossed and typed."

There was a sound of cloth ripping.

"Lauren, can you hear me?"

"O-negative, doctor."

"Forty units. Keep her on half-saline till it's here."

"Catheter."

"Lauren, can you hear me? Lauren, you're going to feel a sharp pain."

"Didn't even feel it."

"She's not feeling anything."

Exactly what she wanted, Peter thought. Six months ago he could not have understood, but now he understood all too well the craving for an end to pain. If he had prolonged her pain by saving her, she would not be grateful.

The emergency team continued acting out their drama beyond the double doors. Their jargon sounded artificial, like dialogue in a radio play.

"Pressure's dropping. Fifty over nothing."

"Lauren, can you hear me?"

"She's acidotic. Pupils are maxed out, deep tendon's minimal. You called in Restoril and Halcion?"

"Bottles are right here."

"She doesn't kid around. We know what time?"

"Least two hours ago, but she vomited. Pink and white caps, looks like, and some white tablets."

"Good. Okay, we've still got a gag reflex, let's get her cuffed and tubed."

Peter looked at his hands. Dried blood had turned as brown and cracked as caked earth. He scraped a fleck of pink gelatin from between his thumb and forefinger.

"Alcohol level, two point one."

"Pump her out and get it to the lab." The doctor continued with a series of mysterious commands for "charcoal" and "lavage" and "peritoneal" something or other. And then he was standing over Peter consulting a clipboard. He was young and unruffled by the drama in the other room.

"Mr. Meehan. You're the friend who found her?"

"That's right."

"Dr. Levine. Does Lauren have a next of kin? Anyone who should be informed?"

"Not that I know of. Will she be all right?"

"Too early to say. At this point we just want to get her stabilized." He consulted his clipboard. "Brought on by a problem with the boyfriend?"

"He disappeared, yes."

"How well do you know this woman? Are you a friend, neighbour, what?"

"I love her."

Dr. Levine accepted this with no particular reaction. "Two things concern me about Lauren. This was not a first attempt."

"No."

"And she's serious—she took a lot of pills, and she nicked the artery in her wrist."

"I know."

"Was she expecting you to visit? When you found her?"

"No. It was an impulse. I live downstairs."

"All right. I'm not a psychiatrist—I'm going to have Dr. Milstein look in on her soon as she's conscious—but clearly something has to change in this woman's life."

"The boyfriend's not a good influence."

"That may be. There's no next of kin?"

"Her parents are dead."

"Well, she's going to need all the support she can get—friends, relatives. Whoever."

"I understand. She needs to know people care about her."

"Exactly," said Dr. Levine. "Don't we all."

DARLING

Darling, when you come
Inside me, then you go away
It's okay, it's okay

I've no idea what you're after
Take whatever you need
I won't bleed, I won't bleed

You are smoke and lightning
I am ashes, skin, and hair
I don't care, I don't care

Forget my name, it's written where
So many dead girls signed
I don't mind, I don't mind

Sink your teeth into my throat
Come in my face, come in my hand
I understand, I understand

But darling, when you come
Inside me, I can see my breath
Love is colder than death
Love is colder than death

—Lauren Wolfe

NINETEEN

LAUREN WAS ADMITTED to the intensive care unit. Peter returned the next morning, and although the doctor warned him, nothing could have prepared Peter for the shock of seeing her in such ruin. Maroon circles ringed her eyes, and a bruise was forming on one cheek where she had fallen. But worse than this, she was shrunken, as if loss of blood had combined with loss of hope to collapse her body inward. Every bone in the pale arms and hands was visible; she looked the victim of famine.

Her breathing was so diminished, the interval between each tremulous rise of her chest so long, that Peter feared each exhalation was her last. He stayed beside her all that day, and all the day after, but there was no change. He vowed that he would stay by her side even if she remained in this half-life for the next thirty years; he would wait through all eternity, if necessary.

A young nurse came in and wiped Lauren's face with a damp cloth. "So pretty," she said softly. She herself was plain, with very thick legs. "Are you the husband?"

"No."

"She's got a bit more colour today, don't you think?"

"I hope to be her husband," Peter added. "One day."

The nurse smiled uncertainly.

Even in devastation, Lauren was beautiful. Perhaps it was the devastation that he loved—responding to it the way a man raised in harsh country will cherish the bleakest vista and be indifferent to lush green hills.

When the nurses bathed her, or when the doctors examined her, Peter went down the hall to the waiting room, a small glass alcove that smelled strongly of Mr. Clean. Here he sat on a vinyl chair beneath a large clock that rattled noisily every time the second hand approached the twelve. When the doctor reappeared, Peter would ask questions.

"Is she in a coma?"

"I don't want to say coma. She's deeply unconscious."

"Is she getting better? Worse?"

"She's breathing on her own. That's a good sign."

"How long can she stay unconscious and still be ..."

"I've seen overdose patients go seventy-two hours with no long-term impairment. We'll have to wait and see."

Peter was dozing under that buzzing clock—was it the second day? the third?— when he was awakened by a woman's voice. As he swam toward consciousness, he thought it was a nurse. Information was being demanded of him.

"You might have at least called me," she was saying.

Peter blinked up at the dark figure before him.

"Naomi Black," she informed him. "Lauren's agent? I think we met."

"Oh, yes. Yes, of course."

"You might have called me," she said again. "Lauren and I have been like sisters since we were five years old."

"I'm sorry. There was so much to deal with."

She jerked her head toward the ICU. "She looks like hell."

"I'm afraid it's pretty serious."

"Doesn't surprise me. The amazing thing about Lauren is she's lived this long."

"I don't understand it. Many people would envy her life."

"Nobody with any sense."

Peter couldn't think of a reply to that.

Naomi sat down, spreading open her coat. An hour passed. They fell into the sudden intimacy of strangers thrown together in crisis. Naomi told him of a summer camp adventure she and Lauren had shared as children.

Peter told her about Lauren at the skating rink—how she had climbed the fence and skated right in like she owned the place.

Naomi asked him, "Would you ever do something like that?"

"Never."

"Me either," Naomi said. "But she's the one with the scars on her wrist."

"It's so sad. They asked for next of kin, and I couldn't give them a single name."

"There's always her mother, I suppose. But she'd kill you if you called her dad."

"No, no. Both her parents are dead. She told me."

Naomi shook her head. "Lauren's father split when she was eight. He's some big-deal doctor in California. Her mother lives in Paris with a Frenchman half her age."

"Why would she tell me her parents were dead?"

"Who knows why Lauren does anything? She hates talking about her parents."

Peter lapsed into silence. It was not the first time Lauren had deceived him, but what did she have to gain by it? Sometimes it was as if she despised him. After a while he said, "I couldn't think of any friends to call."

"There's me. But you're right—she doesn't have a whole lot of friends."

"It's such a shame. She's so sweet."

"Good God, Lauren's not sweet. She's manipulative, suspicious, hostile even. Sweet doesn't enter into it."

"I thought you liked her."

Naomi had been twisting a button on her coat. It came off in her hand, and she contemplated it as if it were a foreign coin.

"I love Lauren the way she is, not some other way I might prefer her to be. You can't go improving people behind their backs. Believe me, I've tried a million times to get her back into therapy, but she's had a bad experience, so ... Anyway, I'm happy if I can sell her work, maybe help her career. But I can't live for her and I can't save her. You're in love with her, I take it."

Peter nodded.

"Poor you."

Lauren awoke the following morning. Peter was dreaming his father was in the hospital, but he had been transformed into a tall red man whose room was a kind of court. Peter was trying desperately to explain something to him when the nurse woke him with a touch on his shoulder.

"She's awake now, sir, if you'd like to come with me."

Peter got up stiffly and followed her down the hall.

The bruise on Lauren's cheek was darker, and the circles under her eyes had deepened. Peter gripped the bar at the side of the bed and said her name once, twice. He took hold of her undamaged hand and warmed it between his palms.

"It's me. Peter," he said, and added, "The mad monk."

The great brown eyes flickered open, unfocused. "Mick?"

"Not Mick. Peter."

He poured her a glass of water from a plastic pitcher. She frowned at him, trying to focus; a gummy white substance clung to her eyelids. Then she was asleep again.

The nurse shooed him out. "Come back tomorrow," she said.

He took the elevator down to the lobby, wandered uptown through the manic bleating of rush hour, and opened the door of Lauren's apartment on what looked like the scene of a violent crime.

Bloody handprints dotted the fridge, the stove and even the walls, vivid as Japanese flags. A palette-shaped pool of blood had turned brown in the middle of the floor. Ezra wandered in and meowed. Peter fed him, then stepped around blood and vomit to get to the next room, Lauren's office. This was where she had cut her wrist. Her computer and keyboard were splashed with blood.

Blood-soaked papers littered every surface. She had apparently torn up her work in a fit of rage. He held a tiny fragment between thumb and forefinger and read, *You are smoke and lightning / I am ashes, skin, and hair* . . .

He stooped to pick up the razor. Lauren's thumbprint was etched into rust-coloured blood. He slipped it into his pocket.

The other two rooms were not so bad. The bed was stained, but the living room was untouched. He went back to the office, gathered her papers into a heap and spent the next two hours cleaning. He changed the bedsheets, wiped down her computer, then found a mop and started on the kitchen floor. The water in the bucket turned pink, then brown. He found a bottle of liquid wax and worked on the tile floor until it shone.

At the bookstore, he kept hoping to turn around and find Molly. Molly would have been all sympathy and common sense. She would have touched his heart and burst this terrible pain he was feeling. For what could be a more forcible rejection than suicide? His mother had done it, and Dominic hated the poor woman to this day. But Peter had always felt himself to be Dominic's opposite; he certainly could never hate Lauren. He had caught her on the brink of death, and nothing, no matter how little she valued his love, could make him let go.

He called the hospital and was told that Lauren was no longer in critical condition.

When he went to visit, he found she had been moved into the psychiatric ward. Her eyes were open, but she lay staring straight ahead, oblivious to her surroundings. She took no notice of Peter's arrival, nor of anything he said, and when he took her hand in his, she did not take it away.

Peter stared at the white cuff on her wrist and, without intending to, reeled off a litany of his feelings. Clichés were all that came to hand, and he recited them in a guilty whisper as if they were sins. *Lauren, you are my life, my breath, my blood; I will do anything for you, I will die for you; I love you more than I love myself; I love you more than the world; I love you more than God.* The truth of this last statement frightened him.

A nurse came in. Lauren accepted a thermometer in her mouth, the glass touching her teeth with a click. Her pulse was taken, the pale hand limp in the nurse's pink fist, and when the nurse returned an hour later with medication, Lauren swallowed it without protest. Her movements were puppet-like. It was a heartbreaking transformation in one whose normal disposition was combative.

Naomi came to visit, and Peter waited in the hallway to allow them privacy. Psychiatric patients drifted in and out of their rooms, stirring in directionless eddies, glassy-eyed. A woman with matted grey hair hobbled up and down the hall trailing her IV apparatus like a figure in a Tarot card. "I condemn you to hell," she said loudly, and Peter thought with astonishment that she was speaking to him. But she muttered the curse over and over—"I condemn you to hell, you son of a bitch"—until it was drained of meaning.

When Naomi came back out into the hall, her all-business facade had deserted her. "I could have sworn—" she sobbed, as she fumbled with her purse. "I could have sworn I had a Kleenex in here."

"Don't be too upset," Peter said. "I'm sure she'll be all right."

"How do you know?"

"I just have a feeling."

"But how do you know? Did you talk to the psychiatrist?"

"Not yet. But ..."

"Then how can you *know*?"

Where do they come from, he wondered, these comfortless women?

Later that afternoon, he did speak with the psychiatrist. "How long will she have to stay here?"

"Mr. Meehan, that depends entirely on Lauren. She'll have to remain under observation until we're sure she's no longer a danger to herself."

All that night and all the next day, Lauren lay mute and staring. Her cheekbones made deep, scalloped caverns in her face, and her eyes looked beaten and dark, the eyes of a refugee. From time to time they filled with tears, and she would lay unmoving, letting the tears roll silently down her face, while Peter made sounds of commiseration beside the bed.

When, on the fourth or fifth day, she did begin to speak, her voice was raw and hoarse. Her speech came in fragments, like snatches of half-remembered verse, sometimes plain statements, at other times exclamations left incomplete. "Oh," she would say suddenly, "how can they hope to . . ." But Peter could never learn what it was, this mysterious hope. Several times she seemed to be describing a family gathering, a party or a weekend trip. "There were a lot of us there. Naomi was there, Dad was there."

Peter would try with gentle questioning to draw her out, but the tears would come, and she would fall silent once more.

The days dragged on and, to the extent his duties at the bookstore permitted, Peter arranged his life around visiting hours at the ward. On his days off, if Lauren was scheduled for sessions with the psychiatrist or social worker, Peter forced himself to go home, returning to the hospital in the evenings. Gradually her appearance improved; colour returned to her cheeks and the bruise began to fade. Peter sat for long hours beside the bed, reading quietly, occasionally talking about what he read. Most often they were silent. He was no stranger to silence, or to devotion.

Eventually, Lauren began to show interest in leaving the ward. The antidepressant medication was beginning to work, and she could now imitate, if not quite be, someone who was not "a danger to herself."

One evening, Peter became aware as he was reading that she was watching him intently. He kept his eyes on the page, waiting for her to speak.

"Why are you here?" She blurted it out like a child. "Why do you come here every day? Sit here every day?"

"Because I love you," Peter said, and this simple answer seemed to him the whole truth of the matter.

"You can't love me. You don't even know me."

"Not as well as I'd like to."

"Well, I don't love you." She picked the book up from her lap and found her place. "It's you they ought to lock up."

Lauren began to talk, of going home, of writing a new novel, of plans to revise abandoned poems. Requests for books and paper followed. Naomi was summoned and a couple of editors, both women, were allowed to visit. They trooped in bearing baskets of fruit, arrangements of flowers or advance copies of forthcoming books.

Even these cool, professional women responded to Lauren's orphan eyes with solicitude. But their offers of help and sympathy were steered to the neutral ground of book-buying trends or the latest gossip of the publishing world.

One day, Peter bumped into—quite literally—an older man as he was coming out of Lauren's room. He had a neat white beard and very dark eyebrows. This was David Cresswell—not a psychiatrist, Peter had learned, but a psychologist attached to the hospital. He had dropped in on Lauren a few times now.

"How do you think she's doing?" Peter asked.

"I think she's doing great. Tremendous improvement."

"Do you think they'll let her out soon?"

"Oh, I think so. My concern is that she get into therapy once she's out—whether it's with me or someone else."

"Well, she seems to put up with you," Peter said. "That's a good sign."

"She's full of good signs lately. I'm very optimistic."

In those latter days of her hospital stay, Lauren made a big push toward health. She became chatty and energetic, and there seemed no lags in her progress, except for one sad afternoon.

On that particular day, Peter had gone back to Ninety-eighth Street to feed Ezra and to collect Lauren's mail. He had cleaned the litter box and was sorting envelopes and magazines at the kitchen table when the telephone rang. It was still ringing when he reached the living room and, without thinking about it, he picked it up. Before he could say hello, the sound of Mick's voice immobilized him. He was leaving a message.

Die, Peter thought, startled by his own rage. *Die.*

"Sorry I took off, babe, but I don't want nobody to know where I am. I mean nobody. So don't call me on the cell. It's not safe."

Mick mentioned the name of a welding shop. The owner was letting him stay there until "business," as Mick put it, calmed down. He left a phone number but no address. Peter found a pencil and scribbled the information on a scrap of paper.

He sat on the sofa with the phone in his hand and contemplated the tiny flashing light that indicated a message. After a minute or two he pressed the voice mail button and listened. The automated voice asked for a password, and he was about to hang up when he heard the automatic beeps and the voice announced the first message. He listened to Mick again. This time the automated voice told him the options. He pressed seven to erase.

Perhaps it was in response to a scowling sky and a mournful wind, but by late afternoon Lauren became agitated. Rain hammered at the windows, and she flipped restlessly through the pages of one magazine after another. Peter sensed that she wanted to say something but was suppressing it with a great effort.

He touched a finger to her forearm.

"Please tell me," he said softly. "It can't be so terrible, can it?"

"I don't suppose," she said, trying to make her voice light, "that there was any message for me from Mick?"

It was as if she had a sixth sense.

"No." He frowned a little to mask this lie. "Not a word, I'm afraid."

"He hasn't come by? He hasn't called?"

"No, he hasn't. I'm sorry."

"You have to wonder how he could survive," she said, turning a glossy page, "without my company. Without my charm, my kindness, my easy loving ways."

"Don't blame yourself, Lauren. He's not worth it."

"As if anybody's worth it. Worth's got nothing to do with it. Look at you, for Christ's sake, hanging around like a spaniel, panting for another kick. I'm nothing, Peter, I'm shit. On my best days I'm barely functional, and you treat me like the Holy Virgin."

"Blessed Virgin. She was never this important to me."

"You're hopeless."

Her eyes dulled, and for the rest of that afternoon her face took on a burned-out look.

But that was the only setback in her otherwise steady progress. Walks became the thing. Interest in the outside world, according to her psychiatrist, would be a sure sign that her depression was on the wane. Peter was dispatched on a series of errands to Ninety-eighth Street: fetching boots, raincoat and umbrella one day; cap, T-shirt and shoulder bag the next. He accompanied her on jaunts to Central Park, to the Frick Museum, and even, one day, to a coffee shop for lunch. She was able to joke again, in her acerbic way, and even—Peter mentally circled this particular date in red—able to laugh.

They were on a path behind the Metropolitan Museum, watching activity on the dog run. One by one, mongrels and purebreds came up to sniff her hand.

"Dogs like me," she said softly, and Peter detected a note of sadness in the observation, as if she could count no admirers among the human species, but only among these shaggy beasts.

A chihuahua took vociferous objection to the attentions of a Great Dane and chased him off—that was when Lauren laughed. Peter had forgotten the sound of her laugh, that sudden throaty staccato, and hearing it again for the first time in weeks, he was moved. He stood off to one side watching her, now rubbing the floppy ear of a sheltie, now tossing a stick for a mutt. He saw how the owners regarded her with bemused expressions, a dark, slender figure amid the colours of the hill.

Their walks became longer each day, until finally her psychiatrist pronounced himself pleased that his patient was spending so much time outside the ward. He was ready to discharge her, provided she came back to see him from time to time so he could keep an eye on her medication. This Lauren promised to do.

Despite her frequent tempers, her deep black moods, the staff on the ward had come to have an affection for her. Nurses stopped by to say goodbye before she left, some with copies of her books clutched in their hands. Lauren had a grateful word for each of them, and it ate Peter alive to see how gentle she could be with people who were paid to look after her when she was so hostile toward undying love.

They took a cab from the hospital, Peter tense the whole way. After all, he was bringing Lauren to the scene of an attempt on her life, even if the attempt had been her own. But Lauren opened the door and stepped briskly into the kitchen as if they were returning from a trip to the supermarket, and not from dark, uncertain weeks in the precincts of death.

There was a disgruntled meow from within.

"Ezra!" Lauren picked up the cat and pressed her face into his fur. "Ezzie, my sweetheart, did you miss me at all, you great fat thing?"

TWENTY

"I'D RATHER NOT treat this as any special kind of day," Lauren said. "I'd like to get things back to normal as soon as possible. Thank you for all you've done." She held out a hand for him to shake.

"Are you sure you want to be alone?"

"I've been surrounded by doctors and psychos for weeks. Yes, I want to be alone."

"I cleaned the place up a little."

"So I see." She put the cat down and went into the office. She switched the computer on, then off again.

"Your papers were a terrible mess, so I—"

"You don't have to explain. No loss there." She continued into the living room and glanced at the telephone. There was no flashing light.

Lauren sat on the couch, but in a tentative way, as if the place, the furniture, belonged to an adversary who might return at any moment.

"Painville," she said. "I live in Painville. Just because I spent a few weeks in hospital doesn't mean my address has changed."

"I'm sure they wouldn't release you if they didn't think you were strong enough."

"What a joke." She pursued the thought as if he had not spoken. "You kill yourself and nothing changes. Everything's exactly as you left it. Maybe you actually *do* die—but the place you end up is identical to the one you left behind."

"Maybe you should write a poem about it."

"Someone with talent might make something of it."

"Lauren, you must know how talented you are."

"Let me tell you something, Pete, old buddy. You think you're kind and loving and that you have my best interests at heart. But you aren't. You don't. You couldn't care less about *me*. You're in love with some idea you have pinned to your forehead. I mention an honest anxiety, like maybe I'll never be able to put another sentence together. Like maybe I've been lucky so far and I'll never sell another line of what I write—a legitimate, realistic worry—and you brush it aside like I'm some hypersensitive dilettante. That's not kindness and that's not love."

"I was only trying to cheer you up."

"You meant to put me down. You need me to be down. It's my misery you love."

"That's a terrible thing to say ..."

She relented a little. "Maybe I'm just paranoid," she said, and gave a deep sigh. Then, in an apparent shift of mood: "Why don't we have a cheerful fucking cup of tea?"

They went to the kitchen. Water was boiled, tea was poured, and Lauren made an effort to talk of inconsequential things—of Ezra's girth, of her overflowing e-mail.

She drank her tea by the spoonful, as if it were soup. "I guess according to you and your brothers I ought to be in hell, right? I mean, if I'd succeeded. If I was dead now."

"I don't know—they're not my brothers anymore. People who try to ... they usually aren't in their right mind. You don't go to hell for that."

He wanted suddenly to tell Lauren about his mother's death, but held back.

Lauren said simply, "I was in my right mind. I knew exactly what I was doing."

"I don't know, maybe that idea is just a kindness to those left behind. We want to believe it was a fit of madness, hysteria. How else could the person imagine that no one cared? That no one would help? It's very painful for those left behind."

"Jesus, don't cry, Peter."

"It's just when I think you nearly died ..."

"Don't cry." Her hand touched his sleeve, then withdrew. "I'm alive, aren't I? Thanks to you."

"But you don't understand how I feel. You can't—"

"Okay, look—I'm sorry for what I said earlier. About your not caring." She stared into her teacup. "But when you hate yourself, it's hard to believe there's anybody on the planet who doesn't. I'd promise to do better, but you don't seem to get it—I'm not a good person."

"Don't be silly. Of course you are."

"You're dismissing me again." She put down her cup. Another sigh. "This thing that's inside of me, this thing that makes me want to kill myself—it's not a separate thing—this blackness, this rage. It *is* me. I could just as easily kill you."

"No, you couldn't."

"Oh, but I could. In a rage ..."

"You're not a violent person. Not that way."

"It's not just me I hate. It's everything." She covered her eyes and started to cry, and when Peter got up to hold her, she clung to him, a drowning woman clinging to a piece of wood.

"I'm so sorry," she said over and over again. "I'm so sorry."

Peter stroked her hair and made soothing noises. A moment ago he had felt utterly worthless, but when she clung to him like this, he was her champion, her saviour, her man.

Lauren at this time was taking a lot of medication and slept much of the day. She also had a lot of appointments with her psychiatrist. When Peter was not at the bookstore, he filled the empty hours by working on the poems Lauren had tried to destroy. He had kept them in a shoebox in his closet since the day he cleaned her apartment. Bloody scraps of paper now littered his table as if someone had used them to blot up brown ink. They were pieces of an intimate crossword puzzle, and whenever Peter worked on it, he was suffused with an almost unbearable tenderness.

Three poems were now complete. The stiff, curled fragments that remained might represent one poem or two, he could not tell. He held up an almost rectangular piece on which the drops of blood were arranged so that it looked like an ace of hearts. Others resembled foreign currency, and there were many no bigger than postage stamps that bore single words such as *baby* or, less poetically, *it*, or *water*. His favourite was a tattered scrap on which a single word was all but obliterated by the rust-coloured blood: *love*.

Still other pieces carried cryptic phrases such as *Don't panic*, or *as if he said*, or *what he meant*. Sometimes Peter had nothing more to go on than a few letters: *ned*, or *pal* or *se*. The bloodstain on this last piece was smudged. He joined it now with a similarly smudged piece and made *This curse.*

His concentration was fierce; remaking her work drop by drop like this made him feel almost like a poet himself. Hours went by and he hardly noticed. Of course, he knew he was not creative, not a poet, but he likened himself to an art restorer, one of those artisans but for whose care great treasures might be lost.

He wanted to tell somebody about what he was doing, rescuing Lauren's poems. He wanted to tell someone how it felt to love a woman who might kill herself at any moment—how it made life tentative, reality suspect—how you had to live with constant fear. But he knew he could never convey what he felt. He had saved Lauren's life, he had survived disaster, but the foundations of his existence had been weakened, and like the owner of a house that has been damaged by a flood, he knew they would not survive another.

TWENTY-ONE

OVER THE NEXT two weeks, Peter devoted long hours to putting together Lauren's shredded poems. As he glued the last broken word into place, he let out a sigh of deep satisfaction.

He threw out the blank pieces, and sifted all the bloodstained scraps into an envelope; this he placed reverently in his cupboard as if it were a reliquary. There remained on the table one coin-shaped fragment of paper, on which a drop of blood had dried in the shape of a crown. He set the wafer on his tongue. Lauren's blood mixed with his saliva, and he swallowed it with a bliss he had not known since his first Communion.

He went to a Xerox place and had the poems photocopied on grey paper so that the stains would not be so vivid; he tucked the originals away in his closet.

When he knocked on her door that evening, he could hear the sound of running water. She greeted him in her bathrobe and slippers in an exuberant mood. No one would have connected the bloodstained relics with the happy woman before him.

"I've finished my chapter," she said, and spun around in her slippers as if she were on skates. "Eleven pages in one afternoon."

"Eleven pages. You're a demon."

"I'm a witch," she said happily, "just like the reviewers say."

He handed her the manila envelope.

"What's this?"

"It's for you. Open it." He was suddenly nervous: what if she had kept spare copies all along? He would look a complete fool.

She opened the clasp and stared at the first grey page.

"This is weird," she said. "I tore this up."

She glanced at him quickly, then examined the other pages. "Where did you get these, Peter? I tore these up."

"I know you did."

"This is impossible," she said, and read a few of her lines to herself. "I destroyed this stuff. I tore them into tiny little pieces."

"I know you did. I put them back together."

She stared at the pages, fascinated. The fresh linen paper made her handwriting look beautiful; the faded stains were only faint outlines.

She looked up at him in wonder. "This is the kindest thing anyone's ever done for me."

"It's not kindness. It gave me so much pleasure."

The small arms circled him and held him tight. "You're so good to me. Why are you so good to me?"

She went into the bathroom to take the shower he had interrupted, and Peter went into the living room. He saw with alarm that the message light was flashing; the phone must have rung while she was running the water. Of course, it might be nothing, it might just be Naomi, but in a panic he snatched up the phone and pushed Voice Mail. Above the muffled hiss of the shower he heard Mick's voice.

"Laur, it's me," Mick said. "I know you're probably pissed off at me, but I gotta see you." His breathing could be heard in the pause. "Laur, I gotta see you. If I don't hear from you before six o'clock, I'll meet you exactly nine o'clock tomorrow night at that place. You know the one I mean, near the park. I need you, babe. Gimme a call—not on the cell."

Peter recognized the number as the one Mick had left before, the welding shop.

He erased the message and sat very still for a few moments. It was the second time he had happened to intercept a call from Mick; how long could his luck hold? He got up and left the apartment and dashed downstairs. He half ran up the street toward the Korean. The corner pay phone was a wreck, but when he picked it up, he got a dial tone. He dialed information and got the number.

"Eighty-first. Sargent Dalsey speaking."

"I need to speak to someone about a murder investigation. The boy who was killed on Ninety-eighth Street a while ago."

"Detective Rossi. Hold on."

The line went blank, and for a moment Peter thought he had been disconnected.

"This is Detective Rossi. How can I help you?"

"I have some information about the murder of that boy on Ninety-eighth Street."

"Uh-huh. Could I get your name, please?"

"The person you need to speak to is named Mick. Mick LeMar."

"Hold on a second. Just give me your first name."

"William. My name is William."

They'd never be able to trace a dead monk. Not from a pay phone.

"All right, William," Rossi said, adopting a more friendly tone. "What's this information you have?"

"The person you want to question is named Mick LeMar. L-e-m-a-r. He's hiding at a welding shop on the Lower East Side. I don't have an address, but I do have the phone number."

"Okay, give me the number."

Peter gave him the number.

"Okay, William. Why should we speak to this Mr. LeMar, in your opinion?"

"Mick is a drug dealer. The boy came looking for him on Ninety-eighth Street one week before he was killed. And Mick knew about it."

"How is it you have this information?"

Peter put down the phone. When he got back to the apartment, the hair dryer was going full blast. A few minutes later, Lauren came into the living room trailing scents of soap and myrrh and found Peter sitting on the couch as far from the phone as possible.

They went to a movie, and later to a café where Lauren bought him an expensive dinner. Surrounded by the soft lamps, the delicate china, she looked happier than he'd ever seen her, and he knew that he had made her happiness possible.

"You know," she said, "at first I hated you for—for saving my life ..."

Peter reached across the table and touched her hand.

"But the way you came to the hospital," she continued. "Every single day. Even when I wouldn't talk to you. When I was nasty to you. You're so loyal. So generous."

"I just always want to be with you. That's not generous."

"Look at Mick, though. He hasn't even called for, what, two months?"

"Maybe he couldn't for some reason."

"No, Peter. Don't make excuses for him. Mick couldn't care less about me. He literally doesn't care if I live or die. Even if he doesn't realize I was in hospital. To just drop out of someone's life like that—it's cruel."

"Forget about Mick. It's such a happy day." He raised his glass in a toast. "To your eleven pages."

Lauren's good mood lasted through dinner and through the long walk home. When at last they stood at the door of her apartment, she held him close, and his heart turned a delicate somersault. But when he kissed her, she pulled away.

"Let's not sleep together, Peter. We made that mistake before."

"You were in love with Mick then. Mick's not around anymore."

"Still. I can't deal with it right now."

"Lauren, always it's either been Mick or the hospital. This is the first time you're actually seeing me, seeing *us*, with clear eyes."

"I'm not sure I'm seeing anything clearly. I'm in therapy right now, and it's going pretty well, I think, but it makes things very confusing. All these thoughts and feelings in the air. I just can't face any more, I don't know, any more *anguish*."

"Let's make a deal, then. I promise I won't rush things, if you promise you won't write me off."

She stood on tiptoe to kiss his cheek. "Deal."

Peter's happiness wafted him through the next two days. Lauren's smile, her goodwill, had such power that he could call it up in the most untoward circumstances—trapped behind a jammed cash register facing angry customers, say—and be comforted. Love made everything so much easier. Molly had still not been replaced, and Peter was constantly overworked, but he refused to let the stress get to him.

Lyle had asked him yet again to work a double shift; it was now the slack period just before the suppertime rush. Vanessa was fooling with a boom-box radio someone had left out on the street, slapping it and cursing each time the signal faded. Long patches of static were interrupted by sudden clear announcements of baseball scores, or a commercial in Spanish.

Then it suddenly began to speak English. A weather forecast—continuing cold with a chance of snow flurries—and then another voice announced that police had arrested a man in the murder of fourteen-year-old Oscar Smalls.

"Don't change it! Hold it there!"

Vanessa had turned the dial and was cruising once more through static. "Stinking news, man. I want music."

"But it's about that murder! Please put it back!"

Vanessa regarded him coolly under drooping eyelids.

Peter added helplessly. "It happened on my street."

Vanessa fiddled with the dial, but all she got was a noise like frying bacon. Then the evening rush began, and they had to switch the radio off.

Let a jury decide Mick's guilt or innocence. Peter had done no more than his duty: you can't have killers running around loose. Yes, he was jealous, and yes, this would get Mick out of the way, but that was not his motive. Not his main motive, anyway; his main motive was to protect Lauren. That Mick seemed to be in many ways a nice fellow could not be helped. Evil, as Father Michael had pointed out, does not necessarily look evil.

On the way home, Peter stopped at a newsstand and bought the evening papers. Then he lay on his bed, unfolding them page after page, looking for news of the arrest. There was nothing. It must have occurred too late in the day. Peter continued idly turning the pages, as his long day began to catch up with him. He could hardly keep his eyes open. He fell asleep breathing the smell of newsprint.

"I *had* to stay gone," Mick said. "I had the bulls on my tail night and day. No peace with those bastards. Rossi and them. No sense of proportion."

He and Lauren were sitting on the couch with Ezra purring between them. Mick was scratching the cat behind the ears.

"It's been months, Mick. You could have called."

"I did call."

His injured expression was so convincing, it threw her off.

"I did call, Laur. Twice I called. You never called me back. I thought you was still mad at me."

"You never called, Mick. Don't lie."

"I'm not lying. I called you twice. You never called me back, so I said hell with it."

"When did you call? When? How long ago?"

"I don't know. Two days ago, maybe."

"Did you leave a message?"

"Yes, Laur, I left a message. You want a sworn affidavit?"

"I never got this famous message."

"So maybe your voice mail's screwed up."

"All my other messages seem to get through. Funny yours don't, wouldn't you say? When was the other time? You said you called another time."

"Christ, I don't know. *Centuries* ago. October, I think. Yeah, it was October. You didn't call back. I figured you was still pissed off. Why are you looking like that?"

Lauren had not finished with Mick, but it was Peter she was seeing in her mind just then. And she was seeing him in a new light. "That devious little ..."

"Oh, blame Ezra now. Good one." Mick rolled the cat over and scratched its belly, which made Ezra curl up like a huge shrimp. "I knew there was something weird about you, Ez. Godzilla, the mega-cat. You don't take messages, do you? Huh? Do you? When you're this fat, you don't *have* to take messages."

"I never got the message, Mick. Peter erased it."

"Petie boy? Naahhh. Petie's a choirboy. He isn't gonna do nothing dishonest."

"He was here two days ago. You must have called when I was in the shower or something. He did seem a little nervous. And he was here all through October. He was looking after the cat while I was in ... while I was away."

"Petie wouldn't do it. Ten to one it's the damn phone company."

A sudden anxiety flickered to life in Lauren's chest. "I know he did it."

"No, Laur. You *don't* know he did it. You *don't* know."

Mick's sudden vehemence surprised her. Why should he defend the man who was trying to win her away?

"Rossi and his guys thought they knew. They thought I killed that dumb-ass kid that got shot. 'We *know* you did it, Mick. Got that? We *know* you did it.' Bastards talking to me like I'm in third grade. Over and over. They must have said it a million times. 'Mick, we *know* you did it.' But they didn't know. They couldn't know. And the reason they couldn't know was because I didn't do it. And now they *know* I didn't do it because they arrested this other schmuck that probably *did* do it."

"They arrested somebody?"

"This afternoon. Found him with the gun he used and half the kid's stuff, is what I heard. I'm in the clear's why I come round. I didn't want you caught up in this shit."

"Who did they arrest?"

"Some asshole he owed money to. That fuck. I hope they nail him to the wall. If he hadn't been so *stupid*—dumping the body in Riverside fucking *Park*—they'd never of bothered me. 'We *know* your alibi's a phony, Mick.' I'm telling you, all you gotta do is get arrested one time: you're guilty of everything the rest of your life, far as the bulls are concerned. Because the bulls are like you, Laur. They *know*."

Mick took hold of Lauren's hand, his way of changing the subject.

"So what's the story, little girl? Did you miss me?"

She yanked her hand away and turned her back. She thought he would touch her again, but instead she heard him getting something out of his canvas bag. Then he went to the kitchen and came back with a bottle of wine and two glasses.

"To the forces of law and order," he said, raising his glass. "Long may they continue to find me innocent."

"Why not continue to *be* innocent?"

"Nah. Not in my nature."

They drank the first glass of wine in near silence. She didn't really want to drink right now, but when Mick refilled their glasses, she didn't protest. She didn't protest when he started to rub the back of her neck, either. Hurt and fury had flooded through her when he had first appeared at the door, big grin across his face. And now, between the red wine and his soothing touch, she was on the verge of purring like Ezra. When he touches me, nothing else exists, *just this, just this* ...

"Laur." He took hold of her hand and held it in his big rough palm. Stroking her fingers, he said again, "Laur."

Lauren still refused to look at him, but her hands apparently knew nothing of this, because the one stayed nestled in Mick's paw, and the other came round to touch his chest. Other parts of her body, she could feel, were also starting to respond.

Mick slid down a little so that he was half kneeling on the floor. He had both of her hands now. Then he went very still and she knew he had seen. His voice was soft, but even so it made her flinch.

"Laur ... You got a new scar on your wrist."

"Very observant. I'm sure Detective Rossi would be impressed."

"It looks bad, Laur. How come you got a new scar?"

"I don't know," she said lightly. "It seemed like a good idea at the time."

"No, tell me. Why'd you do that? Not because of me, I hope."

She pulled her hands away. "I'm sure it makes you feel important to think so. Self-centred pig."

"True. I am self-centred. This is very, very true. You have to go to the hospital and all?"

"I don't want to talk about it, Mick."

"Me either." He raised his glass again. "Here's to not dying."

She clinked his glass. "Until you're ready."

They sipped their wine, and then he twirled a lock of her hair round his finger and gave it a tug. "It's good to see you again, babe. You do something to me. A spell or something. I like seeing you, even when you hate me."

"I don't hate you."

"And when you don't hate me …" He sprang to his feet. "It makes me feel like dancing!"

"Sit down, Mick. I am not going to dance with you."

"I'll dance by myself. I got the legs. I got the moves." He did a very bad imitation of a rapper: "Baby, you know I gots de moves!" He plugged his iPod into the stereo and turned up the Holy Ghost! album. It was great dance music.

"You sure you don't want to dance?"

"Sit down, Mick. You're not going to start dancing at this hour."

"What are you talking about? It's like ten-thirty. Nobody goes to bed at ten-thirty. This is New York."

"Dis is New Yaaawwwwk." She could do a good Mick when she felt like it. "Hey, Babe. I got duh moves."

"Very cute. Remind me to do *you* sometime."

"You do a terrible me. You put on an English accent and stick your pinkie out, like Amy Vanderbilt or something."

"Exactly. That's exactly how you are. Miss Priss. Miss Harvard."

"Sit down, Mick. Have another glass of wine."

Mick sat down and had another glass of wine. So did Lauren.

Mick told her a funny story about the cops. They're driving him to the precinct and they get stuck in traffic when one of them—not Rossi, the other jerk—really has to go. Cops, you gotta understand, drink coffee all day. So here they are stuck on the FDR and the guy's bursting, so what do they do? They pop the cherry on top and crank the siren up, and half the population of Manhattan is pulling onto the shoulder so they can make a high-speed run to the precinct. Just so the guy can make the *can*. This is where your tax dollars go.

They drank the rest of the wine and Mick opened another bottle. "A real Boy Scout, I am. Always prepared. Very sound advice, Laur: always be prepared."

By the time they were halfway into this bottle, the stereo was up full blast and the two of them were jitterbugging around the living room like a couple of teenagers, working up a sweat.

When a slow song came on, Lauren draped herself around Mick. His hands moved over her, into her back pockets, into her shirt, into her jeans. She didn't care, she didn't care. No one touched her the way Mick did—so hot on her skin, his slow, damp hand.

Maybe it was because she was angry with Peter. Or maybe because it had been so long. Maybe it was the wine. Whether it was any of these, or whether it was simply the heat of Mick's touch, Lauren had had no idea she was this ready. Suddenly her jeans were a twisted heap on the couch, and her fingers were tearing at Mick's zipper. When she threw his jeans over her shoulder, they hit a lamp, knocking it to the floor with a crash.

Peter was fast asleep among his newspapers, dreaming of Lauren in a big house. *Their* house. They were in their living room, which was lined with books. The place was bursting with literary folk—agents, editors, writers—a party in progress. A publisher with white hair and a rabbit's face steered him through the crowd into a quiet hall.

"Brother William," the publisher said. "I happen to know that this award would not have happened without you."

"But I'm not Brother William," Peter protested. "I'm not Brother William anymore. My name is—"

He was interrupted by a cry from another room. The hall, the house, swam away as he tried to determine who had cried out: was it one of Lauren's editors? And then a real cry made him sit up in bed.

He was back in his cell: the lumpy bed, the shabby room. Loud music was pouring down the air shaft, but the cry, sharp and clear, still hung in the air. The walls were throbbing with bass notes. Something crashed to the floor overhead, but by then Peter was out of his bed and pulling on his trousers. He didn't bother to button his shirt. He grabbed Lauren's key and ran upstairs.

Zaleski, in rumpled pyjamas, was banging on Lauren's door with a fat fist.

"Doesn't have courtesy to answer. Wakes up whole stinking block and doesn't have courtesy to answer."

"Can't you open the door?"

"Hell with door. I just want no music."

"I heard a crash. She might be hurt."

"Go back downstairs, I will fix." Zaleski banged on the door again. "Miss Wolfe! Turn down music *please*. This is civilized house."

"She never listens to loud music."

"Sure. So considerate, this woman." Zaleski kept banging his fist on the door. "Turn it down, Miss Wolfe! Turn it down or I call police."

Just then the music stopped, the end of the record. Zaleski pivoted away from Lauren's door. "Good," he said. "Finish."

From inside her apartment, Lauren cried out, a long, clear wail Peter had never heard before. He fumbled in his pocket for the key, images rushing through his mind: Lauren stabbed and bleeding on the floor; a dark, faceless thief rooting through her things.

"Is not your business, Mr. Mee-han," Zaleski said. "Why you're hanging around?"

"It *is* my business. Lauren's hurt." He was already turning the key in the lock.

The kitchen was dark. There was a peculiar glow from the bedroom. As Peter hurried past Lauren's office, he could see into the living room at the end of the hall. A lamp had toppled to the floor, casting weird shadows up the walls. He approached the doorway cautiously, hands slightly lifted away from his body. He was ready to subdue any rapist, kill any killer.

Lauren was kneeling over Mick, who lay spread-eagled on the bed. Sensing someone else enter the room, she looked up. Light angling up from the floor gleamed on her face, on the thread of saliva that connected her to Mick. It glittered, dangling between them like a delicate silver chain.

TWENTY-TWO

ONCE AGAIN, despite several attempts the following week, Lauren was unable to reach Mick. And Peter too had fled some-where—perhaps to his brother's place—and she could not blame him for not wanting to see her. If he was gone for good, well, perhaps it was for the best—for both of them.

She began a poem called "Razor," a kind of ode to the one dependable friend in her life, and threw it out. Then she picked up the phone and dialed the hospital. David Cresswell made room in his schedule to accommodate an extra session .

They met in his office away from the hospital, and continued to meet there twice a week. It was in shared clinical space on Twelfth Street West, a place with many potted plants and other grace notes that made Lauren suspect all the other therapists would be female.

"He has this very gentle manner," she told Cresswell, trying to describe how she had come to be entangled with Peter. "Very quiet and self-contained. I mean, he seems that way. He exudes quiet. He's like a cat almost. He can sit in a corner all day with a mystery novel and he doesn't need a thing. Doesn't seem to."

"Tell me more." Cresswell looked at her, pen poised above his notebook. Her previous therapist had never taken a single note.

"Well, he was a monk for ten years. That should give you some idea. He can be so tender. It's like he's suffering with you. Truly. It's like he literally feels what you're feeling. So he'll give me a hug at just the right moment. Or touch my hand and give a little smile. Or suddenly he appears with a cup of tea when I didn't even know I wanted one. I've never met anyone with such ... empathy. It's very ..."

"Very what?"

"I don't know. Seductive."

"Seductive."

"You think that's crazy? I mean, he's a former monk."

"You've been in tremendous pain. Along comes this guy— quiet, good-looking—who's nothing but sympathy. Basically offers to look after you. I can see where that might be seductive."

"He comes on like he wants nothing at all. Like he doesn't need anything. Then, the minute it looks like there's someone else in the picture, he's like, I don't know, all hooks."

"Yes, you've said he's very jealous."

Lauren kept her gaze fixed on the fireplace across the room. There were stacks of books on the mantel, some of them by Cresswell himself. Whenever she couldn't look at him, she found herself looking at the books instead, noting slight variations in their order from week to week.

"What are you thinking?"

"Just ... I don't know."

"What are you feeling, then?"

"Pain." Lauren made a circle around her heart. "Here."

"What kind of pain?"

Lauren tried to reply, but couldn't speak through the storm of tears. This was her third or fourth visit, and it seemed all she did was cry. It took several minutes and several tissues for the storm to subside.

"Why are you crying?"

"Because I never meant to hurt him. He was so good to me and I just hurt him and hurt him and hurt him. I swear I didn't mean to."

"Uh-huh."

"I was aware of it. I knew I was doing it. But I didn't mean to. God, I was awful."

"How?"

"I told you how. By sleeping with Mick."

"Peter interrupted you. You told me he came up to your apartment in the middle of the night and walked in."

"He was worried. I guess I was, uh, pretty noisy with Mick— in bed, I mean."

"Mm-hmm."

"I just can't seem to stop hurting people. Whatever I do."

"How have you hurt Mick?"

"Well, maybe not Mick. I *can't* hurt Mick. He's unhurtable. By me, anyway."

"How's that?"

"Because he doesn't care. I'm just someone to fuck."

"From what you tell me, it doesn't sound like he'd have any difficulty finding women to have sex with, if that was all he was interested in."

"Okay, there are other things he likes about me. He likes it that I'm a writer. He likes it that I come from a wealthy background. He likes it that I'm smart. I guess it makes him feel smart. Or maybe he just finds it exotic. But he really couldn't care less. I'm not exaggerating. It's just a fact."

"So you're wondering why Peter keeps coming back to you all the time, even though you hurt him. And yet you keep going back to Mick, even though he doesn't care about you."

"Believe me, I'm aware of the parallels. I don't know why Peter is crazy about me. And I don't know why I'm crazy about Mick. It's not like it feels good. It's not like I enjoy it. It hurts like hell. So why do I keep doing it? Again and again I go after Mick, and again and again he kicks me in the teeth. It makes me want to die. Is it just stupidity? Why would I keep doing it, if it doesn't even feel good?"

"No, it doesn't feel good—it feels *familiar.*"

"What?"

"It doesn't feel good. It feels familiar."

"Oh, boy. Here we go."

"Here we go where?"

"You're going to tell me how it goes back to my father, right? Don't you think that's a little glib?" Even as Lauren was speaking, the word *familiar* was echoing round her head. She knew she would carry it home.

"Well, you brought up your father," Cresswell said, "not me. He left you when you were eight years old."

"Well, he left my mother."

"You think an eight-year-old makes that distinction? I can tell you right now, children in that situation will automatically blame themselves, no matter how hard the parents try to reassure them. Do you recall any effort they made in that regard?"

"Not offhand. I'm sure they did, though. I mean, I used to go visit my father and everything."

"You've said you've hated him as long as you can remember. Did you hate him before your parents broke up?"

"I'm not sure."

"It's rare for an eight-year-old to hate anyone. Perhaps you were afraid of him?"

"A little, maybe. He had a temper. I probably got that from him. So maybe."

"Why don't you think about it? Our time's almost up. Think about it, and we'll use it as our starting point next time."

Lauren lifted her purse off the floor and pulled out her chequebook.

"Lauren, normally I'm not so—what's the word? Inquisitive? Intrusive? But I need to ask you straight out how you think our work is progressing. I'm not asking for compliments. A few weeks ago you tried to kill yourself, and what matters most to me is that you get the help you need. If I can't provide it, we'll find someone who can. To do anything less would be doing you a disservice."

Lauren scribbled her signature on the cheque and put it on the end table without saying anything.

"Thank you. Lauren, we've had several sessions now. Would you like to try another therapist, or would you like to keep coming here?"

"Don't you think I'm getting any better?"

"I'm asking you."

"If you mean do I feel better generally? Not particularly. I still feel miserable about hurting Peter so badly. I'm still hung up on Mick. I don't see getting over that stuff anytime soon." She slipped her arms into her coat, buttoning it up as she spoke. "But I would like to keep coming here. I'm beginning to think that I really want to fix this. I never did before. I was always afraid that if I fixed whatever it is that makes me behave this way—or even talked about it—it would kill whatever it is inside me that makes me write. And I wasn't willing to do that. Now I am. This last—" She held up her wrist. "It convinced me that I have to change or die. And if I have to give up writing to do that, I'm willing to. Really. I don't know what I'd do for a living, but . . ."

"And have you had to give up writing so far?"

"No. In fact, I'm writing more than ever. Poems, short stories, novel. It's weird, really. And the novel is going amazingly well. I do seven, eight pages some days. Despite the fucking pills. Mind you, it's probably all shit."

"But you always think that, you told me."

"I know. I can't help it. Anyway, even though I don't feel better yet, I can sense that I *might* start to feel better. That maybe I don't *have* to be miserable all the time. That things might actually get better someday."

"I'm glad."

"You realize that's probably the most positive thing I've ever said in my life?"

"That you might not have to be miserable?" Cresswell gave a slight smile.

"It's a start," Lauren said.

"Yes. I think it's a good start."

"So, same time on Friday?"

"Same time on Friday."

TWENTY-THREE

A FRIGID WIND had thrown a sudden turmoil of purple and grey cloud above the north hills. The monks were not dressed for it, wearing only their cowls and tunics, and when the rain came whipping down the slopes, they put up their hoods, but they offered scant protection. It was only a matter of minutes before they were soaked through, and this was a December rain, bone-chilling. The suggestion was made that they leave the field and work in the barn, but Brother Martin had already assigned the barn work and would not hear of them quitting.

"Look at Brother William," he said. "You don't see him complaining."

Peter had cornered a black-faced ewe, backing her up with outstretched hands between an outcropping of rock and the electrified fence. The ewe had an abscess behind one ear and was consequently in a foul temper. The morning had been filled with one disgusting labour after another: a goat had had to be dewormed; a lamb had got into a state of founder and Brother Martin had had to puncture the wretched thing, jabbing a long spike into a spot near the flank. This had produced a long wet noise, accompanied by the stomach-turning smell of methane.

The humped nose gave the black-faced ewe a cross-eyed look. Peter had not forgotten how he loathed the sheep.

"A little discomfort," Brother Martin went on, his one good eye blinking back rain. "Let's offer it up for the souls in purgatory and get on with the job."

Brother Martin, Peter thought, was such a discerning intellectual. As the heavy monk came up behind him, Peter said, "Don't you find it a little funny that we take such care of them? They're only headed for the slaughterhouse."

"We take such care because that's how we get the best prices. Careful, she's getting away."

Martin was slow as a battleship. Peter dodged around him and lunged for the ewe.

"Not like that!"

The warning came too late. The ewe's hind legs came up, and it felt as if he'd been hit in the shin with a hammer. Peter fell back in the mud, cursing.

"Foolish," said Martin, steaming toward him. "Are you all right?"

Peter leapt up and ran for the sheep. When the animal ducked its head, Peter kicked at the dark, stupid face, catching it under the chin. Brother Martin stared in astonishment.

A hundred pounds of living sheep is no easy thing to lift, but Peter picked up the ewe and hurled it down the slope. It landed badly.

"Oh, my Lord. You've broken her leg."

The other monks stared at the sheep with awe. The animal was struggling to stand. A jagged end of bone poked through its hide.

"Both legs," said Martin, kneeling in the mud. "Worried about the slaughterhouse, are you? Such a bleeding heart? She's only three years old. Do you have any idea how many sheep you just cost us?"

A young monk, whose name Peter did not even know, offered to go for the vet.

"She won't survive. She'll have to be killed." Martin pointed to the barn. "Brother William will fetch the axe."

Father Michael came out of the main building just as Peter was heading back to the field carrying the axe. He stopped him in the lee of the barn.

"You're going back out, William? I was just on my way to call everyone in."

"They'll be in soon."

"What are you doing with that?" the priest asked, pointing to the axe. "Oh, of course. You'll be clearing that stump. Another storm like that and the whole place will blow away. I don't know what Brother Martin's thinking. You're soaked through."

"I'd better get back. They're waiting for me."

"Just a moment. There's something I want to say."

Peter waited, gripping the axe.

"It's very brave of you to come back here," the priest continued. "To face all this again. Everything you see must remind you of the early days, when a vocation is a bright new flame."

Peter nodded.

"You'll have to close up your place in the city soon. I know it's only been a couple of weeks, but clinging to it will only make things harder."

Peter nodded again. Taciturnity was the only aspect of a monk's character that came easily these days, but his silence was now a shield from man, not an opening to God.

"Careful with that thing." Father Michael pointed at the axe. "You're liable to amputate a foot." As Peter strode away, the priest called after him, "Tell them I said to come in, will you? Martin will have everyone down with the flu."

The monks were still in their ragged circle, but when Peter approached with the axe, they looked off into the distance as if something of interest were happening on the far hills. The ewe lay on its side, legs flickering now and again as it tried to stand. Agony was a new experience, and the black, stupid face bore a look of incredulity.

"Give her a good one on the crown and get it over with," Brother Martin said.

Peter raised the axe and brought the flat end down, smashing the skull. The legs jerked spasmodically, the glistening black eyes filmed over, and the animal lay still.

"Just be thankful I don't make you carry her to the shed and hang her up to bleed. It has to be done right."

When Father Michael began the Mass, Peter thought of the pain he had caused that innocent ewe. It was too bad Lauren could not have ended his own pain as quickly. Brother William had died for her, and now Peter too was slowly dying. The sight of her bending over Mick should have finished him off, but instead it ate at him, boring its way slowly through his intestines. Uncertainty and doubt had made him miserable, but he would have given anything to have them back. As long as he had been uncertain, there had been hope. Peter's lips mumbled the liturgy, but his thoughts could not have been further from God.

Father Michael had said it must be hard to see again the place where one's vocation first caught fire, and it *was* hard, but not, Peter considered, because he had ever really had a vocation. Back in college, Cathy McCullough's rejection of him for another young man had simply driven him over some kind of precipice.

After reading the note she had left for him in the dorm—reading it for the ninth or tenth time—he had become a very sorry creature indeed. He had taken to hanging around outside the women's dorm, skulking in doorways, watching Cathy go by with her new boyfriend, even following her at a distance. He had sensed that this was wrong; he had watched himself do these things as from a distance, powerless to stop himself.

Contrary to Peter's imaginings, his replacement in Cathy's affections was no great specimen of male beauty, and when Peter investigated, he discovered the youth was not even a good student: he was a drinker, a sports fiend, and belonged to a fraternity best known for its all-night parties.

For Peter, Luce College was transformed overnight from Arcadia into a district of hell. Sleep abandoned him, his grades plummeted, he lost his scholarship.

One night, he waited outside Cathy's dorm. He had not slept for days, he had eaten nothing: he was an unshaven wreck, running on caffeine and nerves. For three nights in a row, he hid in the shadow of an elm, waiting. Finally, one night, Cathy came home alone.

He stepped out of the shadows, startling her.

"Hello, Peter," she greeted him, trying to sound gay and carefree, although he could tell she was alarmed by his appearance. She breezed by as if he were nothing more than a casual acquaintance. He took hold of her wrist before she could open the door.

"You said you loved me," he accused her.

"I wasn't lying," Cathy said. "I thought I did."

He glared into her eyes. He wanted to explain true love to her. He was just beginning to gather his thoughts when Cathy had tried to extract her wrist from his grip, and that was when he hit her. It wasn't until she was curled up on the sidewalk that he realized he held a rock in his hand. He ran into the night, into blackness.

There was a blank space in Peter's memory where the next few minutes should have been. He did not remember crossing the quad, or entering the men's dormitory, or taking the elevator to the top. He had no memory of the stairs he must have climbed. His next memory was of looking out across the campus from the roof. There was no moon, and the trees were bare, lit only by the small yellow lamps along the paths.

He remained perched on the edge of the roof, trying to work up the courage to jump. But he could not. There were a few moments then when he seemed to be two people: one at the edge of the roof, another watching him from slightly behind and above. This second self, a wraithlike being not fully formed, watched him climb down.

The strange sensation had passed by the time he came out from the stairwell into the dorm. He was about to call the emergency number from the pay phone when he heard the sirens. The last bus into Southampton went by the front window, and Peter ran to catch it. An ambulance raced by in the opposite direction as the bus was pulling onto the highway.

When he rang the doorbell of the small rectory beside the Catholic church, it was answered by an elderly priest who was not at all pleased to be wakened at this late hour. He left Peter in a small parlour that smelled of furniture polish, and a few moments later Father Gage entered, wearing a plaid dressing gown.

"Father, you have to hear my confession," Peter said, suddenly kneeling before him. "I don't deserve to live."

Father Gage went to fetch his stole, heard his confession right there in the parlour, and so began—before he even knew it—Peter's career as Brother William. Father Gage could see that he was truly remorseful, and so there had been no question of withholding absolution. It was Father Gage's forgiveness—or rather God's forgiveness conveyed through this balding, plaid-gowned human instrument—that almost overwhelmed Peter with gratitude. He was less overwhelmed with Father Gage's urging that he go straight to the police.

Peter visited Cathy in the local hospital, but she had not regained consciousness and was soon removed to a rehabilitation centre that was too far away. He was consumed with remorse, but could not bring himself to confess to the police. Father Gage repeatedly urged him to do so: he had a duty not just to his own soul but to Cathy, to her family, to society. Peter refused, descended into a maelstrom of guilt and failed his spring mid-terms.

In the end, Cathy survived, though she was left with a slight slurring of speech, and a slowness of response down her right side. The head trauma was grave enough, however, that she had no memory of the attack, or of the events immediately surrounding it.

Peter was questioned, but many people were questioned. Cathy had been attacked at eleven-thirty. He told the police he had been in the college library until it closed at midnight. The library staff were so used to seeing him there that they confirmed his story. Certainly, there was nothing in Peter's character that pointed to guilt. By all reports, Cathy's included, he was a gentle young man.

Father Gage suggested he attend a monastery for a retreat of a week or two, to collect his thoughts and discover for himself the right path to take. He recommended Our Lady of Peace. Peter went the very next day and, once there, confessed to Father Michael and spent the week praying for guidance. He believed his prayers were answered, and a new life would begin.

Now, as Father Michael moved with a rustle of vestments about the altar, Peter looked up across the pale oak benches. The faint smell of incense brought back the first searing moments of his love for Lauren. He stared at the back of the chapel where she had sat and remembered the dark crescents of her eyelashes when she had gazed down at the Psalm book. The scent of myrrh lingered in the soft grey air.

Even the library was no longer a refuge. An older monk was librarian now, but thinking it a kindness, Father Michael had allowed Peter to assist him. Within half an hour, Lauren's book was in his hand. He kept it on the little trolley as he trundled it among the shelves, and her orphan eyes called his name. Here was the table where she had studied with such passion, there the spot on the floor where he had found her pencil. He even leafed through the Abelard biography that had caused her first indignant outburst. He asked to work in the fields instead, a place where Lauren had never set foot.

And now Father Michael would learn about the sheep; Peter would be expected to tell him himself. Surely he had come to the end of his brothers' patience, he thought as they sang the Kyrie. I am fouling their serenity. I am the beggar who spoils dinner with his hollow eyes, his gaudy marquee of sores. Lose the gift of faith and you are no longer human but mere animated flesh, lurching toward the grave. Beneath the sung responses and the muttered prayers, he could almost hear their flesh rotting, their bones crumbling. *You are smoke and lightning / I am ashes, skin, and hair.*

A terrible image flashed into his mind: Lauren torn and bleeding. He nearly cried out, right there in the chapel. But it was like a first faint flash of lightning, perceived in the corner of the eye. He was not even sure what he had seen.

Father Michael stepped to the lectern for the sermon. "There is much that seems like love that is not love," he began, "kindnesses that are not kindnesses. It is easy to be fooled, but we must always remember that these flights of fancy, these gusts of emotion, those things that seem most beautiful, those things that seem most real, often turn out to be the most dangerous illusions, the kingdom Satan offered to Christ."

But *this* is the land of illusion, Peter thought, right here in Our Lady of So-Called Peace. A collection of misfits locked away in an asylum.

"It is difficult to judge the difference between illusion and reality in the behaviour of others; it is the work of a lifetime to learn the difference within ourselves."

Lauren is real, Peter thought, the only real thing I have ever known. The taste of her sweat, her skin, her tears, her blood—that's the only reality I need; to have her love for one split second the only eternity I want. The rest of the Mass was lost to him; reveries of Lauren dazzled him, as if the interior of his skull were a dome of beaten gold.

"I hope you're feeling a little better," the young monk said to him on the way into the refectory.

Peter did not reply. Nothing is more intolerable to the man in pain than unwanted encouragement.

Mealtimes, at least, were made bearable by the cessation of talk. As the food was passed along the table, Brother Conrad resumed reading from a biography of Pope Francis, a chapter concerning his college days. The food was better than Peter remembered, but as the sonorous voice droned on, he could not bear the insufferable contentment of his brothers, slurping their soup while this ex–disc jockey read to them as to a group of children. Their simplicity, which he had once striven to emulate, now sickened him.

The rain had slowed to a drizzle, and after dinner Peter walked up to the cemetery and knelt in the mud at Brother Raphael's grave. A white metal cross had been planted at the head of it, making it indistinguishable from all the others. Peter shivered. To think he had once admired this deluded old man. Forty years locked away in this barnyard—never knowing real love, a woman's love—why not kill yourself at twenty and get it over with?

Beside it there was a newer grave, no cross on it yet. That would be Clement Smith's, the lay brother. Clement Smith. Not even a monk, but he chose to waste his short life here, to die here, to be buried here. Clement had been about the same age as Peter.

He stood on a rise and watched the rain softly falling over the chapel and the refectory, slanting in cross-hatch patterns across the barn and over the fields, hovering in a pale blue mist above the wreckage of his life.

He had a dizzying perception that the hills were actually moving, rolling beneath his feet, surging around him like ocean swells. These must be waves of pain, he thought—yes, he was adrift on an ocean of pain. And yet the waves were crashing around him, outside him, not within—as if they were someone else's emotions, the rage that someone else, a lesser man, might feel, having lost everything.

A man who loses everything can always turn to God; Peter had believed that once. He had believed it for ten years. He had hoped that by coming back to Our Lady, by going through the motions, as Father Michael had said, his faith would return. But it showed no sign of returning, and without it, the monastic life was not only excruciating but ridiculous. He had lost his faith when he had found Lauren, and now that he had lost Lauren, he had nothing. The word tolled through him like a knell: he was nothing. Nothing.

The monastery itself had not changed in any detail; it was the identical place he had left more than a year ago. Nothing in his cell had changed: the same Bible with the same stain lay in the same corner of the same shelf. The same crucifix with the same chip hung from the same wall. When he woke in the middle of the night, the room was dark as a coffin; inch by inch, the walls closed in.

He lay staring up into the darkness. Another horrific image came to him: Lauren with her heart cut out, a black, gaping hole in her chest. But it was just a flash, not really a thought, gone in a split second. And then there was Mick.

He was not angry with Mick: Mick had done nothing he himself would not do; Mick had not even killed the boy, as it turned out. Mick had been a rival, not a friend, and rivals, unlike lovers, cannot betray.

Later, he had a nightmare. A hooded figure worked a pump handle up and down, sucking the air from Peter's cell. "One of these days ..." it said in a snide, reedy voice, "one of these days, Brother William, I'm going to teach you a lesson." He was awakened by the noise of a squirrel on the roof; it sounded like Lauren's fingers scurrying over her keyboard.

He wished he were dust—a fine white powder that could be scattered over mountains and waves, over islands, trees and farms, as light as snow—and not this hard, bitter lump that swelled in his throat but would not burst and would not kill him.

His monk's habit hung on the back of his door like an exhausted brown ghost. The city clothes he had worn here, except for the shoes, were gone; he had burned them in the incinerator upon his arrival. Peter Meehan, after all, was dead. Again. A faint voice inside him had been praying for the resurrection of Brother William, but that gentle monk was never coming back.

He got out of bed and put on the cowl and tunic. He slipped into his shoes and walked silently down the corridor and out into the quadrangle. *What am I doing? Where am I going?* A small part of him wanted to know. *What is this?*

This is love, he told himself as he entered the kitchen, dead silent except for the drip of a tap. Carving knives gleamed in the moonlight. He took one down and felt the sharp edge with his thumb. How many lambs, he wondered, had it carved? He pulled out bread and cheese from the fridge and made himself a couple of sandwiches.

This is love, he said to himself as he crossed the quadrangle once more and entered the chapel; the dull red glow seemed to beat softly in the air as if he were standing inside the Sacred Heart itself. The red lantern hung near the altar, the small constant flame signifying the presence of God.

This is love, Peter said as he walked up the aisle. He paused before the lamp, then reached out and twisted the tiny stopcock shut. Behind the red glass, the steady flame dimmed, then sputtered, then died. The chapel was dark. It was as close as he could come to killing God.

This is love, he said to himself as he walked along the grass border of the front drive so his footsteps would not crunch on gravel. He entered the front lobby, passed the gift shop and continued along the hall to Father Michael's office, where he lifted a set of keys from a peg.

This is love, he said, outside once more. He got into the blue station wagon and shifted into neutral, letting the car roll backwards down the gravel incline. He turned the key, and the motor caught with a roar. He headed down the drive toward the highway. Eyes of hidden animals glittered in the hedges. The dashboard clock said twelve-thirty.

The sign on the curve swung into view: "New York City 285 miles."

This is love, he thought as he settled in for the long drive. They can spend the next forty years in that prison and never know the difference between love and fear. One of the monks would come for the car eventually, but they would not ask Peter to come back. His misery was a reproach to them, just as their serenity was to him.

This is love, he thought hours later as the George Washington

Bridge rose out of the hills. Dangling chains of lights were reflected in the river. He thought of that delicate silver chain that had hung glittering between Lauren and Mick. That, he knew, was not love.

A length of time went by that felt like space because he had no sense of it passing. Three weeks? Surely not four. He sat in his tiny room with no firm idea of when he had arrived. The place stank of the garbage he had neglected to remove before fleeing to the monastery. He sat on the edge of his bed, trapped in his body, clenched tight as a fist.

Time passed, and then he was on his side, still clenched tight. He tried to cry, but could not. Tears were not available in this place.

More time passed. Perhaps he dozed. It was still dark. He should have been hungry, but he was not. He went to the window. It must be very late; there was not a soul on the street. It was snowing heavily, and an eerie quiet had descended. He stood there a long time.

The next thing he was aware of was turning on the light. He observed himself opening the cupboard under his tiny sink and taking out the hammer he had bought when he had first moved in. He saw his hand pluck Lauren's keys from the little hook by his door. He observed himself going down the hall, a hooded figure, his face a blot of darkness.

Peter Meehan was dead, Brother William was dead, and now all that remained of them glided up the stairs.

He opened her door without making a sound. He walked through the kitchen, keeping close to the walls. The centre of the floor creaked—who could know this better than he? Had he not lain one floor below like a man buried alive and listened to her footsteps creak across the lid of his coffin?

A dull glow filtered from her office as he walked past; she had left her computer on, as she often did.

His feet made no sound on the bedroom carpet. The room was stifling. The number-twelve jersey lay on the floor. Ezra was curled up on a chair. Peter moved toward the bed, yet stood apart, watching himself move closer.

A book about the fashion industry was splayed face down on the night table; beside this, a stenographer's notebook, marked with Lauren's neat, square handwriting. Setting it down, she had knocked over a small bottle of sleeping pills. She had cut one of them in half, trying to keep her dosage down; it lay like a half moon, miniature and blue, beside the bottle. The hammer hung heavily in Peter's hand.

Lauren lay under a thin sheet, sleeping peacefully on her side. Her small breasts moved slightly with the rise and fall of her breath. Her mouth was open slightly, showing the small teeth. The pale hair was tucked behind her ear, the scarred wrist upturned against the pillow. He did not want Lauren to suffer; he had never wanted Lauren to suffer. The hammer rose. Beneath the skin of Lauren's temple, a vein was beating like a tiny lilac heart.

TWENTY-FOUR

WOOD FROM THE small pile on the floor spat and crackled in the stove. Smoke curled in streams round the edges of the lid, thickening the darkness. Peter made himself a cup of instant coffee. He clutched the hot mug in both hands, but still it could not warm him. He shivered beside the stove in his wet cowl and tunic.

He had been miles out of the city by the time dawn broke. All the way here, snow had fallen in heavy grey sheets. It clung to the few cars and buses that crept along the streets, muffling their motors to a damp throb. Peter had been driving north on the highway by the time dawn finally did break, and it broke dark as Good Friday. Clouds lowered on the hills as if some divine plan were coming to fruition. But Peter no longer believed in anything divine; it was a snowstorm, nothing more.

He opened the stove lid, dropped in another piece of wood, and sparks flew up like fireflies. The cabin was even darker than it had been when he had come out here with Dominic. One entire side was buried in snowdrift; the only light squeezed in through a tiny window on the other side. Although it was not yet noon, outside it looked like nightfall. Snow tumbled heavily past the window, but the winds had dropped and it fell straight to earth.

He had driven for three hours. All along the highway, cars were pitched at strange angles where they had slid onto the shoulder. Peter had inched his way north to the hypnotic flap of the wipers. The storm had destroyed his plan: to kill himself by driving at high speed into a bridge support or off a cliff. He did not want to risk hitting another car. It was only when he recognized the dim hump of Fire Mountain that he had come up with this secondary plan.

The country road had proved to be impassable. When the car got stuck, he had spun the wheels until they sat on highly polished patches of ice. He abandoned the car and waded in the direction of the cabin through a trackless, waist-high meringue.

Despair, he discovered—trying now to warm his hands over the stove—was not at all the same as misery. Misery was torment, misery was raw emotion. But despair, he found, had its bleak attractions. Despair was another country altogether, a place with its own distinct landscapes, its own lunar climate. Emotion did not exist in this atmosphere; all was clarity. Objects took on a sharp, stark beauty, as if observed through a lens.

Peter stood before the scorching heat of the stove with his hands spread apart like a priest saying Mass. Steam rose from the front of his tunic, damp with snow and Lauren's blood.

The surrounding silence filled him with peace. It was as if a terrible engine that had clanked and howled throughout his life had suddenly ground to a halt. Was this what Lauren had experienced, he wondered, in those moments before she set blade to wrist? He did not think so. He had seen in her none of the calm that was building inside him like the snowdrifts outside.

When he had stood over her, watching the pulse beating beneath her skin, he had found calm enough for them both. His arm had remained cocked for some time like a mechanical figure on a clock, poised to strike the hour. The hammer came down squarely on Lauren's temple—came down with such force that it broke through the thin bone and lodged there. He had expected her to remain utterly still, but she had flipped over on her back. After this, he remembered only flashes: the whites of her eyes jerking rapidly back and forth, the rushed intake of breath that sounded like whooping cough, the hammer slamming down on her forehead, the coin-shaped indentation above her eyebrow.

He remembered only those two blows, but he must have hit her more times, because the hammer became so slick with blood that it finally flew from his hands, crashing into the corner behind him. And Lauren, previously so ready to discard her life, had clung to that life ferociously; the whooping cough had seemed to go on and on forever.

The frail scarred wrist, the delicate skin, the exquisite crescents of her eyelashes—Lauren had been a creation perfectly conceived for love, yet somewhere in her life pain had entered in and broken that perfection. Peter now knew that she had been right about one thing: that it had been her pain, and no other aspect of her character, that had drawn passion from him like blood from a wound. So he had lied to Lauren when he said he loved her. He had lied all his life: to himself when he had become a monk, to God when he had taken his vows. But he was clear of the lies now.

He looked around the cabin at Dominic's things. The shotgun propped in the corner, the row of traps that hung from the wall. The traps, gleaming dimly in the red light of the stove, gave the place the look of a torture chamber. Torture had been a specialty with monks a few centuries ago.

"No salvation without pain," Conrad of Marbourg had claimed as he ordered another twist of the rack, another spike inserted, another finger crushed. It was not without logic, as religious beliefs go. It was like picking a lock: if you found the exact combination of torments, the imperilled soul could only respond by leaping across death into the arms of God—a God who waited like a lover to catch him on the other side.

Peter opened the cabin door. Whiteness fell away on every side—a whiteness made of the grey of ash, the blue of razors. He remembered the deer that had wandered into the clearing; there had been so many colours then. He remembered Dominic's rifle.

It was easy to believe that the snow would never stop falling. It was falling now in flakes so fat they hit his face with an audible impact. He had the sensation he was fixed inside one of those toys children love, a hemisphere of glass. A little boy had shaken it up in his fist, and Peter was the tiny figure inside—a miniature monk beside a miniature cabin in a miniature blizzard. From here, inside the toy, it looked as if the snow would fall forever, though only the boy who held everything in his hand could know for sure. He might shake it up again, or he might toss it aside—cabin, monk and blizzard—in favour of another, more amusing, toy.

TWENTY-FIVE

DOMINIC MEEHAN AND Detective Frank Rossi were driving along the exact route that Peter had taken the previous day. The highway had been plowed, and they had made pretty good time until the turnoff near Fire Mountain. Someone—probably the state troopers—had plowed an ineffective and extremely narrow track through the drifts.

Rossi had slowed the car to a crawl, and Dominic Meehan was slumped on the passenger side, his puffy eyelids nearly closed. Between the slits his eyes occasionally swivelled left or right, like ball bearings. His brother was just a gentle fool. He, Dom, had always been the violent one. Everyone else must see that too. Certainly Rossi must know that.

"So, the guy packs everything up," Rossi was saying, "ten years of his life—his entire universe, you might say—and comes to the big city after the girl. When was this, exactly?"

"November, December, a year ago—before Christmas. How should I know?"

"I thought you said he stayed with you."

"It was a year ago, for Christ sake. Tell me about the medical examiner, Frank—he any good?"

"Grigson? Hold on a minute—we got something here."

Rossi rolled down the window as he spoke, and yelled to a state trooper parked in a cruiser. Dominic waited while Rossi got out of the car. A blue station wagon had foundered in the drifts. Rossi was a small man with dark, curly hair that clung to his skull like moss; the rest of him was all but hidden in trench coat and sunglasses. Next to the trooper (a six-footer bundled in a regulation parka) he looked miniaturized.

Rossi stepped around the station wagon, examining it. The trooper kept talking while Rossi bent to peer in the car window, hands in pockets, careful not to touch anything. Dominic watched the steam issuing from the trooper's mouth, and Rossi nodding his head.

A few minutes later, Rossi got back into the car. A blast of winter rolled through the interior.

"Grigson's okay," Rossi went on as if their conversation had not been interrupted. "I mean, they're all nuts, MEs—that's understood. But Grigson's okay. Twenty years in the business and kind of a RoboDoc, if you want my opinion. Only thing Grigson gets excited about is maggots. What kind of person chooses to work with maggots?"

"Matter of taste, Frank. I've worked with some very personable maggots."

Rossi gave a dark little laugh. "Don't talk about your clientele that way, Dom. It brings disrespect to our parole system."

"Some people, I'm telling you, it's like when they were a kid they couldn't wait to grow up and live in the penitentiary. They get out for a couple of weeks, they find a way to bust back inside. It's like they have a vocation."

"That the story with your little brother? Lost his vocation?"

"Oh, very subtle, Frank. Didn't see that one coming."

"Sorry, buddy. I know you're upset and all, but I'm just trying to understand."

"You're asking the wrong guy."

"What are you talking about? He was your brother, for Christ sake."

"Different planets. I didn't know the guy. Different planets, you know what I'm saying? Never says a bad word in his life. Doesn't drink, doesn't smoke, doesn't swear. He's nothing but sweetness and light, okay? He'd never hurt a fly."

"Dom, please. Remember who you're talking to. He may not have a record, your bro, but you weren't at the scene, you didn't see her apartment, and you didn't see the—well, I'll spare you the details. Let's just say it was one of the worst, okay? Something like this—Jesus—something like this does not drop from a clear sky. You quit the force because you thought you'd end up killing a malefactor, right? That's what you told me, Dom. You were afraid you'd end up killing somebody."

"Different planets, remember? Pete was exactly the opposite of me. Frank, the guy was a *monk*."

"Not to play Detective Freud or nothing, but what about the thing with your mother? A mother taking her own life, thing like that could unhinge a guy."

"You can blame anything you want on the bitch. No skin off my ass. But Pete and I had the same identical mother, and I don't see you coming to arrest me."

"I don't expect to be arresting anybody today, Dom."

A long silence filled the car. Dominic remembered the small, intense woman his brother had brought to visit, her relentless questions. He was sorry now that he had not liked her.

Rossi flicked a hand at the windshield, the blue station wagon. "*Was* a monk, you said. *Was* being the operative word. That Taurus is registered to Our Lady of Peace monastery outside Corning. The steering wheel is covered with bloody prints."

"Yeah? So what about her lover boy? The dealer. You check him out?"

"First guy we talked to. He didn't do it. Took it real hard, too."

"That doesn't mean he didn't do it."

"Dom, you come down to the shop with me later, I'll show you his statement. You can watch the tape of the interview. Mick LeMar is a low-level dealer, not a player, and at the relevant time he was miles from the place. Rock-solid alibi."

"Don't tell me: he was watching the game."

"Actually, he was burying his mother. Very nice guy, LeMar. You'd like him. Wanted to know if he could have the girl's cat."

"I'm touched."

"Tell me something, Dom—your brother ever tell you exactly *why* he joined a monastery?"

"Same reason anybody does. He had a vocation—and he was pretty clueless about how to get on in the world."

"He ever mention a girl named Cathy McCullough to you?"

"No. Who's she?"

"Month before your brother joined the monastery, he was questioned in an assault that took place at Luce College. Cathy McCullough—his girlfriend, by all accounts—was bashed in the head with a rock. She had no memory of the assault, but it permanently affected her speech."

"Jesus, how the hell'd you get on to his college career already?"

"Things have changed since your day, Dom. Soon as we had

his name, all it took was a cross-check with unsolveds. Narrow it down to blunt-force trauma, ten years ago . . ."

"But he was questioned, right? Not arrested."

"Not arrested. But maybe he played judge and jury and sentenced himself, so to speak. Ten years."

"Jesus."

Dominic was resisting the idea of Peter's guilt, but it was a feeble resistance, an attempt to hold down the nausea that climbed in his throat. Something cold and heavy was turning over in his stomach, a long denial melting into reality. His brother had always had the potential; that was why he had joined the monastery: because he had known—how consciously, Dominic didn't care to guess—that he should not be at large. He could not remain in the world, any more than Dominic could remain a cop—and for the same reason. It had nothing to do with vocation. Part of Dominic had always known this to be true, but another, more conscious part had always, despite his sarcasm, wanted to believe in the gentle, innocent monk.

The coroner's yellow tent looked like a half-inflated balloon lit up on the side of the hill. Early that morning, a hunter taking his new snowmobile out for a spin had dodged a tree and nearly run over an outstretched arm. He had taken one look at the pale blue hand—a male hand, bloody—and headed his snowmobile back to the highway and the nearest telephone.

The detective from the state police told all this to Rossi as soon as he had introduced himself and Dominic (*Detective* Meehan, Rossi had called him). The hunter was sitting very co-operatively in a nearby cruiser if they wanted to question him, but Rossi declined for the moment. He and Dominic stepped under the flap of the yellow tent.

Rossi went straight up to the body, but Dominic held back. He prided himself on his coolness, his ability to withstand pretty much anything, but this was not a sight for which anyone could be prepared.

Dr. Grigson continued with his examination of the body. Every few seconds he made a comment into a miniature tape recorder, clicking the machine off again each time. The phrases sounded as if he was mentally filling in a form, which in fact he was.

"Skull appears intact." *Click.*

"No trauma to trunk." *Click.*

"No trauma to trunk," Rossi interrupted him. "The guy's covered with blood, and there's no trauma to trunk?"

The coroner looked up at him, the eyes partially hidden by fogged lenses.

"The blood on the trunk appears at first glance to be older than that on the extremities. I could be wrong, but I suspect there is another body somewhere."

"There is."

Rossi and the coroner looked at Dominic, who remained just inside the flap of the tent.

"You don't have to watch this, Dom."

"It's okay. It's not a problem."

Grigson turned once more to his work.

"Massive fracture to the right fibula, which is clamped in a large leg-hold trap." *Click.*

"I brought him out here once," Dominic said quietly. "I told him about the guy who ate his gun. Remember Lopez? It may be the only thing we ever had in common—thinking of this cabin as a good bet for suicide."

"We don't know yet that it *is* suicide," the coroner said without looking up. And then, into his tape recorder: "Time of death difficult to estimate owing to temperatures well below freezing." *Click.*

"It's true, Dom. He could've stepped into that thing by accident."

"You think I leave bear traps lying around outside my cabin? Besides which, it's got a foot of snow under it. Obviously, it had to be set up well into the storm."

"Maybe someone else. Maybe somebody forced him into it."

"Frank, I don't need to be comforted. I hardly knew the guy. Different species."

"You're a cold bastard, Dom."

"Better cold than dead."

"Tissue appears frozen well into the muscle. You'll have to wait for the autopsy for time of death." *Click.*

"Trooper says there's a shotgun in the cabin," Rossi said, "along with a box of shells. Why stick yourself in a trap so you can freeze to death? Why choose the most painful way available?"

"Oh, that's often the case," Grigson put in without looking up. "People set themselves on fire. Hang themselves with piano wire. Suicides do often go in for maximum pain."

"That's my brother," Dominic said. "He was always looking for maximum pain."

The coroner spun round. "This person was your brother?"

"Yes."

"Well, Jesus Christ, you can't stand there. It's not proper procedure."

"Ease off, Doc. He's not touching anything."

"I don't care. You should have informed me at once of his relationship to the victim. His presence constitutes contamination of the scene."

"I can see how you made coroner, Doc. It's your bedside manner. All your chatter about maximum pain."

"He has to leave. I won't proceed until he's gone."

"Suits me," Dominic said with a sigh.

"One thing I can tell you," Grigson said in a milder tone. "The trap didn't kill him, though it must have hurt something awful. Ten to one this man died of exposure."

"Really, Doc. Is that supposed to make him feel better? That trap nearly bit the guy's shin off."

"Look for yourself."

The three of them looked down at the frozen features. Ice crystals weighted down the eyelashes, and the skin was mottled grey and blue, but for all that, Brother William's features were set not in agony but in something close to contentment.

"I have to admit," Rossi said, "he looks pretty good, considering."

Then he spoke over his shoulder to Dominic. "Looks like your brother got lucky for once. Before it was over, he must have gone completely numb."

But Dominic had thrown open the flap of the tent, and was already bending to step into the cold.

GILES BLUNT grew up in North Bay, Ontario, and spent twenty years in New York City as a novelist and a scriptwriter for such shows as *Law and Order*, *Street Legal* and *Night Heat*, before making his home in Toronto. He is the author of the six novels in the bestselling Cardinal crime series, featuring Algonquin Bay's John Cardinal and Lise Delorme, which he is currently adapting as a television series for CTV. He is widely considered "one of Canada's top crime novelists" (the *Globe and Mail*) and among "crime drama's elite" (*Publishers Weekly*). He is a two-time winner of the Arthur Ellis Award for Best Novel and a recipient of the British Crime Writers' Macallan Silver Dagger.